A SMALL TOWN, ENEMIES-TO-LOVERS ROMANCE

FOR YOU I'D BLOOM

BOOK 3 OF THE PEACE FALLS SERIES

HANNAH JORDAN

ABOUT THIS BOOK

Peace Falls Series **Reading Order:** *For You I'd Bloom* is a stand-alone novel; however, Lauren and Aiden are featured throughout the first two books of the *Peace Falls Series*. *For You I'd* Bloom occurs chronologically after *For You I'd Break* and *For You I'd Mend* and contains spoilers for both books.

Content Warning: This book contains potentially upsetting subject matter, including references to self-harm, sexual assault, child abuse, and accidental death. It also contains multiple blush-inducing sex scenes, so if you're looking for a sweet, small-town romance, best put this one down.

Published by Hannah Jordan Books 2025

Cover Design: Kaytalin McCarry, Duskbound Books

ebook ISBN: 979-8-9905868-4-0

Paperback ISBN: 979-8-9905868-5-7

www.hannahjordanauthor.com

To all the what ifs that become our forevers.

Chapter One

Lauren

Karma is real. I was a believer long before Taylor Swift touted its power. But honestly, I never cared how it came around for others. If living in foster care taught me anything, it's to focus on what I can control and not give a flip what other people did. The best revenge has always been a great life.

And my life was great. I loved being part of a tight-knit community. My coffee shop/bookstore, appropriately named Karma, was thriving. I had wonderful friends and two adorable cats who kept me warm at night, plus a third I'd eventually convince to love me.

Just not today.

Dido hissed when I opened my closet door. She'd curled herself into a tight ball on my favorite suede boots, leaving flecks of fur all over them. Hopefully she hadn't clawed any of the dresses within reach of her vengeful paws. Even if I had far too many for someone who wore a t-shirt and yoga pants to work every day, I loved them all. I'd be checking for damage later.

"Good morning to you too," I said, reaching inside the closet to grab an old pair of sneakers to replace the coffee-soaked ones I'd left downstairs.

Dido growled and arched her back. Her calico fur stood on end, and she lifted the stub of a tail she had remaining.

"Stop that," I said, retreating as fast as I could.

I'd already peeled off my soggy socks before rushing up the steps to my apartment. My colorful aqua Karma apron had taken the brunt of the spill, saving my shirt and my skin. Luckily, I'd gotten my shoes off before the hot liquid burned my feet. My black leggings were a little damp, but I needed to get back downstairs. I grabbed a pair of Jane Austen socks, pride for my right foot, prejudice for my left, while Dido gave me the stink eye. I yanked on the shoes as fast as I could and sprinted out of my apartment, down the steps, and through the back room. By the time I reached the counter, the line was out to the sidewalk.

"I'm so sorry," Wyatt said again while I tied a fresh apron around my waist. He pushed a mop through the area behind the register where he'd dropped a full pot of dark roast, smearing coffee and broken glass everywhere.

"It's ok," I said, taking the mop from him. It wasn't like Wyatt to be so agitated unless his blood sugar was off. I grabbed his hands and looked him in the eyes. His palms were sweaty, which instantly made me anxious. "Do you need to eat something?"

He shook his head. "I'm fine. Just clumsy."

His complexion didn't look off, or I'd have made him check his blood sugar. He was probably just embarrassed. "No one was hurt," I said, giving his hands a squeeze. "And anyone who can't find patience for us right now can leave."

I said that last part loud enough for everyone in line to hear. No one moved.

"See," I said. Wyatt squeezed my hands back before dropping them and reaching for the mop. "Focus on the glass first, OK," I said, handing him a dish towel. "Then mop after. I'll take care of the line."

He nodded and began picking up shards with the towel. Something was definitely off with Wyatt. He wasn't clumsy by nature and going straight for the mop while glass littered the floor didn't match the common sense I admired in him.

I made a mental note to check in with him the next time we had a lull. After grabbing a full pot of breakfast blend and a stack of to-go cups, I stepped around the counter and faced the crowd.

"OK, everyone," I said, loudly. "Drip coffee drinkers in front of me. Everyone else form a line to the left. For those in my line, I'm pouring black coffee and you'll fix it however you'd like at the self-serve station. You can drop your payment in the tip jar or pay next time. If that doesn't work, please get in the other line. Anyone ordering food should join that line as well. After we clear out the regular coffee drinkers, we'll help everyone else as fast as we can. Got it?"

Everyone shuffled into position. Within a couple minutes, I'd served coffee to over half the customers in the original line, and Wyatt had cleaned the area behind the counter.

We worked together making espresso drinks and hot chocolate for the remaining customers, who were all pleasant and grateful after I announced they'd all be getting a free cookie with their order. A few, like the town pharmacist Mr. Wilson, refused it outright.

"I don't need a freebie, Lauren," he said, handing me the full amount for his cappuccino and cookie. "Nobody else did either."

I leaned forward so Wyatt wouldn't hear me. "I wanted to smooth over the situation as fast as possible. If people got nasty, Wyatt would have felt worse. Plus, it helps Rowan and Poppy's bakery."

Mr. Wilson shook his head but smiled at me. "You're too generous, young lady."

"Pot, kettle," I said, pointing at myself and then him. He smiled, shoved a five in the tip jar, and left.

By the time we had a handle on the line, I had three minutes to spare before story time. Wyatt was still knocking out drinks, so our chat would have to wait. I grabbed my extra-large mug of black coffee and headed toward the bookstore portion of Karma. No matter how many times I walked through the shelves, it felt like stepping into paradise.

I'd never met my grandpa before he pulled me out of foster care. To this day, I don't know if the state found him or if Mom realized she'd never get her shit together and asked her estranged father to step in. During the first awkward weeks Grandpa and I lived together, I spent most of my time in the bookshop, reading. Neither of us wanted to talk about Mom or my life before I came to Peace Falls, so we talked about books. Books we'd both read. Books we recommended to each other. Our little book club of two lasted until he passed away a year after I graduated high school.

When I took over the store, I removed the cards and glossy magazines to make room for the coffee bar that now accounted for seventy percent of my profit. I'd crammed in as many tables and chairs as I could, but judging by how fast they filled, it wasn't enough. I would probably make more money if I removed a few bookshelves and expanded the café menu and seating, but I couldn't bring myself to make any more changes to the shop.

I'd kept the ornate tin ceiling throughout but painted it a light blue. Most of the comfy leather seating scattered between the bookshelves had been in the store for years. Grandpa was a hipster before his time and had fully embraced the exposed brick trend decades before it became popular. I'd added works by local artists to the walls but kept all his historical black-and-white photographs of Peace Falls. Overall, the bookstore remained familiar and cozy, with enough additions to make it my own.

As I waited for the kiddos to arrive, I gulped my coffee and enjoyed sitting down for the first time since 4:30 am. A half-dozen children flopped at my feet while I read and tried to avoid rocking on their tiny fingers. I liked children in small doses. I started Sunday Story Hour because I loved watching kids fall in love with books. Adding Tuesdays and Thursdays for Tots so harried stay-at-home parents could enjoy a cup of coffee and a chat while I read to their toddlers and preschoolers was for karma's sake and why, instead of doing payroll, I was reading *The Very Hungry Caterpillar* to a group of wriggling children, one of whom had sneezed on me twice.

"Another?" a little boy named Max asked as I finished the last book I'd intended to read. The other kids looked ready to bolt from the carpet after four stories, but Max sat calmly by my feet with my blind cat Medusa in his lap, his thick glasses magnifying his cornflower blue eyes.

"I'm sure Ms. Lauren has a lot of work to do," his mother, Brandi, said, crouching down to his level. She gave his back a gentle rub, and he looked up at her with so much love in his eyes, my breath caught.

For as long as I can remember, I've watched parents with their kids. Sometimes with envy when I was little, sometimes with anger when I recognized something of my own mother in their behavior, but always with interest. I'd have envied Max if we were both kids. He may have an unfair share of health problems, but he'd won the parental jackpot. Brandi and her husband were the best mom and dad combo I'd ever seen. Good thing too, since Max needed more support than most kids.

"OK," Max said, agreeably. "Thank you, Ms. Lauren."

Brandi smiled at him, and her tired face glowed with happiness. "I still need to do a little work on the computer, but Ms. Lauren has coloring sheets and crayons in the front."

He flashed a crooked grin and gently set Medusa on the braided rug before he used the arm of my rocking chair to pull himself to his feet. Brandi reached for him, then drew her hands back as he took one uneven step after another. I scooped up Medusa and held her close to my neck so she could smell me and know who was holding her. I walked beside Brandi, whose arms were as tense as a pair of cobras ready to strike should Max lose his balance as he limped to the front.

"Thanks so much for letting me use your computer, Lauren," she said without taking her eyes from her son. "Our internet provider said it'd be another week before they fixed our service, and Max's doctor sent over a ton of forms he wants completed before our next appointment."

"Use it any time," I said. "Medusa loves when Max visits." At the sound of her name, my cat purred against my neck. I gave her head a scratch and she rumbled louder.

"That's because we understand each other," Max said without turning around. "I don't see well without my glasses, so I know how scary it can be if something moves too fast or makes a loud noise. She likes that I'm quiet and don't move much when I hold her."

I didn't miss the sheen in Brandi's eyes. If I didn't love Medusa so much or think Brandi already had an overflowing plate, I'd offer to let Max take the cat home. Instead, I told Brandi to print out as many forms as she needed.

"Are you sure?" she asked as Max took a seat at one of the bistro tables by the career center, which Brandi had claimed earlier with their jackets. "I'm happy to pay you."

I shook my head. "Someone dropped off paper and ink this morning."

The career center wasn't much. Just a couple computers I'd salvaged from a lawyer's office in town and a 3-in-1 printer/fax/copier shoved in the corner beneath a corkboard where local businesses posted job openings. It may not be state-of-the art, but I'd seen a lot of good happen there. Single moms applying for work. High schoolers printing out term papers. Retirees writing editorials for the town's newspaper.

"Huh," Brandi said, glancing at the front door, where without fail supplies appeared whenever I needed them. "I wonder if it's the same person or a bunch of different people paying back your kindness."

I shrugged. "I'm just happy the printer stays stocked."

My three-legged cat, Desdemona, ran-hopped to my feet and began weaving around my legs. Dido jumped on the table beside Max and hissed at me.

For a cat who hated people, she sure made use of the cat doors throughout the building to find me when she wanted to unleash her attitude. "Be nice," I said to her.

She plopped down on the far side of the table, beyond Max's reach. Her stub flicked at a steady tempo that seemed more pissed off than happy.

"Would you mind if I left Medusa with you?" I asked Max.

"Sure," Max said, holding out his arms for her. He laid her gently on his small lap and waited until she'd curled into a contented ball before he started petting her.

Desdemona stopped weaving between my legs and let out a desperate meow, clearly seeking more affection herself.

"Think you can handle two?" I asked Max.

"The one without the tail doesn't like me," he said in a quiet voice.

"Dido doesn't like anyone, but Desdemona would appreciate some love. If I put her on the chair beside you, can you pet her too?"

Max beamed at me. "Yes, ma'am."

I lifted Desdemona onto the chair and gave her ears a couple scratches before I headed for the counter. If I didn't submit payroll in the next hour, I'd have to pay additional fees to ensure Wyatt and my friend and part-timer, Cammie, got paid on time.

When I walked behind the counter toward the back, I found Wyatt twisting a dishtowel in his hands and pacing. Yep, something was definitely up.

I put my hand on his shoulder. "Everything OK?"

He opened his mouth to speak when the bell over the front door clanged, and Dr. Evers stepped inside.

"Mocha latte?" I asked the doctor.

"Yes, please," he said, approaching the counter.

I grabbed the coconut milk, Dr. Evers's favorite, and poured some in a frothing pitcher. Like the well-oiled machine we were, Wyatt started making two espresso shots.

I bumped his hip once he had it set to brew. "What's up?"

He waited until I started heating the milk to speak. "Aiden offered me a job."

"You're quitting?" I screeched over the blast of the milk frothier.

Karma was definitely paying me back. Why else would a meathead like Aiden O'Malley be super glued in my life to wreck it every chance he could?

Over the years, I'd perfected the art of sleeping with someone and cutting them loose without hurt feelings or lingering awkwardness. Unfortunately, my singular sheet tango with Aiden happened right out of high school, when I wasn't yet skilled in the art of the one-night stand. Things have remained weird between us ever since.

To make matters worse, Aiden was best friends with Cal, my best friend Rowan's fiancé, so of course we're thrown together all the time. Once Cal's other best friend, Theo, started dating Rowan's sister, Poppy, Aiden and I became a default pairing in our group of six. Fortunately, Cammie was coming on this weekend's bachelor/bachelorette trip, so at least there'd be a buffer between Aiden and me.

Wyatt had the decency to duck his head like a teenager caught getting handsy with his date in the back of a movie theater. "I'm not quitting," he said. "I just want to cut back my hours. I can still cover weekends and evenings."

"I have Cammie for those," I said, dumping hot milk over a double shot of espresso and adding an obscene amount of chocolate syrup.

Wyatt shuffled from one chuck to the other while I stirred the mocha latte hard enough to whip cream before adding a mountain of actual whipped cream on top. "You work more than any person I know, Lauren.

If you let Cammie and I work together and add someone to the day shifts, you could finally have time off. You need it."

True. But I loved Karma. It only felt like work when my feet ached and the espresso machine acted up. More importantly, I didn't trust anyone to run my business.

I fought the urge to glare at Wyatt and plastered a smile on my face as I walked to the register. "Here you go, Dr. Evers," I said, handing the man his to-go cup. "Would you like a brownie as well?"

The good doctor looked at the glass case with all the delicious baked goods supplied by Rowan and Poppy's bakery and sighed. "I better not. I gave up dessert for Lent."

Because I want to be nice, I didn't point out that his drink of choice probably had more sugar than a brownie. "In that case, your first brownie after Easter is on me."

We both knew he'd pay for his next brownie, whether he put the money in the tip jar or the drawer, and that I'd end up putting two brownies in his bag when he asked for one. He winked at me and started drinking his latte before he reached the door.

As soon as Dr. Evers was out of earshot, I whirled to face Wyatt. He'd crept as far from me as possible while I had my back turned. Either I hadn't hidden my annoyance well or the espresso machine really did need his attention. And damn it, Wyatt was the only person who could coax that beast into a better mood.

I took a moment to get my emotions in check. Wyatt was more like family than an employee. Even better, since the relationship was chosen. He was one of the sweetest and most reliable people I knew, which meant I shouldn't be screeching at him. "What's Aiden paying you?" I asked, forcing my voice to sound calm.

"Twenty-five dollars an hour with benefits."

My stomach sank. I paid my workers above minimum wage and slid every tip their way, but even so, Aiden's offer was a huge jump for Wyatt. Karma did well, but we didn't have the profit margins of a construction company. And if I upped Wyatt's pay, I'd have to up Cammie's. It was only fair. With pay rates like that, I wouldn't be able to hire additional staff.

"I can't pay twenty-five, but I can bump you to eighteen. With tips, you'd only be a few dollars an hour short. I can up the coffee prices again and give you another raise in a couple of months."

"I'd rather you raise the prices, hire someone at my current rate, and give yourself some time off."

Wyatt wasn't wrong. We desperately needed more employees. I rarely had over five hours of sleep a night. As much as I hated to admit it, I was burning out.

"Plus, I need the health insurance."

"I thought you were on the college's plan."

He shook his head. "I lost coverage when I became a part-time student. My COBRA is about to run out."

Damn it. No way could I offer him health insurance. I could barely cover my own premiums, and as a diabetic, Wyatt needed coverage.

He stared at me with those earnest brown eyes, the ones that convinced me to hire him even though he was a stranger at the time, and all my irritation melted. Well, at least all my irritation at Wyatt. I still had plenty for Aiden. If I couldn't have Wyatt full time, keeping him with fewer hours was better than not at all. "It's a great opportunity for you."

"It is," Wyatt said, beaming. "I learned so much already on the projects I helped with before, and everyone on Aiden's crew likes working for him." He paled slightly. "It's not that I don't love working here. And you're the best boss I've ever had, it's just—"

I held up my hand to stop him. "You'd be crazy to turn it down." I opened my arms, and he rushed forward to hug me, lifting me slightly off my feet. "You'll always have a place here, Wy."

"Good," he said, stepping back. "Cause I don't want to leave Karma or you."

"Especially if it means sharing shifts with Cammie."

He smiled like I knew he would. The poor guy has had a crush on Cammie since the day he walked in the door. I've tried my best to discourage him since she's sworn off men and was actually afraid of most, Wyatt included. But he'd remained hopeful without pestering her.

"Maybe she'll finally talk to me," he said with a self-deprecating laugh. "I'm hoping she'll be in a good mood after your trip. Aiden said he didn't want me to start until after you and Cammie get back from St. John. So don't worry about that."

Of course I was worried. I'd be leaving Karma in the hands of Rowan's seventeen-year-old brother, Chris, and Wyatt, who'd just informed me he needed to be replaced. Even worse, I'd be spending four days on a tropical island with Aiden O'Malley.

He'd likely run around shirtless the entire time. It'd been almost a year since my last one-night stand. Long enough that Aiden, who had always been annoyingly handsome, was starting to make my pulse jump every time he bought coffee. And not just because he pissed me off.

He had the most piercing blue eyes I'd ever seen, the kind of ice blue that snagged your attention, whether you wanted to give it or not. I knew exactly how great his full mouth and trim beard felt against my skin. The muscles he'd carved through hours of work with his skilled hands. His thick — I did not want a repeat of that rodeo. Don't get me wrong, the sex had been great. Honestly, the most mind blowing, toe curling, best I'd ever had. But we'd fallen into bed with very different expectations. I'd assumed the former quarterback of the football team wanted to add me to his long list of hookups. Imagine my surprise when he wanted more. He didn't take the brush off well. And after years of avoiding me, he'd made it his mission to irritate me ever since Rowan started dating Cal. I'd tried to keep my calm, but he inevitably drew out the worst version of me.

As much as I wanted to get away and soak up the sun, part of me dreaded spending so much time with Aiden. Since he just poached my only full-time employee, I now had the perfect excuse to stay home.

"Let me know your new schedule, and we'll fit you in here whenever you can," I told Wyatt.

"Thanks, Lauren," he said and turned back to the espresso machine, which gave a steamy sigh when he loosened something and thumped the side.

The next thing I knew, it was afternoon. Payroll was late, the inventory hadn't been unpacked, and someone spilled the half-full mug of coffee I'd left in the children's section all over the carpet. I started counting all the tasks I needed to complete and the hours left before we opened again at 5:00 am.

I'd be lucky to get four hours of sleep tonight. No way could I manage without Wyatt full time. If I didn't post the job and start interviewing tomorrow, I'd have to cut Karma's hours.

I texted Rowan and explained that I couldn't make the bachelor/bachelorette trip. When she asked why not, I replied:

Aiden.

Because karma's a bitch.

CHAPTER TWO

Aiden

I LAID THE LAST line of caulk where the backsplash met the counter and stood back to admire my work. The shape and shading of the blue tiles in the backsplash gave a 3-D illusion that would look great in small spaces but felt too busy in my oversized farmhouse kitchen. The beechwood cabinets were the lightest I'd ever used and my favorite so far. They made the entire space feel brighter, almost welcoming. I ran my hand across the smooth wood the color of sand before I took a crowbar and yanked a cabinet from the wall.

Once it hit the floor, I grabbed a sledgehammer and started swinging. As splinters filled the air around me, the white-hot anger burning in my chest cooled to blue. I stopped when my shoulder throbbed.

I wanted to smash everything to bits, but my foreman, Sam, was re-doing his grandmother's kitchen and asked me to keep an eye out for second-hand cabinets. Usually, I salvaged the cabinets for my kitchen from job sites, but I'd seen these and thought they'd look nice in Mrs. Sanchez's house.

After I busted the one cabinet, I used my electric screwdriver to remove the rest, which should be more than enough for Sam's project. But I was beating the shit out of the tiles. No surprise I'd found those heavily discounted.

As usual, I'd left the beige Formica counters and stained porcelain sink alone. Not that I needed either. I lived on takeout and mooching meals off my mom and sisters. But sinks and counters were too expensive to destroy every couple months.

Once I placed the cabinets on a drop cloth in the relative safety of the dining room, I started chiseling the tiles from the wall. Each time one smashed on the floor, my anger cooled a degree. When my shoulder tightened enough to make me groan, I put the chisel down and looked out the window over the sink.

Across my back field, which should come out of winter dormancy any day now, and beyond the pitted dirt road, sat an old barn framed by a copse of trees. At this distance, it looked tiny, insignificant. It was neither.

"At least I only destroyed one cabinet this time, Logan."

I didn't talk to him often, and never when anyone could hear me. But every time I tore apart something that had taken me days to build, I indulged in a little one-sided conversation.

I imagined him giving me shit for wasting so much time and materials but stopped short of admitting, even to myself, that he'd have been pissed that I'd aggravated my shoulder. Logan had protected my ass on the field and off, which was the only reason I was alive enough to tear apart my kitchen, and why he wasn't here to stop me.

"I'm trying. We all are. It's just taking me longer than Cal and Theo."

I really had tried to get it together. I'd moved next door to the barn where Logan spent his last hours and then bought it. I'd forced Theo and Cal to go there with me because none of us had worked through losing Logan enough to live our lives.

It didn't take a shrink to know spending hours and a sickening amount of cash to remodel a house only for the satisfaction of tearing it down was seriously fucked up. Not as fucked up as Theo and his self-harm tendencies, which had thankfully abated since he committed to therapy and Poppy, but fucked up nonetheless. Add to that the fact I kept all the destruction a secret, and I was neck and neck with Theo for being the most mental in our trio. Cal had simply buried himself in school, then work, and ignored his grief and every other intense feeling until he fell for Rowan and had to pull through to be with her. Theo had taken longer, keeping Poppy in the friend zone for over a year before he sorted his shit.

"Good job, by the way, with those Stevens sisters. Maybe you need to send me a woman too."

I laughed, the sound hollow and pathetic in the still kitchen. I might be a jaded asshole, but I honestly believed Logan had somehow orchestrated Rowan and Poppy Stevens into Cal's and Theo's lives. They were doing well now. Better than well. Which meant I was the only one who hadn't yet pulled my head out of my ass, despite being the one who'd pushed my friends out of their grief. Logan would have wanted me to help them, and I owed him that much, but that didn't mean I was ready to move on.

"I'll leave you alone now," I said, picking up my chisel. "There's only so much crazy I'll allow myself and these tiles need breaking."

I'd just finished scrapping the last of the tiles onto the covered countertop when my doorbell rang. I froze. Living this far out of town, I rarely had solicitors. I wasn't expecting a delivery. I certainly wasn't expecting visitors. I hadn't allowed anyone in the house since I moved in two years ago. How else could I hide five kitchen remodels and half a dozen bathroom updates?

The doorbell rang again, followed by someone pounding on the heavy oak door. I crept into the center hall and peered through the peephole.

"Open up, asshole," Cal yelled. He was still in his scrubs, his brown hair standing on end like he'd yanked it the entire ride over.

Theo smacked Cal's arm before saying, "We just want to talk, Aiden. Stop pretending you're not here. We can see your truck."

Well, fuck.

I unlocked the door and opened it a crack. "Ever heard of texting?"

"Ever heard of texting back?" Cal snapped. "Or picking up the phone when someone calls you?"

"Yeah, even I don't do that," Theo said with a smirk.

OK, so Cal was pissed, and Theo was trying to calm his ass down because he thought Cal was overacting. If I'd upset Poppy, they'd both be mad, since Theo was dating her and Cal was marrying her sister. Theo hadn't been with Poppy long enough to think of Rowan as family, so I figured I'd ticked off Cal's pint-sized redhead, not Theo's goth pixie.

I blew out a breath and rubbed my forehead. If sweet Rowan wanted my balls, I'd royally screwed up. And I could only think of one reason. It was the same reason I'd turned my phone off before demoing my kitchen.

I squeezed through the front door and pulled it shut behind me. Theo took a step back and leaned against the railing, giving me space on the narrow porch. Cal didn't budge and looked ready to take a swing.

"I need Wyatt," I said, crossing my arms over my chest and tucking my hands under my pits. Slowing my block time would make Cal think twice about hitting me, and I didn't feel like bruising his pretty-boy face right before we left for a four-night trip together with the Stevens sisters, who would no doubt inflict revenge on my ass in some creative and terrifying way for upsetting Lauren. "I'll have three job sites going when we get back from St. John, one of which is a massive housing development on a tight deadline."

Cal rubbed his forehead, his anger deflating a little with my very rational explanation. "And you couldn't hire anyone else?"

"Wyatt's a hard worker, a fast learner, and bilingual."

"And the only full-time employee at Karma," Cal said.

"You and I both know Lauren can teach someone to steam milk faster than I can teach carpentry skills."

"Not someone she trusts," Theo said, quietly.

I leaned against the door while a heavy knot of guilt slammed into my stomach. "Not my problem."

Cal narrowed his eyes at me like he believed my bullshit, but Theo stood there reading every damn emotion I had like a tattooed Dr. Phil.

"It's your problem now," Cal said. "Lauren can't go on the trip because she needs to find a replacement for Wyatt. So Rowan's upset, which means I'm pissed."

I didn't want to think about Lauren, let alone talk about her. "Lauren's being difficult. Four days won't make a difference. She can put the ad online and set up zoom interviews from the island if she's in that much of a hurry."

Which was exactly what I'd texted her in reply to her six texts—all in caps—before I turned off my phone.

"Would you hire someone you've never met in person?" Cal asked.

"For a trial period, sure," I said, shoving my hands in my pockets and telling my feet not to shift. The last thing I needed was Theo picking up on how much the conversation agitated me. "Why not? So what if someone spills coffee or snaps at a customer? Big deal. She can fire the rude klutz and move on."

"He has a point," Theo mumbled.

"If she wanted to keep Wyatt, she could pay him what I offered." Doubtful. I paid my crews well above market rates, and construction workers typically made more than baristas.

Cal nodded. I'm pretty sure he'd upped Cammie's pay significantly when he bought his physical therapy practice from his boss, not that his office manager wasn't worth every penny. Truth be told, I'd like her to run my construction company, but I wasn't about to get into a pay pissing match with Cal for his pseudo sister. How he landed on that relationship with the hot blonde before he started dating Rowan was beyond me.

"Did you have to steal him the day before we leave?" Cal asked.

"No, but then Lauren wouldn't have a reason to stay behind," Theo said.

I jabbed my finger at him. "I told you I needed Wyatt as soon as we got back. At least this way Lauren has some notice."

"So she could stay behind and find a replacement," Theo said.

"He's right, isn't he?" Cal said, glaring at me. "You did this on purpose because you don't want her on the trip. What could you possibly have against Lauren?"

Plenty. Besides, I needed another full timer, and Wyatt had been working for me part time on a project-by-project basis. It made sense. Pissing off Lauren was a bonus, but did I want to avoid seeing her stretched out on a beach in a bikini, her perfect curves taunting me for days? No. Yes. Maybe.

Just thinking about her filled me with the usual combination of lust, longing, and a hefty dose of self-doubt. Sex with Lauren was unlike anything I'd experienced before or since, but if we'd just shared a bed for a night, I wouldn't still be fighting the simultaneous urges to avoid her and be with her as much as I could without looking like a damn stalker. Cal and Theo stared at me, waiting for an answer, so I blurted out what I'd been too embarrassed to tell them for eight years. "I slept with her."

Neither of them looked surprised. "Recently?" Theo asked.

"When you were away." I never used the word prison. I wasn't sure if that was for my benefit or Theo's since I'm the reason he went.

"How is that a problem?" Cal asked. "No offense, but you and Lauren are Peace Falls's king and queen of one-night stands. It's inevitable you'd sleep together at some point. What's the big deal?"

"Fuck, brother, you're dense," Theo said, laughing.

As usual, the nickname felt like a tiny pinprick. Theo and Cal had called each other brother long before Logan died. It'd never bothered me then because, despite how close we were as a group of four, Logan and I had the same tight relationship Cal and Theo had. We might not have called ourselves brothers, but that's what we were. We grew up next door to each other. I slept at his house as often as I did my own and vice versa.

"What am I missing?" Cal asked Theo. For all his book smarts, Dr. Cardoso really was a dumbass sometimes.

Theo ignored him. "Did she want more or did you?"

I rubbed my forehead. Might as well lay all my pathetic cards on the table now that I'd started. "I did."

"Oh shit," Cal said, finally getting a clue. "That's why you're always ripping up napkins whenever she's around. You still like her."

I shrugged because I didn't want to say it out loud. What's the point? I wasn't good enough for Saint Lauren and never would be. Maybe if I'd gone to college or joined the league, she'd have wanted more than a single, unbelievable night. But I wasn't an NFL star or even a college grad, just a contractor with a bum shoulder and anger issues.

"It's not about you," Cal said, surprising both me and Theo. "She's scared."

Once the asshole got a clue, he focused his big brain on an issue like a pig sniffing truffles. Theo nodded like Cal's idiotic statement made sense. Lauren was a lot of things: irritatingly beautiful, kind, fucking sunshine and rainbows to everyone except me. She wasn't a badass like Poppy, who didn't give a shit what anyone thought about her, but Lauren didn't strike me as scared. Not like Cammie, who avoided men whenever she could, which I guess went a long way toward Cal stepping into an overprotective brother role.

Lauren wasn't afraid of men at all. In the years since we'd slept together, she'd continued having hookups at a pace similar to mine. Some of those lucky bastards bragged about it, others seemed as hurt as I was by her ride-and-ditch act.

"Makes sense," Theo said. "It's the same reason she hasn't hired more staff at Karma. She doesn't trust anyone."

"Bullshit," I said, getting angry. "She's the Pollyanna of Peace Falls. She sees the best in everything and everyone."

"Except you, apparently," Cal said with a chuckle.

"Or only him," Theo said. "Which would explain why he rattles her so much."

"She's rattled because I rattle her every chance I get," I snapped. I wasn't about to consider the possibility that Lauren was like some ten-year-old boy pulling my hair because she had feelings she didn't know how to handle.

"So, you're scared of her," Cal said. "Got it. Now I have something to tell my fiancée that might earn you a smidge of sympathy."

"I'm not scared of anything," I yelled.

"Great, so you won't mind if we tour your house?" Theo shot forward like he was about to physically move me from the door but stopped when he saw my face. "Whenever you're ready, A," he said, gripping my shoulder.

At the rate I was going, that'd be never.

Chapter Three

Lauren

Wyatt dumped a scoop of roasted beans into the grinder and rubbed his forehead. "I feel terrible you're missing the trip because of me."

"Don't." I held up the notepad I'd been carrying everywhere since I flipped on the café lights. "Only one item on this list is to post a job ad. I'm using the time to catch up on all the things I've been meaning to do. You won't even know I'm here."

"Yes, we will," Chris said as he slid the cookies Rowan delivered last night into the display case. "You'll be the Energizer bunny, like always, working your tail off, while Ann cries into her pina colada because her best friend isn't with her on her bachelorette trip."

"You aren't going either," I said.

"I'm seventeen, and my mom won't let me. So I'm here at the butt crack of dawn theoretically so you could enjoy yourself on a tropical island with my sisters. So remind me again why you're here?"

"She's a control freak," Rowan said, flinging open the door to the back. "And I prefer mango daiquiris. Pina coladas are too sweet."

She had on an ivory eyelet dress paired with thermal leggings and a bulky green cardigan, her red hair piled on top of her head in a bun that somehow looked more artful than messy. That was Rowan. Always thinking ahead. The moment she stepped off the plane in the Virgin Islands, she'd strip off the warm layers, let her hair down, and be ready for vacation.

I dropped my pen and notepad on the counter where I'd been doing a tea inventory and stared at her. It was just before five in the morning, way too early for visitors, even ones who had keys to the back door. "Why are you here?"

Before Rowan could answer, Cammie burst through the swinging door, flashing her signature smile, her blue eyes dancing with excitement. "I love pina coladas. Anything coconut, really."

I pictured them lounging together in beach chairs with frozen drinks, soaking in every moment of each other's company before they returned to their busy lives, Rowan to her fledging bakery and wedding plans, Cammie to her jobs at Cal's office and here. I fought a sharp pang of regret and smiled at them. "Not that I'm not delighted to see you both, but what's going on?"

"I was hoping I could borrow some clothes from your awesome wardrobe," Rowan said. "I don't have many sundresses."

"I'm here to teach Chris how to make the specialty lattes," Cammie added.

Wyatt raised an eyebrow at me. I shrugged. I had no idea why Cammie assumed he couldn't teach Chris.

"Help yourself to whatever you want," I told my bestie. She pulled me into a brief hug and ran off to raid my closet.

Rowan may or may not have been telling the truth. I could see her jolting awake on the morning of the trip, worried she didn't have the right clothes. But Cammie was full of it. No one got up this early unless they had to or were neurotic like Rowan. I put my hands on my hips and stared at her. "Now, tell me what's really going on."

Cammie glanced at Chris and Wyatt, who had both given up all pretense of working, and stood waiting for her reply. "Let's go to your office."

She grabbed my arm and tugged me to the back, pushing me into the squeaking swivel chair behind my cluttered desk before she closed the door and leaned against it.

Cammie was a wisp of a thing who probably weighed a buck ten soaking wet. I wasn't worried about moving her if I needed, but the fact she'd blocked the door to tell me something had my heart racing. "What's happened?"

"Rowan wanted to make a PowerPoint, but I figured that was overkill. Give me three minutes."

"OK," I said, my heart still thumping at an odd rhythm.

"I'm staying here and you're going on the trip.

I blew out a relieved breath. "Geeze, Cammie, I thought something was wrong. You scared me."

She shifted uncomfortably on her feet. "I didn't mean to worry you, but honestly, you ditching this trip is wrong. You're Rowan's best friend. I've known her less than a year and Cal only two. If I stay behind, there's no reason you can't go."

"I need to find a replacement for Wyatt."

Cammie smiled at me. "You know I love you, right? You're one of the best people I know, and I wouldn't change you for the world."

"Um, thanks," I said, unsure how she was going to turn the compliment into an argument for why I should jet off to the Caribbean while my business faced a staffing crisis.

Cammie straightened to her full height and gave me a look I'd seen her give Cal a time or two, but only when he really needed to hear what she had to tell him, which was usually something critical and a hundred percent accurate. "You hire with your gut, not your head. The chances of you finding a replacement for Wyatt any time soon are next to nil."

"I hired you. And him."

"Because your gut told you we could be trusted."

"And that's a problem because?"

"Your gut's standards are too high. You don't need that level of faith in every person who works here. Sure, you want to trust they won't spit in the drinks or steal from the till, but that's not the same level of trust you have for the people you allow close to you. You don't have to be friends with your employees. Let me help you hire someone."

She wasn't wrong. In fact, she was being generous. Wyatt and Cammie were more than friends. They were my family. And not like a toxic work culture "family" whom I expected to work endless unpaid hours to improve my bottom line. I liked working with people I could trust enough to put my guard down slightly.

"You're right, but I need more than that to let you stay here instead of me."

Cammie smiled and held up one finger. "Besides the two excellent reasons I already gave, Cal will be more relaxed on the trip because I'll use my number as the emergency contact. I'll be able to field all his patient calls and only reach out to him if it's absolutely necessary." She put up another finger and continued. "I've never flown before and I'm honestly terrified. If you make me go, I'll need to get roaring drunk to board the plane and then everyone will be worried about me." Another finger. "I don't know how to swim. Someone will always be staying behind with me when they'd rather be snorkeling or whatever people do in the ocean, and I'll feel guilty."

"You don't know how to swim?"

"Focus, woman," Cammie said, holding up another finger. "You work harder than anyone I know. No one on this beautiful earth needs a vacation more than you."

"That's—"

"And finally," she said, holding out her thumb. "I need to get used to working with Wyatt, since we'll be covering evenings and weekends together. You trust him, so I know I should too. Honestly, I'm only nervous around him because I can tell he likes me, and he's kind of cute and sweet, which is a lethal combination. But if you tell him I said that I'll catnap Desdemona and Medusa and never speak to you again. You'll only have Dido for company, and she hates you."

"You like Wyatt?"

"I said he was kind of cute and sweet, which makes him dangerous because I'm never getting into another relationship. But it's time I put on my big girl panties and stop avoiding him. Call it exposure therapy."

Damn it. I couldn't argue with that last reason. If Cammie was ready to swallow her fear of men, or at least of Wyatt, and take a brave step forward, I wouldn't stop her. "OK."

She clapped her hands and did a little hop. "Great! Because Rowan is upstairs packing for you right now. Better hurry if you want to add anything. Your ride gets here in ten minutes."

"What?" I said, standing. "I thought the flight left this afternoon."

"Aiden traded in my ticket and some points he had to upgrade everyone to the direct morning flight from Charlotte instead of the connecting one from D.C. Plus, now you don't have time to change your mind." She flung open the door and laughed.

Rowan was standing just outside with a roller suitcase and a huge grin. "I might have pilfered through your summer wardrobe after my delivery yesterday while you were power cleaning the café."

"Where'd you get the bag?" I asked, stepping around the desk and spinning the navy suitcase in a circle. It glided with ease across the industrial tiles on four unblemished wheels. It looked brand new and expensive.

"I ordered it when Aiden started planning the trip and was going to surprise you last night. You've had that cloth tote bag since our high school sleepover days. The seams are busted. Consider this an early birthday gift."

"I never go anywhere," I said. "And my birthday isn't until October."

Rowan shrugged.

I ran my fingers along the hard case but stopped when I saw my initials stamped on the side in gold letters.

"That's so you know it's yours if you ever have to check it," Rowan said, watching me closely. "But it's carry-on size, so you won't need to do that today. I can help you set a combination for the lock at the airport."

It was just a suitcase. If I told myself that enough, I might keep the tears from slipping down my cheeks. By the time I came to live with Grandpa, I'd lost count of the number of black garbage bags I'd used to move everything I owned from one foster home to the next or back to wherever Mom was living, only to put everything in another garbage bag a few months later and do it all again.

"Better open it and make sure I got everything you need," Rowan said softly. I glanced at her but looked away when I saw the sheen in her eyes. She knew. Somehow, without me saying a word, she understood what having something like this meant to me. I guarded my pre-Peace Falls childhood like a dog with a rotten bone. But time and time again, sweet, empathetic Rowan somehow guessed the rawest pieces of my past.

I tipped the bag gently on its side and opened it to find all the clothes I would have packed for a four-day trip to the tropics neatly folded in packing cubes in a way I'd never have managed, including my favorite gold sandals, a black bikini, and a book I'd wanted to read for months. I pulled out a toiletry bag that matched the suitcase and peeked inside. "Seriously?" I said, lifting out an impressive ribbon of condoms.

Rowan shrugged. "I know it's been a while. Maybe you'll meet a cute guy on the beach."

Cammie smirked. "Or you could go for another round with Aiden." Her eyes were a little red, which meant she'd caught on to the significance of the suitcase. Chances were, she'd moved everything she had in garbage bags a time or two herself. Not that we ever talked about it.

"Forget I ever told you about him," I said, shoving the condoms back in the bag and zipping the suitcase closed. A couple months ago, in a moment of extreme weakness, I'd blurted out to Rowan, Cammie, and Poppy that I'd had a one-night stand with Aiden. I hadn't told them it was the best sex of my life or that I still found him annoyingly attractive, despite his obnoxious personality. But ever since, they'd never missed an opportunity to suggest I revisit that mistake.

"Oh my word," Cammie said, laughing. "You and Aiden will be a default couple in St. John."

My stomach dropped. The original plan had been for Cammie and me to break off together whenever the couples wanted their alone time. I figured I'd have to put up with Aiden some, but now he was my travel partner by elimination. That alone was reason enough to stay behind.

"No," Rowan said, shaking her head. "You're going, Lauren. Either you walk to Aiden's truck or Theo and Cal carry you."

"I'm not riding with him. I'll drive myself, thank you." And be conveniently late for the flight.

Rowan put her hands on her hips. "Your car couldn't make it to Charlotte."

"Of course it would." Doubtful. But what better excuse for missing a flight than a broken-down car?

"Is the check engine light still flashing?" Cammie asked.

"Of course it is," Rowan said. "Don't worry. I told Chris to hide her keys where she'll never find them."

"That's evil," I said, but I couldn't help laughing. I loved how the Stevens siblings came together whenever one of them needed help. When

Rowan left her ex-husband, Poppy filled his apartment with poop that Chris collected from Cal's dog, Skye. Rowan and Chris almost shattered a sliding glass door to enact revenge on Theo when he broke Poppy's heart. They were fierce in their love for each other, and I never tired of seeing the Stevens Suicide Squad, as I called them, in action.

Rowan's phone vibrated in her hand. "They're here," she said with a face-splitting grin. "Come on, Lauren."

Cammie yanked me into a tight hug. "I've got everything covered here. Promise you'll relax and have a pina colada for me."

I nodded into her shoulder, my throat suddenly tight, and gave her an extra squeeze before stepping back and grabbing the handle of the first suitcase I'd ever owned.

Chapter Four

Aiden

I paced behind the truck, breathing into my cupped hands to warm my fingers. The sun wouldn't rise for another hour, and the March morning felt more like January than the cusp of spring. As much as I was looking forward to a long weekend in the tropics, my stomach bunched in knots. Part of it was guilt, but that I could manage. I'd figure out Cammie's dream vacation somehow and pay for it. Probably somewhere that didn't involve flying. When I called Cammie to apologize for being the dumbass who created this mess, she admitted she was relieved she had a good excuse not to fly. I believed her. I'd still be buying her a kick-ass vacation package. The knots in my gut were because any minute now, Lauren would be settling into my life for the next four days like a nasty virus.

Cal leaned casually against my truck while I wore a hole in the pavement. "You OK, A?"

Asshole knew I wasn't. He played wide receiver to my quarterback, and despite having the emotional intelligence of a gnat sometimes, he always knew when I was nervous before a game. Back then, he'd suggest some ridiculous prank to take my mind off the nerves, and we'd spend the pre-game minutes planning its execution. Half the time, we never enacted our idea. But the other half were some of my best memories from high school. Whether we were stealing the opposing team's mascot costume or setting off a stink bomb in their locker room, Logan and Theo always joined us, mostly to keep Cal and me from getting our asses kicked off the team or arrested.

"You want me to drive, so you can sit in the back?" he asked.

"You couldn't handle my truck."

"Bet I could handle it better than you could handle Lauren," he said with a smirk.

"Bet you don't want me cuddling with your fiancée." Cause no way in hell was I sitting next to Lauren if Cal doubled down on his dare.

That wiped the smirk from his face. Rowan might as well be one of my sisters at this point, which I figured he knew. Still, Cal and I loved a good competition and spent most of our twenties chasing the same women who were down for a good time and nothing more. If we ever compared lists, I'm sure we shared a few, but Cal has always been a gentleman.

"I get this is awkward for you," Cal said, placing his hand on my shoulder. "But can you please try to be civil with Lauren? For me."

"When have you ever known me to be civil?"

Cal shoved my shoulder. "You know what I mean. Try not to goad her."

"I'll do my best," I said, which could either be taken as a promise to leave her alone or take my jabs to the next level.

Karma's backdoor opened with an irritating creak and Rowan stepped out, dragging a suitcase behind her. Cal ran over and grabbed it before looping his arm in hers and helping her to the truck like she was made of glass. I'd have done the same. It was cold enough for black ice, and one fall would probably move up the spinal surgery she had scheduled after their wedding.

"Lauren's coming," Rowan said, smiling. "She's just grabbing a few things."

Cal looked relieved. The knot in my stomach tightened.

"Give me that," I said, motioning for the bag.

"Be careful with it," Rowan said as the back door creaked again.

"Princess Lauren doesn't want her suitcase scuffed?" Good thing I hadn't promised Cal I'd behave. Truth was, I enjoyed getting Lauren riled up, especially since I seemed to be the only person who could.

Rowan glared at me, which was kind of adorable and scary at the same time. With her red hair and small features, she looked like one of the fairies from my gram's stories, but I'd seen firsthand how feisty Rowan could be while defending someone she loved.

"She just knows you're an oaf," Lauren said behind me.

Rowan turned her glare toward her best friend while I carefully lifted the suitcase into the truck bed and secured it. "Good enough for you?" I asked, finally turning around to face her. And fuck me. Even at this hour, standing in a dirty alley under crummy street lighting, she looked radiant.

Her long brown hair was in the thick braid she always wore while working. It'd grown since the one time I wrapped it around my wrist and took her from behind. Her full lips were set in the frown she always aimed at me. Her usually warm eyes narrowed to steely slits like they always did whenever she looked my direction.

"Thanks," she said. "I'd have driven myself, but Rowan and Chris hid my keys."

"Sorry to hear it. Hope you don't mind the back seat."

She glanced at my truck, which was brand new, top of the line, and the largest on the market. I'd needed more seats to haul my guys to and from job sites, so Sam started driving my old truck, and I found a six-seater large enough to fit three full-grown men in the back. Yeah, it got dirty from time to time, but I'd had the entire cab detailed before the trip. She'd be more comfortable in my back seat than driving her piece-of-shit sedan.

"It's fine," she said, walking to the rear driver's-side door and climbing in. Of course, she'd chosen the seat where I couldn't see her unless I leaned into the middle to look in the rearview mirror.

"Your best sucks," Cal said, fighting a laugh. He put his arm around Rowan's waist and pulled her close for the walk to the rear passenger side.

I yanked a tarp over the entire truck bed and secured it while I took a few calming breaths. Lauren and I would ruin this trip for everyone if we didn't at least attempt to play nice. I needed to get a grip. We both did.

I climbed into the driver's seat and couldn't help smiling. Poppy and Theo were curled into each other on the front bench like a pair of emo kittens, fast asleep. I closed the door as softly as I could. Theo and Poppy were both night owls, and everyone would be better off if they got a few more hours of sleep on the way to the airport. I questioned whether Poppy would even remember climbing into the truck. I half expected her to jolt up at some point during the drive, confused why she and Theo weren't in bed.

Rowan and Lauren chatted quietly as I drove to the interstate, but once I merged onto the highway and hit seventy miles an hour, even their murmurs disappeared. There's a stillness to the blackest hour before dawn that I've always appreciated. Working construction, I'm often awake before sunrise, savoring the calm before another hectic day of pounding hammers and power tools. But the quiet today felt odd, heavy. It wasn't often I was surrounded by other people, yet completely alone.

Twenty minutes into the three-hour drive, after the sky had lightened behind the dark mountains, I glanced in the rearview mirror to check if anyone was still awake. Lauren glared at me.

"Eyes on the road," she said, loud enough for me to hear.

Poppy let out a disgruntled huff and burrowed closer to Theo. He tightened his inked arm around her, and she settled back to sleep.

"Try not to wake Hell Cat," I said, only slightly softer than Lauren had spoken. "I'm not in the mood to get scratched."

Lauren gripped my headrest and leaned close enough for her breath to caress my neck. "Stop calling her that."

I turned toward her voice, wishing there wasn't a seat between us, so I could bury my face in her hair and whisper in her ear. "Jealous I haven't given you a nickname?"

"You're a jerk," she said. "That name's offensive and Poppy is more sensitive than she lets on."

"You think I don't know that?" I asked, my voice far too loud.

Poppy let out another groan and flung a large straw hat over her face like it would protect her from noise.

Lauren stuck her arm through the space between my seat and the door and pulled herself closer. Too close. "You don't strike me as—"

"Sit back," I yelled. "Buckle your fucking seatbelt."

Theo shot awake, his breathing loud enough for me to hear. We both waited in tense silence until we heard the click of Lauren's belt.

"Never do that again," I yelled.

"I need to tinkle," Poppy said, breaking the tension that had settled like molasses inside the truck. "Mind pulling over, Stud Man?"

If I wasn't so pissed, I would have chuckled at the nickname she'd given me just this week when I hung a shelf at her bakery. Instead, I put on my signal and moved to the right lane to take the next exit.

As the truck slowed on the ramp, Poppy reached over and rubbed my arm. I loosened my death grip on the steering wheel and blew out a breath.

So I guess Theo had told Poppy everything about the accident. How I'd unbuckled my seatbelt and climbed into the front seat to show Cal something on my phone moments before Theo wrapped the car around a tree while trying to avoid a deer. How seconds before the crash, Logan had unbuckled his seatbelt to pull me back into my seat and buckled me in, saving my life and costing him his own. Logan was dead and Theo spent a year in prison because of my stupid mistake.

I wondered if Cal had told Rowan. If so, had she told her best friend or was Lauren fuming in the backseat, pissed that I'd yelled at her without understanding how terrified I'd been when I realized she wasn't buckled in. I decided she didn't know. Lauren didn't like me, but she'd never be carelessly cruel.

When we pulled into a gas station parking lot, Poppy twisted around and said, "Lauren, Rowan, you're coming with me."

Doors opened. Theo and Poppy slid out. The door behind me slammed shut.

"Shit," I said, resting my head on the steering wheel.

Theo walked around the front of the truck, opened my door, and motioned for me to get out.

"I'm fine," I said, sitting back in my seat.

"I'm not," he said. "I need to drive."

"Let him," Cal said from the back seat.

I glared at him. "You know I will." Because I'd show Theo, any chance I could, that I trusted him to drive me despite the accident that wrecked my shoulder and ended my football career.

I climbed from the driver's seat, and Theo pulled me into a one-armed hug. I pounded his back twice and crossed over to the passenger side. Cal launched into a conversation about the different hiking trails on St. John, and by the time Rowan, Poppy, and Lauren returned to the truck, most of the tension had left my body.

I stepped out for Poppy to slide into the middle, but before I could climb back in, Lauren grabbed my hand. I hadn't touched her since that night. Despite the years of venom between us, my chest ached when she curled her fingers around mine.

"I didn't know," she said in a voice so gentle I wanted to kiss the words from her lips.

I pulled my hand from hers and held it up. "We're good."

She nodded but looked so close to tears it took everything in me not to reach for her.

"Truce," I said, holding up my pinkie like we were third graders in a playground spat. "At least for the rest of the trip."

She stared at my pinkie a moment before finally aiming those kind eyes at me. "Truce," she said, twisting her slim finger with mine.

The truce lasted all the way to the airport and through the flight, where Lauren and I somehow ended up seated together and where she immediately fell asleep after takeoff and drifted onto my shoulder. I tortured myself with her ginger and coffee scent for a good hour before I eased her against the window and told my dick to calm down since no way in hell was I jacking it in a tiny plane bathroom to thoughts of a woman who hated me.

CHAPTER FIVE

Aiden

THE TRUCE ENDED LESS than ten minutes after we arrived at the villa.

"Why should I take the kiddie room?" Lauren asked, crossing her arms over her chest.

I wanted to tell her that the room suited her because she acted like a child. "You and Cammie were supposed to share. I figured you'd want your own beds."

To her credit, Lauren had backed me up when I'd suggested the couples take the two rooms with ocean views. The villa sat on the side of a mountain overlooking Cruz Bay. The two rooms at the back of the house faced a wall of vegetation. One had a double bed and the other had twin bunk beds. Unfortunately, they shared a bathroom.

"Well, Cammie's not here, and we all know whose fault that is. Besides, who made you king of the house?"

Me. When I forked over two-grand a night to rent it. Not that Lauren knew that little detail. I'd told everyone it cost that much for three nights, which split three ways, since no one thought Cal and Rowan should pay for their room, came out to a devilish $666.66 per room, which Lauren and Cammie had planned to split between them.

"I'm six-one. It makes sense I'd take the double bed. I'd bump my head whether I slept in the top or bottom bunk, assuming I could even fit."

"Trust me, I've slept in enough bunk beds to know I'll whap my head just as much as you would. I'm not fun size like Poppy and Rowan."

"I've got a good seven inches on you."

"Five at best," she said, letting her eyes roam to my shorts and back up again.

I took a step closer and leaned down until our eyes were level. "Feel free to measure anytime, Princess. You're welcome to share that double bed with me."

"Don't call me Princess. What is it with you and nicknames?"

I shrugged. "You seemed pissed I'd given Poppy one and not you. You're welcome, by the way. I could think of a lot less flattering things to call you."

Lauren waved her hands toward herself in the universal motion for bring it on. "Go ahead. I'm sure nothing you could come up with would sting."

Of course she'd think that. But I grew up with three sisters. Three older sisters. My verbal barbs were fine-tuned and sharpened to slice. I tapped my chin like I was trying to unravel string theory or compose the next great American novel. "My favorite is SPAM."

Lauren tilted her head. She always did that whenever something confused her. I hated myself for knowing that, and I hated her for looking so fucking adorable every time she did it.

"Like junk mail?"

"Like canned ham. Might be tasty, but full of unhealthy crap. Highly processed, low nutritional value piece of meat. Though calling it meat is generous."

"You think I'm fake?" she asked, her eyes widening.

"It's made of ham," I said back pedaling.

"But you think I'm fake?" she asked again. "And just a piece of meat?"

I wish. I wouldn't be this hung up if my attraction to her was purely physical. I thought she was SPAM. Something I craved on the regular, but knew wasn't good for me. "No. Not really."

"No or not really?" she asked, her voice rising with each word.

"Hey," I said, taking an involuntary step toward her. Shit, I was trying to be funny. I lived to irritate her, but I never wanted to hurt her feelings. "Why do you care what a dumbass like me thinks?"

"I don't," she yelled. But the tears forming in her eyes suggested otherwise.

"Everything OK?" Rowan asked, sticking her head into the hallway from the primary suite.

"All good," I said, walking past Lauren into the room with the bunk beds. When I turned, she was still standing in the hallway with her back to me. I closed the door and leaned my forehead against it replaying our conversation. Had I really called her a piece of meat? Fuck, I had. I wanted to punch myself in the face. Who said that to a woman? Me, apparently, to the girl of my dreams.

A moment later, someone beat on the door, which sounded fantastic with my face pressed against it. I braced myself for a well-deserved round two with Lauren, but instead, Poppy shoved her way into the room, almost knocking me on my ass, and shut the door behind her. She had on the ridiculous hat she'd been carrying around all day and enough sunscreen to cover an elephant, which I guess was necessary since her hair was as red as Rowan's beneath the black dye.

"How much did this place really cost?" she asked, putting her hands on her hips.

"The girls look great in that suit," I said, pointing to her chest. "Even with all that white crap." OK, so ours was kind of a weird friendship. I looked after her like she was one of my sisters and ribbed her like one as well. And since we weren't actually related, I considered her smoking body free fodder.

"Cut the crap, Stud Man."

"Two thousand, like I said."

"No way in—" Her green eyes doubled in size. "Crap on a cracker," she mumbled. "It's two thousand a night, isn't it?"

I pretended I didn't hear her.

"Aiden."

I didn't like how she'd said my name. Hell Cat was a force of nature who stomped through bullshit with her combat boots and sass, but she was most dangerous when she pulled in her claws.

And she knew my soft underbelly. I had so many medical expenses after the accident, my parents had no choice but to sue Cal's and Theo's parents. Just their insurance companies, not them personally. Even so, friends shouldn't sue each other. Theo's parents bailed on him right after the case settled and moved back to Greece. Cal's parents never discussed the suit with me until I tried to pay them back, so there's a good chance they didn't mention it to Cal either. As far as I knew, neither of my friends were aware that I'd built my career on money I'd taken from their parents. After paying the bills, mine handed me the rest of the settlement to start my construction company. I'd taken that $50,000 and doubled it, then doubled that, and so on until I had a multi-million-dollar operation. Even with all that, Cal's parents tore up the check I wrote them. I figured Theo's parents owed him, but I couldn't exactly hand over a stack of cash to him without an explanation. Which meant I either fessed up to the lawsuit or paid Cal and Theo back whenever I could, usually without them knowing. Like upgrading plane tickets "with points" and finding an "excellent last-minute deal" on a vacation villa.

"Have you seen this place? No way anyone would believe this is five hundred a night."

"Honestly, I haven't seen much of it. I've been fighting with Lauren over bedrooms."

Poppy glanced at the bunk beds and the dancing seahorse wallpaper and smiled. "Guess she won."

"This round," I said and winked at her.

"I'm serious, Aiden. There's no way the others will buy it."

I shrugged. "They've never noticed before. I've covered way more than my share of stuff in the past. Nights out. Things like that."

"Like buying the building for our bakery, remodeling it for free, and charging way less rent than you should?"

"Exactly." I kind of regretted that one since Poppy figured it out and confronted me. Though it was kind of nice that someone knew I wasn't always a selfish prick. "But you paid for materials."

"Maybe the things we shopped for with you, like the sink, but don't pretend you charged us for all the drywall and other stuff you used."

"Rowan said I could have free baked goods for life. We're even. And for the record, Cal never suspected a thing."

"Cal's clueless, but are you sure Theo hasn't caught on? You bought him a house."

"I'm renting Theo a house."

"For the price of a storage unit."

I shrugged. "I'm the reason he went to jail. I'd owe him whether or not I sued his parents."

Poppy bit her bottom lip and tiny creases formed on her forehead. "I don't like keeping this from him," she said, quietly. "It feels dishonest."

The knots in my stomach pulled taunt. Based on the pain in my gut, I either needed food ASAP or an antacid. "His parents left him right after the lawsuit, Hell Cat. He'd never forgive me if he knew."

Poppy's eyes hardened. "He'd never blame you. His parents left because they suck. Period. Fuck them. Or at least his dad. His mom might be coming around, but I'm holding judgment until after I meet her. Honestly, Aiden, Theo probably knows. I'm sure the lawyers had to interview witnesses, and he was the driver."

"Shit," I said. I wished I could sit on the bed without knocking my skull. I settled for leaning against the wooden bunk frame.

"You OK? You're really pale."

"You're right," I said, my chest aching. "I never read through the suit, but he'd have to know."

"Just talk to talk to him," Poppy said, gripping my arm. "Please."

That was a hard no. The last thing this trip needed was more drama on top of the tension between Lauren and me. "Come on," I said, wrapping my arm around Poppy's slim shoulders. "Show me what 2K a night gets us."

She let out a sigh but walked with me to the main room where Cal and Rowan were already snuggled together on the plush sofa.

"The kitchen is insane," Rowan said. "We should grab groceries today. I can't wait to get in there."

"Not until breakfast," Poppy said. "You deserve at least one day out of the kitchen. Plus, if we don't get lunch or dinner or whatever you want to call it soon, I'll have to dig into my emergency beef jerky, and that will leave me at risk for being hangry at some point on this trip."

"I'm all for going somewhere to eat," I said. "Give me the abbreviated tour, Hell Cat."

I knew from the online photos that the couples' rooms had king-sized beds and top-of-the-line bathrooms, so I skipped those and headed for the sliding door leading to the deck.

"Definitely worth $2K," I said, admiring the view of the ocean and the town below.

The grief hit me like a rogue wave. One minute I was enjoying the paradise before my eyes, the next I was reminded of all the views I'd seen with Logan when we hiked the Bay Reef Trail back in high school.

"Walk to the edge and take a peek at the pool," Poppy said, hopping beside me and bringing me back to the present. I'd never seen her so peppy. That alone was worth the price tag.

I walked to the plexiglass wall surrounding the deck and looked over. A story below, an infinity pool stretched off the side of the mountain, the water the same stunning turquoise as the Caribbean.

"It's incredible," Lauren said, stepping out from under the deck and walking around the pool to the stairs that led up to us. The sight of her in a short yellow dress, her brown hair cascading freely down her back, made me grip the railing. I wanted to scoop her off her feet and show her exactly how we could share that double bed.

Poppy chuckled. "Close your mouth, Stud Man."

Theo let out a whistle at the view and joined us on the deck at the same time Lauren did. "Great job finding this place, man," he said, slapping me on the back. "It's a steal."

Poppy glared at me. "An unbelievable deal."

I cleared my throat. "Let's grab some food before Poppy gets hangry."

"Oh, what level are we at?" Lauren asked. "I have a granola bar in my purse, but I'm saving it for a level three or higher." She started digging into the faded tote bag she'd kept at her feet on the plane. Of course, she'd packed an emergency snack for Poppy. As if I needed more proof of how thoughtful she was with everyone but me.

"I'll be good if we leave now," Poppy said. She looped her arm through Theo's, and they headed for the sliding glass door.

Lauren started after them, but I laid my hand on her arm. Her smooth skin had already soaked up some heat from the sun. She shrugged off my hand and kept walking.

"Hey, can we try that truce again?" I called after her.

"Depends," she said, without stopping or turning to face me. "Can you try not to be an asshole?"

"I'll do my best," I shouted. And this time, I meant it.

CHAPTER SIX

Lauren

SINCE I'M PROGRAMMED TO wake early, I'd snuck into the kitchen before dawn, brewed a cup of coffee in the fancy machine on the counter, and settled in a chair on the deck. The sky over our slice of paradise lit with gorgeous oranges and pinks as the sun rose on the other side of the island.

The sliding glass door opened behind me and I groaned. Rowan was an early riser, but only one other person in the house kept the same insane hours as me.

"Sunset will be incredible," Aiden said, pulling out the chair beside me. He had his own mug of coffee, which he took with a little bit of cream, no sugar. I knew because he pestered me at Karma at least three times a week. His blue eyes were already alert pre-caffeine, but his dark blonde hair with that fresh-from-bed tussled look made my stomach dip.

Stop it, Lauren. He called you SPAM. I'll admit, I'm not the saint people believe I am. Far from it. Don't get me wrong, I'm not a serial killer or anything. It just takes a lot of effort to be the person everyone likes. Well, almost everyone. Before I came to Peace Falls, I'd lied, stolen, and fought my way through most of my childhood. I'm not proud of the things I did, which was why I worked so hard to be a good person now. But sometimes,

I worried my kindness might be more about earning good karma than actually being kind. Aiden's nickname hit a little too close to the voice in my head that called me fake.

"What would you like to do today?" he asked.

Two sentences without an ounce of snark. Maybe he was really trying to keep the truce, which meant I needed to at least treat him like an annoying customer. "I'll do whatever Rowan and Cal want. It's their trip."

"So, the Reef Bay Trail before lunch."

"Um, is that what they want to do?"

Everyone in our group, except Cammie and me, enjoyed hiking. I'd already researched all the island's trails and figured out which ones I could reasonably do without holding everyone back. The Reef Bay Trail was a strenuous five-mile hike across the island, which was about four miles beyond my comfort level, maybe less depending on how outdoorsy people defined "strenuous." Cammie was supposed to be my lounging companion while the others tackled that trail. We'd planned to lie out by the pool and meet up with everyone else after.

"I think that's the plan," Aiden said. He placed his mug on the glass-top table beside us and stretched his muscled arms over his head. His green t-shirt rode up, showing a peek of his abs. My stomach bottomed out and my breath caught. His abs were by far the most defined of any man I'd been with. I remember running my tongue over the crests and valleys that spanned from his ribs to the deep-cut v at his hips. I buried my face in my coffee mug to hide the rush of heat to my cheeks. I'd say he was putting on a show for me, but his eyes remained glued to the view, and he lowered his arms after a brief stretch.

We'd spent our first afternoon on the island feeding Poppy at a harbor-side restaurant and exploring Cruz Bay. Then we'd rented snorkel gear and gone grocery shopping at the local market. We'd missed the sunset entirely, pulling into the villa's parking area at dusk. I knew we'd have to cram in as much fun as possible before catching the ferry back Sunday afternoon for our evening flight. I just didn't think we'd start out with the toughest trail on the island.

I sipped my coffee while trying to think of a decent excuse for skipping the hike other than being a liability. "What's the plan this afternoon?"

"Snorkeling at Trunk Bay."

That sounded more like it, even if I'd never been snorkeling before. Unlike Cammie, at least I knew how to swim, but the only other vacation I'd ever taken had been a trip to Washington, D.C., to visit Rowan when she lived there.

"Then I guess we'll come back here so the couples can ditch us again," he said before taking another sip of his coffee.

I couldn't help but laugh. The couples had retired ridiculously early. Rather than stare at Aiden all night, I'd curled up in my double-sized bed and attempted to read while he took the world's longest shower. And sang. I hated to admit it, but his shower singing wasn't terrible. I'd pressed my ear against the wall when I realized he wasn't singing in English or to any tune I'd heard before. Goosebumps rose on my arms as his voice wrapped around me.

"What language were you singing last night?"

He glanced at me and his cheeks reddened. "You heard me?"

"Of course I heard you. The shower is right next to my bed."

"Sorry. I'll try not to do it again."

"No need to apologize. It's not like you sounded bad. I was just curious because I'd never heard the songs before, and it didn't sound like English."

"It wasn't," he said, pulling on his neck. His biceps tightened and so did my stupid vagina. "My gram taught us a bunch of songs in Gaelic. Honestly, I don't know what I'm singing. I never picked up the language like my sisters did."

I tore my eyes from his bulging muscles to his face, which didn't help cool me down. Those slicing eyes cut straight to my core. "Probably because they practiced more. I bet they used it whenever they didn't want their baby brother listening in."

He smiled at me and my stomach flipped. Aiden O'Malley hadn't flashed that panty-melting grin in my direction in years. The best I'd gotten were cocky smirks that didn't reach his eyes.

"Probably," he said. "It's OK though. All my nieces and nephews are learning Spanish in school. Pretty soon, we'll be able to have full conversations my sisters won't understand. I intend to take full advantage."

The smile slipped from his face, and he cleared his throat as if remembering he was talking to me and not someone he liked.

We went back to admiring the view, but a few minutes later, he spoke again. "I'm sorry about Wyatt. I really needed someone who could communicate with everyone."

"Same," I said, glaring.

He shrugged. "Have him write down the menu in Spanish and English. Problem solved."

Typical Aiden. Karma was more than a coffee shop. Wyatt helped people who came in to use the career center or who needed help filling out school registration forms. Word had gotten around Peace Falls that he was a patient translator and that I didn't mind when he stepped away from the counter to help someone. Many people relied on their bilingual children to get by, but sometimes they needed help with things their kids were too young to comprehend, like legal documents or medical forms. I opened my mouth to tear into him when Rowan pushed open the sliding door.

"The cinnamon rolls and bacon are in the oven. Breakfast should be ready in twenty minutes." Aiden got up from his seat facing the view and motioned for her to take it before pulling a chair to the other side of mine and sitting so close I could smell his woodsy cologne.

"How much damage do you think Hell Cat would inflict if I pinched her?" he asked.

"Why would you pinch Poppy?" I asked.

Rowan flinched at the tone of my voice, and I took another gulp of coffee to keep from saying anything else to Aiden.

He shrugged like I hadn't just screeched at him. "I figure she won't wear green today."

"That's right," Rowan said. "I forgot it's St. Patrick's Day."

I glanced down at my blue pajama set and shot him a daring look. "You should keep your hands off anyone who doesn't invite you to touch them."

Aiden narrowed his eyes and opened his mouth, then seemed to think better of it and nodded.

Damn, he really was sticking with the truce. "What time are we leaving for the trail?" I asked.

Rowan laughed so hard she snorted.

"What?" I asked.

She shook her head. "I love you, Lauren, so don't take this the wrong way, but I really hope you'll do something else this morning. Go to a beach or just lie by the pool. We both know you'd hate every minute of the hike."

"Are you sure? This trip is supposed to be about you and Cal."

"And you can spend all afternoon snorkeling with us."

Thank you, universe. "Sounds great," I said. "Text me when you're done, and I'll pack a cooler for the beach."

"Or me," Aiden said, rolling his mug in his hands. "I did that hike the first time I was here. I wouldn't mind taking it easy this morning."

"You seemed eager enough a few minutes ago," I said.

He glared at me. "I'd have struggled through it, same as you."

"I highly doubt that," I huffed. "Don't you hike all the time?"

Rowan dug her nails into my arm but kept her eyes on Aiden. "You came to the island with Logan, right?"

He nodded. "I tagged along on his family's vacation our sophomore year. We liked it so much, we wanted to come back with Theo and Cal."

Rowan relaxed her fingers, and I silently thanked her for stopping me from putting my foot in my mouth again.

"Well, that makes this trip even more special," she said with a kind smile.

He nodded.

"We better make sure the cinnamon rolls aren't burning," I said, shooting from my chair. Rowan winced as she rose from hers and followed me. I glanced at Aiden as I slid the door closed. He'd left his mug on the table and had walked to the plexiglass wall where he stood staring out at the view, gripping the railing.

"Thanks for saving me out there," I said once Rowan and I were in the kitchen. "But a little heads-up that this trip was a gigantic grief trigger would have been helpful."

Rowan peeked into the oven and closed the door softly. "Cal told me last night after we went to bed. I know you and Aiden don't get along but try to keep in mind that being here might be hard for him."

"I will." I watched her straighten with a grimace and frowned. "Are you sure you can handle that hike?"

Rowan gave a little shrug. "Walking isn't that painful. And other than snorkeling, the Reef Trail was top of my list of things to do."

"I wouldn't be sad if you stayed behind and acted as a buffer between me and Aiden."

Rowan chuckled and shook her head. "I'm sure you can manage half a day together. Just give him a little grace."

And I did. Aiden and I were polite to each other throughout breakfast. We even worked together to help the couples pack up for the hike. But the moment I stepped onto the pool deck in my bikini, Aiden tested my patience.

I'd hoped he'd walk into town or just wander the vegetation so I could be alone, but of course he'd stretched out on a lounge chair by the pool while I changed into my swimsuit.

"Hope you brought something with more coverage than that," he said, flicking his eyes over me. "The sun's brutal here. I'd hate for you to burn your tits or ass."

Not that it was any of his business, but I had a rash guard to wear when we went snorkeling that would cover my back, shoulders, and arms. My bikini bottoms were cut a little high, but it wasn't like I was wearing a thong. "Why don't you let me worry about my own skin and focus on yours. You're so pale I can see your veins from here."

"That's it," he said, rising from his lounger and stomping upstairs. Good. If I'd had known calling him pale would piss him off that much, I'd have done it sooner. I'd just gotten comfortable in the lounger he left behind when he returned with a bottle of whiskey and two shot glasses.

"OK, Princess," he said, pouring a shot and handing it to me. "I was saving this for later tonight when we could all celebrate St. Patrick's Day together, but I figure we have a good four or five hours to kill without murdering each other. Every time you or I say something mean, we take a shot."

"You sure you're up for alcohol poisoning on this trip?" I threw back the shot. At least it wasn't crappy whiskey. The liquid rolled down my throat like warm silk. "Cause my tolerance for liquor is a lot higher than my tolerance for you." I held out my glass for a refill.

He watched me take a second shot and then threw back two of his own. "Bring it, Princess."

Three more insults and shots later, we decided to cool off in the pool, which really meant splashing each other like a pair of kids.

"Hope you wore waterproof sunscreen, so your pasty shoulders don't fry," I said when he was good and soaked. Aiden wrapped his thick arms around my waist and tossed me into the deep end. I came up sputtering and pissed.

He laughed as I lunged toward him. "You have zero chance of knocking me off my feet, Princess."

"Want to bet?" I said, wading close enough my breasts brushed against his hard chest. The warmth of his skin seeped through my thin bikini top, making my nipples peak and an ache form low in my belly.

His eyes filled with heat and something far more dangerous. "Lauren," he said, brushing a clump of wet hair from my face. He stared at my lips as his rough fingers traced a line down my face.

I panicked and stepped back.

He turned before I could see his reaction and waded to the edge of the infinity pool. My breath came in rapid bursts. I tried to get my body under control, but once the panic dissipated, I was left so turned on I could barely stand. Aiden wasn't a random match on a dating app. I couldn't just sleep with him because I was horny. Could I? The muscles in his shoulders and arms tensed as he gripped the plastic wall. Damn, he looked incredible. I wanted to feel the weight of him above me, which wasn't something I typically liked during sex.

Maybe we could sleep together again. As long as I was clear it didn't mean anything, we could have a little fun, and no one would get hurt. I ignored the part of my brain that wanted to unpack why I'd panicked in the first place.

Maybe releasing the sexual tension between us would make it easier to keep the truce for the rest of the trip. I found myself leaving the shallow end and making my way to him.

"I don't want a boyfriend," I said swimming up beside him.

He nodded, not taking his eyes from the harbor below.

"But I can have fun, if you can. Just this morning."

He faced me and smirked. "You want to scratch an itch."

I rolled my eyes. What the hell was I thinking even suggesting we let off steam together? "That has to be the least sexy way to describe it."

He gripped my hips, his thumbs making lazy circles near the elastic band of my bikini bottom. "Well," he said, raising an eyebrow.

I placed a chaste kiss on his lips. He groaned and pulled me against his hard length. "Yes or no, Princess?"

In that moment, nothing felt more important than quieting the ache between my thighs. I wrapped my legs around him and kissed him hard. His rough hand slid into my bottoms and found my throbbing clit. I threw my head back with a gasp. "Not here," I said, panting. The last thing I wanted was our friends coming back early and finding us banging it out in the pool.

"Lead the way," he said, taking his hands from me.

The longing I felt when he withdrew his touch was almost enough for me to forget why I'd wanted privacy. I swam as fast as I could to the ladder with Aiden right behind me. As soon as we climbed onto the pool deck, we ran. Without stopping to dry off, we dripped water down the villa's tiled hallway. I shucked my bikini as soon as we got to my room. Aiden yanked down his swim trunks, freeing his thick cock. The next moment, we were on the bed, moving frantically together.

Sex with him was even better than I remembered. He filled me with each thrust, his hands and mouth finding every spot on my skin that drove me wild. Pleasure coiled tighter and tighter until my orgasm thundered through me. Aiden let out a roar and swelled inside me moments later. We collapsed on the mattress together, our bodies still joined.

The sound of a car door woke me. My head throbbed as I opened my eyes and found Aiden O'Malley in my bed, holding me. Everything that had happened came rushing back, the drinks, the pool—the sex. What the hell had I done? I wished I had time to freak out, but the front door slammed shut and voices filled the main area of the house.

"Wake up," I hissed, jabbing his toned stomach with my finger. He let out a groan and squeezed my boob. Why did his hands have to feel so good? Warm, with just the right amount of roughness to ignite a longing so deep and strong it took my breath away. I jabbed him again and he pulled me close, so close I could feel his erection against my stomach.

I shoved him again. "Get up." His eyes opened slowly and for a moment, he looked happy to see me. Then his eyes widened, and I watched him realize where he was and what we'd done

"You need to leave before anyone sees you," I said, shoving him toward the side of the bed. "Go through the bathroom. Move it."

"Wow, you're getting rid of me even faster than last time," he said, throwing back the covers and standing without an ounce of shame.

"This didn't happen," I said, closing my eyes. "Don't talk about it. Don't even think about it."

"Got it, Princess. We scratched an itch. I can be cool about it if you can."

"Get out before someone sees you," I said without opening my eyes. As if none of this would be real if I didn't see him gloriously naked and hard.

He let out a huff and slammed the bathroom door closed. Moments later, the shower turned on, and I fought back tears while he washed himself clean of me.

Chapter Seven

Aiden

Usually I can hold my liquor, but Lauren and I had tossed barbs and shots at lightning speed. When I finally made my way to the main room after a failed attempt to sober up with a cold shower, I had to focus to walk in a semi-straight line.

"How much did you two drink?" Cal asked with a laugh when he saw me.

Lauren sat at the kitchen table wearing a pair of oversized sunglasses and a frown. "Too much," she said. She'd thrown on a pale blue coverup over her still-wet bikini, making the fabric cling to her every curve.

Rowan worried her bottom lip with her teeth, her gaze ping ponging from me to Lauren. "You sure y'all are up to snorkel?"

"Yes," we said at the same time.

As if to prove her point, Lauren pushed back from the table and shuffled to the door. I followed, hoping to grab a moment to talk before everyone else joined us, but the couples were right behind me, loaded down with snorkel gear, beach towels, and a cooler. Clearly, everyone had been waiting on my ass.

Lauren climbed into the front passenger seat—the one place in the entire vehicle I had zero chance of sitting beside her since we both knew I wouldn't be getting behind the wheel in my current state.

I was relieved when Poppy and Rowan crawled into the third row together, since a booze-filled gut and winding mountain roads did not make a winning combination. Theo climbed into the driver's seat, and I sat behind him while Cal finished loading up the trunk. The good doc tossed me a bottle of water when he buckled into the seat beside me, and I dutifully drank.

Lauren stared straight ahead through the windshield the entire drive to the beach. Maybe she needed water too. I should have offered her some of mine before I chugged it down, but knowing Cal, he'd already pushed her to hydrate before I dragged myself from the shower.

"Good job not hurling in the car, Stud Man," Poppy said as we headed toward the sand with all our gear.

"Please don't talk about hurling," I said as my stomach twisted.

She laughed. "Serves you right for starting the party without us."

"Trust me," Lauren said. "It wasn't a party worth attending."

I let the couples get a few feet ahead of us before I leaned toward her and said, "Based on the sounds you made when I was buried inside you, I'd say you found it worthwhile."

She stopped abruptly, yanked off her sunglasses, and glared at me. "What are you talking about? Nothing happened."

She sounded so convincing I started to question if she remembered. Shit, how drunk was she? We both passed out after, but I thought she was sober enough to know what was happening. Parts of what we'd done in her room were fuzzy, but I had a crystal-clear memory of asking for her consent and the kiss she laid on me.

"Lauren," I started. "I'm sorry, we—"

"Won't ever bring this up again," she said. "Because nothing happened." She must have caught a glimpse of the worry on my face because she cleared her throat and added, "That we need to talk about. Ever."

With that she shoved her sunglasses on her face and double timed it to where Theo and Cal were setting up chairs in the sand. She chatted with Poppy and Rowan about their hike, ignoring any attempt I made to get her attention. Her obvious desire to forget I existed zapped most of my lingering buzz. By the time we'd sorted our snorkel gear, my hangover loomed, but I entered the crystal-clear water with the group. Thankfully, I'd been snorkeling in the Bahamas with my family since Logan died, so while familiar, being back in Trunk Bay with a tube in my mouth and flippers on my feet didn't punch me with grief.

I let the others swim ahead toward the underwater snorkel trail. Watching them point out things to each other brought a smile to my face. A fish swam right up to Poppy, and she let out a yelp I could hear underwater before remembering she was badass. She kept completely still, and we all watched the fish swim circles around her until it dove deeper than we could go without flooding our breathing tubes. As if we'd planned it, we all surfaced after reading the trail's first underwater marker.

"Oh, my word," Rowan squealed as she treaded water. "It's like swimming in an aquarium."

"Incredible, wasn't it," I said staring at Lauren. Because damn, it was. Holding her in my arms, tasting her, brought back every moment of the night we shared before. Only this time was better, the passion between us having boiled beneath the surface like a volcano waiting to erupt. Sex that intense required both people to be into it. I'd heard her loud and clear when she said she didn't want a relationship, but to pretend nothing had happened was bullshit. It also stung more than I cared to admit.

Poppy, Theo, and Cal talked over each other to agree with me, even though I wasn't talking about the fish. Without a word, Lauren pulled her mask over her eyes, lowered her face into the water, and swam away.

CHAPTER EIGHT

Aiden

"THAT'S ENOUGH, KIDS," MY oldest sister Kayleigh shouted to the nine kiddos attempting to tackle me to the ground. "We get to play with Uncle Aiden now."

A chorus of whines filled my parents' backyard. My oldest niece, Aubrey, put her hands on her hips. "He likes playing with us more."

Kayleigh shot her the mom look, a masterful copy of the one our mother used to keep us in check, the one that made my balls shrivel and still did on occasion.

"Sorry, Mama," Aubrey mumbled.

Kayleigh retreated indoors, and I crouched down to get as close to eye level to as many kids as possible. "Aubrey's right, I'd much rather be out here with y'all, but they're my sisters and it'd be mean not to spend a little time with them. They'll get tired of me soon enough, and we can play four square."

That perked everyone up. They headed as a group toward the driveway, where my parents and two of my brothers-in-law were talking with Logan's mom and dad. As usual, Kayleigh's worthless husband had some excuse not to be here. I heard Aubrey yell for sidewalk chalk as I walked inside the house and made a mental note to take her and her siblings out for ice cream later this week since their dad couldn't be bothered to spend time with his kids.

"Here you go, baby brother," Kayleigh said, handing me an ice-cold IPA as soon as I entered the living room. "Figured you'd need this."

I took a seat next to her on the couch and twisted the top off the bottle. The dark circles under Kayleigh's eyes had deepened since I last saw her, but I knew better than to bring it up in front of everyone since she'd just brush it off.

My youngest older sister, Fiona, sat in Dad's duct-taped leather recliner with her feet up, rubbing her pregnant belly. A couple Christmases ago, my sisters and I bought him a new chair, but he insisted it wasn't as comfortable as the one he had and made us take it back.

"Y'all are mean," Fiona said. "You know that's my favorite beer."

My middle older sister, Ciara, plopped down beside me with her own bottle. "So stop getting pregnant," she said, taking a swig.

"Says the woman with four kids," Kayleigh laughed.

"You don't even like beer, Ci," Fiona said.

Ciara shrugged. "Talk to me when you have four kids. Mom and Dad are watching mine tonight, so Mark and I can finally have time for ourselves. To Logan."

We held up our drinks, even Fiona, who had a tall glass of strawberry milk garnished with a pretzel rod. Between my three sisters, I'd lived through nine, almost ten, full-term pregnancies. I knew better than to ask.

"So tell us about St. John," Kayleigh said. "We need all the details of your glorious vacation to the tropics while we froze our butts off here."

Logan's sister Everly flung open the front door without knocking. "Are you telling them about your trip? Maddie and I want to hear about it too."

Sundays were my favorite day of the week for this very reason. All my sisters and Logan's together, just like when we were kids. Seeing them always made me miss him, but I liked to think he'd have wanted us to keep acting like one big family. Plus, I didn't really have a choice since our parents still lived next door to each other and both demanded Sunday family fun days. Last week's trip to St. John was one of the few times I'd ever missed our weekly gathering.

"Did you hike the Reef Bay Trail again?" Maddie asked, running through the open door and pulling it closed before plopping onto the floor by her sister. They were both long-limbed like Logan and had his warm brown eyes.

You'd never guess seeing them sprawled on my parent's ancient beige carpet that Everly was a kick-ass lawyer on track to make partner before she was thirty or that Maddie had taken up Logan's dream of becoming a pediatric oncologist and was almost through her second year of medical school.

"Was that the one that went across the island?" Everly asked.

I didn't want to think about the day the others hiked the Reef Bay Trail. Waking up with Lauren in my arms felt like a dream that morphed into an episode of the Twilight Zone.

Lauren had meant it when she said it never happened. For the past week, she'd pretended like nothing did. Still, my days since were filled with thoughts of touching her, of her touching me, and one memory of sinking into her wet heat that made me harder than steel if I thought about it too long.

"What happened?" Ciara asked.

They were all staring at me with concern. I didn't want to tell them about Lauren, but these women were relentless. Three of them had mom radar and the other two shared the protective instincts that had made Logan such a great offensive guard. They wouldn't rest until I explained why I looked like someone had crapped in my cereal every morning this week. I went with part of the truth.

"Honestly, I stayed back and got trashed while they did the trail. I underestimated how much it'd hurt being there without Logan." And fuck did it hurt.

I should have lied and said I got food poisoning or something since now they were all emotional, especially Fiona, who let out an audible sob and then chugged the rest of her strawberry milk.

Sometimes I wondered if I set off my sisters and Logan's because I found it impossible to cry myself. Despite missing him so much it hurt to breathe, I'd only cried twice since we lost him. The first when I woke up in the hospital and learned he'd died and the second at his funeral. I came close on the ten-year anniversary of the accident. Cal and Theo blubbered all the time, especially now that they were both loved up, but my primary emotion had always been anger.

When Everly came up with the idea to build a tree house in the old oak by the barn to honor Logan, just like the one where we'd spent countless hours of our childhood, I'd had to leave her in the field with Cal and Theo, so I could take a hammer to my living room wall. I'd been pissed he wasn't there. Just like I'm pissed Logan wasn't here to rib me about Lauren. I wanted to take a sledgehammer to the bathroom I was halfway through remodeling instead of waiting until I'd finished it. I know Logan wouldn't want my anger any more than he'd want our sisters crying over him a decade later, but sometimes it felt good knowing I wasn't the only one still mourning him.

Kayleigh and Ciara wrapped me in a sister sandwich while Everly and Maddie wiped their eyes. I let their hug ease the anger enough to save my bathroom, then patted their arms. They let me go, but Ciara rested her head on my shoulder.

Everly took a deep breath and blew it out. She'd always gotten herself under control the fastest. "He'd have loved that you took Cal and Theo there. He always said he wanted to go back with them. And you, of course."

"Did you enjoy the trip at all?" Fiona asked, not even bothering to wipe the tears from her face.

"I could have done without snorkeling half drunk. I almost threw up on a parrot fish. Zero out of ten. Do not recommend."

Kayleigh chuckled and the mood in the room lightened slightly.

"The rest of the trips was great." Other than Lauren avoiding me. "We hit every beach on the North Shore." Lauren put on her snorkel mask and dunked her head in the water every time I tried to talk to her. "Hiked a few other trails." Without Lauren. "And enjoyed the villa, which was awesome." Except for all the times I had to listen to Lauren shower and try not to picture her naked. "Rowan cooked amazing dinners, and we ate on the deck watching the sunset over the water." Lauren seated as far from me as possible.

Ciara lifted her head from my shoulder and narrowed her eyes. "Y'all made Rowan cook on her bachelorette trip?"

"She wanted to, and we all pitched in to help."

"Sure you did," Kayleigh said. "Eating a third helping so she wouldn't have leftovers to enjoy the next day isn't helping, Aiden."

"I only do that to you," I said. "It's not like you'd ever have enough leftovers to feed all your kids."

"He's got a point there," Maddie said, smiling. She'd moved over to sit on the arm of Dad's recliner and was rubbing Fiona's shoulder. Maddie glanced at the soggy pretzel rod in Fi's glass and shot me a look. I shook my head. She took the glass from Fiona and set it on the floor without questioning why my sister had landed on such an odd combination.

"He should be making all of us dinner for giving him so many nieces and nephews," Ciara said. She jabbed me in the side, and I jabbed her back.

"I'll buy you dinner anytime. Just name when and where."

"OK," she said, with a smile that made me a little nervous. "Next weekend. Your house."

"I said I'd buy dinner."

Kayleigh shook her head. "You buying us dinner would be like me handing you a bagel and calling it a gourmet meal."

"Bagels are great," I said, trying not to squirm. "I promise I'll have everyone over once I finish the remodel." Which, at the rate I tore through kitchens and bathrooms, would be about when I had to move into an old folks home.

"So none of you have been inside either?" Everly asked. "Good to know he wasn't just excluding Maddie and me."

I glared at her. "You're as much family as they are."

"I know," Everly said, smiling. "I'm just doing my younger sister duty and annoying you."

My nephew Bryant opened the front door and toddled in.

"What do you need, baby?" Fiona asked, swiping the tears from her face. Bryant pointed at me.

"Oh, look at them sending in the youngest to get what they want," Kayleigh said, laughing. "Even I can't say no to Bryant."

"Duty calls," I said, swooping Bryant up and plopping him on my shoulders.

"Send us pictures of the trip in the group chat," Ciara called after me.

I bounced up and down, and Bryant let out a happy squeal. "Didn't take any."

Fiona sighed. "Figures. I'll text Cal later."

"Does anyone have Rowan's number? I want to make sure she really wanted to cook for my idiot brother and his friends."

I'm not sure which sister said that since I was already headed out the front door and to the best part of my week. Obligatory grilling complete, I now had the entire afternoon to play with my nieces and nephews. The kids cheered when they saw me. Their excitement felt a hell of a lot better than being ignored by Lauren.

With Cal and Rowan's wedding only a month away, she had to speak to me at some point. I was walking her fine ass down the aisle. Until then, I'd go to Karma three times a week like I always did. She'd pretend I wasn't there, like she always did, but would shove my usual order across the counter and put my money in the tip jar for Cammie or Wyatt. I'd pretend my memories of us together were as old as the tension between us until she cracked and spoke to me again, and then I'd try my best to make more of those memories. Ones she'd never want to forget.

Chapter Nine

Lauren

"This never happened," Aiden said, trailing kisses from my neck to my belly that had me arching beneath him. I gripped his hair as he continued down my stomach and — the alarm woke me. Again. Typically, I'm up and out of bed before it goes off, but without Wyatt, I no longer had time for the cat naps that accounted for half my sleep. I wanted to burrow under my comforter and not move all day. Maybe fall back into the dreams that had plagued me since St. John, because my subconscious had zero issues getting naked with Aiden over and over again.

I slapped the alarm off and dragged myself out of bed. By the time I shuffled through getting dressed, braided my hair, and scarfed down a granola bar, I had less than fifteen minutes to get everything ready before Karma opened at five. I'd be lucky if the coffee had finished brewing by the time the first customers arrived.

I flipped on the lights in the back room and stepped around the pile of boxes that had accumulated all week. Thank goodness it was Saturday. Cammie and Wyatt should arrive soon, and I'd be able to sort through the new inventory while they worked the front.

I quickly ground some of our signature roast and started brewing. Next, I scooped decaf beans into the grinder for those special souls who drank decaf first thing in the morning.

The rich smell of coffee filled the air. But something wasn't right. It smelled burnt. I checked the brewer for any spills or smoke. Everything appeared to be working fine. The back door creaked open like a coffin in a horror movie and a moment later Cammie stepped out from the back.

"Morning," she said brightly.

I opened my mouth to respond but the coffee smell became so overwhelming and awful, my stomach did an ominous flip. I ran past Cammie and into the customer bathroom, making it just in time.

"Oh no," Cammie said, standing in the open doorway. "You must have caught that bug going around town."

I flushed the toilet and nodded, suddenly dizzy from my dash to the bathroom and losing what little I'd eaten. "I think I'll go upstairs for a while."

"Don't worry," Cammie said, giving me a wide berth to pass her. "I'll disinfect before we open."

The coffee smell was even stronger now, and my stomach gave another quiver. I ran through the café, not realizing I'd held my breath until I gasped in a lungful of air on the staircase to my apartment.

I'd felt fine when I went downstairs. Tired but fine.

Dido growled at me from my grandfather's chair when I collapsed on the sofa and rested my head on one of the brightly colored throw pillows. I did not have time for this. I needed to unpack inventory, finish reconciling the quarterly accounts, and work on the daunting list in my phone's note app. There wasn't much I could do lying on the couch, but I could check off a few things while my stomach settled.

Desdemona and Medusa pushed through the cat door. Desdemona hopped onto the couch arm, then meowed so Medusa would know where to jump. They laid down on either side of my head like two purring pillows.

I'd taken pictures of the gorgeous spring-themed cookies Rowan and Poppy sent over yesterday and took a couple minutes posting them to Karma's social channels, tagging the Stevens sister's Red Blossoms Bakery. Next, I opened my calendar app to see if I needed to cancel anything if my stomach didn't cooperate. The day was pretty clear, but something niggled. I looked through my schedule leading up to the wedding next weekend and realized I hadn't yet made an appointment for my next birth control shot. Since the end of the quarter was always busy, I typically scheduled it for midway through. I'd had to reschedule February's shot because of an ice storm, so everything got shifted. Now was as good a time as any to use the online scheduling tool to set my second quarter shot, but I wasn't sure when I'd gotten the last one.

I scrolled back to February and noted the appointment I'd missed. But as I flipped through the weeks after, panic built. I'd rescheduled the first quarter shot. Hadn't I? By the time I'd arrived at the current week, my palms were sweating, and my stomach lurched again.

When I finished dry heaving into my kitchen sink, scaring all three cats from the apartment, I sank to the linoleum floor and leaned against the beat-up cabinet.

I'd missed a shot.

That'd never happened before. Whenever I'd had to cancel an appointment, my doctor's office always contacted me to reschedule. I thought back to the past couple of months and the many calls and texts I'd missed from my suppliers and friends. I opened my text app, which had an embarrassing number of unread messages, and searched for my doctor. Three. I'd received three texts reminding me to make my appointment. One of which I even opened at the beginning of March.

Sex had been so far from my mind, I guess the reminder slipped through the cracks like so many other things I thought could wait. I hadn't slept with anyone in almost a year before —

"Oh, shit."

It happened so fast, we hadn't stopped to grab a condom. At the time, I wasn't worried because I was on birth control. Or supposed to be. My stomach gave another twist. I'd gotten sick. Twice. Once, for no other reason than the smell of coffee.

This can't be happening.

Since starting the shot, my periods had been unpredictable, disappearing for months at a time. I had no way of knowing where I'd be on my cycle or if I was late.

I rose from the floor slowly, not wanting to set off another dizzy spell, and grabbed my purse and keys. I couldn't wait another minute to find out if I'd brought back an unintentional souvenir from the Caribbean. Sneaking down the back stairs was easy, but when I opened the exit door, it let out a loud groan, and Cammie called my name.

I thought of pretending I hadn't heard her, but I didn't want her to worry that someone had gotten in from the street. "It's me," I said.

"Where are you going?" she asked, pushing through the door from the café.

"I just need to get some things to, um, settle my stomach."

Cammie frowned. "I can run out and get whatever you need as soon as the morning rush ends, and Wyatt gets here. You shouldn't be out and about spreading germs."

"Actually, I don't think I'm sick."

"Sure sounded like it to me."

"I mean, I'm sick. But I think it's something I ate. Or drank. I probably had too much wine last night with Rowan. I'm going to grab some rose bay willow."

"Is that a tree?"

"It's an herbal remedy."

Cammie held up her hands. "I can't keep up with your woo woo ways. If you think you can get to the store and back without hurting yourself or sickening someone else, I'll leave you to it."

Which was exactly what I figured she'd say. "I'll be back in less than an hour. The health food store is in Jericho." Not that it was open this early.

"Whatever works for you," Cammie said, shaking her head. "I'm happy to grab you some soda and saltines from the grocery store later. Just text me what you want."

"Thanks, Cam," I said, pushing out the door, which screeched like a pissed-off banshee.

Because I knew everyone who worked at the grocery store, pharmacy, or anywhere else that would sell a pregnancy test, I headed out of Peace Falls. I may have bought condoms from Mr. Wilson a time or two at the town's pharmacy, but no way in hell was I buying a pregnancy test from the man.

Climbing into my somewhat-trusty beater, I asked the universe to please get me to Jericho and back without breaking down. Karma was on my side, and I pulled into a 24-hour pharmacy fifteen minutes later and headed straight for the family planning aisle. The young woman at the register glanced at me when she rang up the pregnancy test, but since I didn't know her, I pretended buying a pregnancy test before six in the morning was no big deal. Or tried to.

"There's a bathroom in the back, if you need it," she said.

"Thank you," I said, touched by her kindness. My eyes stung. For goodness' sake, she'd offered me a toilet, not a kidney. I turned and pointed to the back of the store. "Where?"

"Right corner, by the adult diapers. It's just through the door."

I headed in that direction and pushed through an unmarked door next to the Depends. The bathroom sat on the other side of a narrow hallway. I went in and locked the door behind me, thankful I had the entire room to myself.

My hands shook as I tore open the cardboard box and peeled the plastic from both tests. I'd gone with the idiot-proof version. This was not the time to decipher how many lines meant what, and I wanted both tests to confirm whatever answer the other gave.

As I hovered over the surprisingly pristine toilet, I contemplated whether I should call Rowan. This felt like the kind of thing best friends helped each other through. And wasn't I always getting on her for introverting when she should lean on others, namely me?

I decided best friend or not, Rowan didn't need to hear me pee. When I finished, I placed both tests on the back of the toilet and washed my hands. After setting a timer on my phone, I paced with it, watching the seconds tick down.

No sense telling Rowan about a false alarm. She'd want to know who I'd been sleeping with, and despite all odds, neither Rowan nor Poppy suspected anything had happened between Aiden and me, other than drinking too much whiskey before lunch.

Definitely no need to call Rowan because the test would be negative. The shot had lingering levels of protection. I'd only had sex once. I imagined both tests flashing "Negative" and sent it into the universe.

I paced the closet-sized room until the timer went off. When I picked up both sticks and read the results, I had to lean against the wall to keep from falling on my ass.

Pregnant.

Both tests had the same result. But they could be from a faulty batch. I tossed them both in the trash and hurried back to the family planning aisle, where I grabbed one of every type of test.

This time Melissa—I took the time to read her name tag—rang me up, then handed me a bottled water from the refrigerated case by the register. "You might need this."

She was right. My bladder felt completely empty. I unscrewed the cap and chugged the full bottle. My stomach did not approve. Thankfully, I made it outside before I watered the bushes by the front door.

"You can return those tests, if you want," Melissa said, handing me a paper towel.

I wiped the tears from my eyes, then my mouth. "Maybe," I said, my voice shaking.

"You can exchange them for some ginger tea. That really helped me."

I nodded. "OK."

I followed Melissa back inside the store where she gathered tea and a box of Pedialyte frozen popsicles. "Make sure you stay hydrated. Would you like to keep one test? You could take it tomorrow morning. Just to be sure."

I nodded again, my throat too tight to speak. After she'd completed the transaction, she gave me a small smile, and I burst into tears.

"Are you a hugger?" she asked.

I nodded, and she walked around the counter and wrapped me in a tight hug. It's the kind of thing I would have done, and had done, whenever I'd crossed paths with a stranger who clearly needed some support.

"Thank you," I said, taking a step back and grabbing my bag from the counter, "for being so kind."

She shrugged. "What goes around comes around, right?"

I nodded, but for the life of me, I couldn't think of anything I'd ever done bad enough to deserve being knocked up by Aiden O'Malley.

Chapter Ten

Lauren

The bridal suite looked like a tornado had torn through dropping makeup, hair spray, and rhinestones. Rowan's gorgeous dress hung off the bathroom door, the full tulle skirt sweeping the floor. Our bridesmaid dresses hung all over the room, from curtain rods to closet doors. The pale pink lace complimented the delicate off-the-shoulder bodice of Rowan's gown, and the jeweled rose gold belts we'd added elevated our dresses from pretty to stunning.

I couldn't wait to see Rowan in her gown with her hair and makeup done, but we still had an hour before the photographer arrived. Rowan wore a white silk robe with the word "Bride" stitched on the front pocket while the stylist fussed with finding the perfect "effortless" look that would hold up through the reception.

Poppy, Cammie, and I sported pale pink robes, our hair and makeup complete. The robes were a surprise gift from Poppy, who'd insisted ours be plain so we could wear them again without feeling like idiots. I'd have worn mine even if it had the word bridesmaid stitched on it. The silk felt like a soft caress and was the only thing I'd worn this week that hadn't made my boobs ache more than they already did. I planned to stay in the robe until the very last minute before pictures.

The bridesmaids' nude pumps were lined against one wall beside Rowan's bedazzled rose gold sneakers, which looked more mirror ball than shoe. I was not excited to be in heels for six hours.

"I love Rowan's shoes," I told Cammie, who was sitting on a small couch with Poppy, enjoying the view of the mountains outside. I wanted to sit down with them, but Poppy kept bouncing her knee. Nerves or excitement. Probably both. I'd propped myself on the wall beside the couch, doing my best not to move and set off my stomach, again.

Cammie smiled. "Thank you. When Cal asked Rowan not to wear heels, I knew she needed something special."

"And by special you mean shiny," Poppy said. "How many rhinestones did you use?"

"The perfect amount," Rowan said. She shifted on the folding chair we'd set up for the "hair station," a slight grimace on her face.

I pointed to the lovely afternoon tea that had just arrived, compliments of the hotel. "We should eat soon." Not that I'd be having anything, but Rowan's back probably needed a break from sitting. Cal's request for sensible shoes meant his bride would be a good foot shorter than him in all the pictures, but hopefully in less pain.

"That's a good idea," Cammie said, plucking a strawberry from the service cart, which we'd rolled against the coffee table in what had been the only remaining free space in the entire suite. "You don't want your stomach growling during the ceremony, and you should eat now, so we have time to touch up your makeup."

"Y'all should get started without me," Rowan said as the stylist doused her with another round of hairspray.

Poppy grabbed a scone and shoved half in her mouth. Cammie chose a small pimento cheese sandwich and handed Poppy a plate to stop the cascade of crumbs. Poppy only ate like an animal when she was level three hangry. The bouncing knee made sense now.

"Go on, Lauren," Rowan said.

"I'll wait. I want to make sure there's one of everything for you to choose from."

Cammie and Poppy both stopped mid-chew, and a sprinkle of guilt blended with the hormone-induced nausea swirling my stomach. "Honestly, I'm not hungry."

The morning sickness had only intensified as the week progressed and was unfortunately not confined to the morning. It arrived with little warning, but I'd learned certain things set it off. The brunch spread the hotel sent up earlier had come with an urn of coffee that sent me running from the room. And yes, being a café owner with a coffee revulsion was a special kind of hell.

"Done," the stylist said, standing back to admire her work. "I'm going to take a quick break, but I'll be back right before pictures for touchups."

"Help yourself to anything here," Rowan said, standing with obvious difficulty.

"That's generous of you, but I like to leave this time for the bridal party to have some moments alone. I'll be back in thirty."

"Does she expect us to have a sobfest or a pillow fight?" Poppy asked once the stylist had left the suite.

"Pretty sure she'd want us to avoid both since either would wreck her work," Cammie said.

"You look absolutely gorgeous," I told Rowan as she made her way through the cluttered room to me. Her green eyes danced, and she hadn't stopped smiling all day.

"I can't believe I'm marrying Caleb Cardoso in an hour." She pulled me into a hug that made my stomach lurch.

I'd never seen my best friend so happy, including her first wedding, and as much as I wanted to celebrate this moment with her, my stomach had other plans.

"I forgot something in my room," I said. "Be right back."

I bolted from the suite and down the hall into the room I shared with Cammie. Even a modest room at the resort was a fortune, so we'd decided to split the cost. If only I'd known when we made the reservation that I'd need privacy to hurl.

"That's it," Cammie said, closing the door to our room. "Brush your teeth and get out here. We need to talk."

I brushed my teeth, doing my best not to mar the makeup the stylist had painstakingly applied, but I didn't have time to talk. Neither did Cammie.

"We need to get back to help Rowan," I said, walking from the bathroom.

"Rowan's fine," Cammie said, standing directly in front of the door to the hallway. "She's having the best day of her life. She won't notice if we're gone five minutes. Sit."

I collapsed onto the bed where I'd slept the night before, fighting the urge to sprint into the bathroom again. Cammie lowered herself gently beside me as though she knew any movement would upset my stomach.

I took a couple deep breaths, and my nausea eased slightly. "I'm fine."

Cammie shook her head. "I've seen you throw up too many times this week for you to be fine."

"Stomach viruses can last awhile."

"But they don't disappear and come back, day after day."

I didn't say anything. Cammie grabbed my hand and gave it a squeeze. "Whenever you're ready to talk, I'm ready to listen."

She stood to leave and the panic that had been building for days erupted out of me. "I can't be a mother."

Cammie sat back on the bed and took my hand.

"I can't," I said, sitting up. "I'd never get it right, and I won't put a baby through a childhood like mine."

Cammie nodded. "I can tell you've given this a lot of thought."

More like obsessed over it 24/7. And every time I came to the same conclusion: I wasn't mom material.

"How far along are you?"

"Five weeks."

"And you're sure?"

I nodded. "Based on the date of conception."

Cammie gave me a sad smile. "That's not what I meant. Are you sure you don't want this?"

I nodded, trying my best not to cry and ruin the six-shadow job on my eyelids.

"OK. But you're not going alone. We can look for a clinic after the wedding, if you haven't already."

I shook my head. "I know that's an option, but I've decided to find an adoption agency."

Whatever Cammie was thinking or feeling, she kept her expression completely blank. "What about the father?"

"What about him?"

"If you're putting his child up for adoption, he has a right to know."

"Believe me, he's no more able to take care of a baby than I am, but you're right. I'll have to tell him. It's not like I can hide being pregnant forever."

"So, he's local," Cammie said, carefully.

"It's Aiden."

Saying his name hurt. Seeing him hurt. And unfortunately, he'd popped up at Karma the usual three times a week since the trip last month. At first, I'd been embarrassed to see him. Waking up naked next to someone after a drunken hookup was awkward enough, but the way I'd treated Aiden for years made what happened on St. John so much worse. I'd ghosted him, as much as you could ghost anyone in Peace Falls. Then, after mere hours alone together, I'd gone and slept with him again, initiated it even.

Despite his snark, I knew I'd hurt him both times. Which, now that I think about it, was probably why karma had gotten me back with this pregnancy. Once I found out I was carrying his child, seeing him and keeping the information to myself became physically painful. I knew I'd have to tell him about the pregnancy and my choice to put the baby up for adoption, eventually. But our best friends were marrying each other today, and I didn't want to do or say anything that would take away from their happiness or Aiden's.

Cammie didn't seem at all shocked. "For what it's worth," she said, standing and pulling me from the bed. "I think you'd be an amazing mother. And I wouldn't underestimate Aiden. He might just surprise you."

I breathed through my nose and out of my mouth a few times. Any sudden change in position amped up the nausea. "He's surprised me enough, don't you think?"

"How long have you two been—whatever you are?"

"We aren't anything. Just two people who took too many shots and made a baby."

"Oh, Lauren," Cammie said, placing her hand on my arm. "I wish you'd told me sooner. Sitting alone with something like this isn't healthy, you know that."

I nodded. Helping people had become my life's mission. Not in any grand way. But in small doses, spread to as many people as possible, I hoped to make my mark on the world. A kind word. A smile. A helping hand. A sympathetic ear. Despite how much I wanted, even needed, to help everyone around me, I had a hard time asking for help myself.

Cammie started toward the hallway. "Let's get you some ginger ale."

"It won't help," I said and burst into tears.

Cammie grabbed a tissue and did her best to minimize the damage.

"I'm ruining Rowan's wedding. I'll probably throw up during the ceremony or on her dress. Then I'll have to tell her, and she'll insist I tell Aiden immediately. He'll probably go old school and make us get married today too."

Cammie laughed so hard her eyes watered. "Sorry. It's just, I don't think that will happen. Run to the nearest receptacle if you need to be sick, and I'll tell everyone you got food poisoning."

I sniffed. "That could work."

She wrapped me in a hug and my tears slowed. "Of course it will. And no one can make you do anything, Lauren. Though, I have to admit, your worst-case scenario surprises me."

"Throwing up on Rowan's dress?" I said, stepping out of the hug. "That's kind of a no brainer."

"Marrying Aiden."

I waved her words away. "Don't read too much into that. I'm dehydrated."

Cammie frowned. "You do look pale. Ok, new plan. We're telling Rowan you have food poisoning now, and you're going to suck on some ice cubes and rest as much as possible."

I shook my head. "She'll worry if you tell her that."

"Sorry, Lauren. Once Rowan sees the tear-stained makeup and how bad you look under it, she'll know something's up. Food poisoning or pregnancy. Take your pick."

"OK, but nothing I ate here. I don't want her to feel guilty."

Cammie nodded and pulled her phone from the pocket of her robe. "You ate some—not that," she said, scrolling. "Recalled spinach. Does that work?"

"Um, sure."

"Don't worry," Cammie said. "I've told my share of lies to keep the peace, and I have a feeling you have too. If anyone can pull this off, it's us."

Unfortunately, I knew she was right. No one can lie like a foster kid.

Chapter Eleven

Aiden

"There," Rose said, pinning a cluster of pink flowers to Cal's lapel.

They matched his tie. Only Rowan Stevens could get Caleb Cardoso to wear baby pink and smile about it. Fortunately, she'd gone with light green for the groomsmen. Not that I'd have complained. I wore purple for Fiona's wedding and fucking polka dots for Ciara's. Thankfully, Kayleigh eloped or I'd have been the same age as Rowan's brother in her wedding and just as nervous.

I gripped Chris's shoulders and gave him a little shake. "You got this, kid. You face down cornerbacks who want to shove you into the field every play. This is easy. You stand behind me, watch your sister get married, then copy what I do when we walk out."

He nodded, but he still looked like he was headed into the most important game of his life. "I don't want to mess up."

"Even if you do, Rowan won't care. That's one of the only perks of being the baby brother. If you fall on your face, she'll be worried you got a boo boo, not that you screwed up the wedding video."

Chris smirked and some of the tension left his face.

"Your turn, Chris," Rose said.

Someone knocked on the door.

"That's probably the photographer," she said around the pins in her mouth. "She's coming here before she goes to the bridal suite."

Since Cal was fussing with Theo's tie, I got the door.

I hadn't expected to see Poppy before the ceremony. Like Theo, she'd somehow managed to keep her bad-ass-goth vibe in formal wedding attire. Even more impressive, she'd pulled it off in head-to-toe pink. "Hell Cat! What can I do for you?"

Her mask slipped and my stomach sank. "Is my mom in there?" she asked in a small voice.

I stepped into the hallway and pulled the door shut behind me. "What's wrong?"

"Not much," she said, twisting her hands. "Lauren got food poisoning and looks like death; my sister is bawling her eyes out because Dad's not here to walk her down the aisle; and Cammie's running around like a crazy woman trying to take care of them both. I mean, I get it, but it's kind of a weird tradition, don't you think? It's not like he'd really be 'giving Rowan away.'"

Adrenaline spiked through my body. "Does Lauren need to go to the hospital?"

Lauren had seemed off last night during the rehearsal. Even more than what had become our usual. Since we got back from the trip, she'd actively ignored me. Last night, she'd looked too tired to pretend I didn't exist. She'd taken my arm as we practiced walking down the aisle from the altar without hesitation or a single sarcastic jab.

Poppy gave me an odd look and shook her head. "Even if she did, there's no way she'd miss the wedding. So head's up since you're escorting her. Is my mom inside or not?"

I pushed down thoughts of Lauren and focused on the problem in front of me. "Yeah, but if you tell her Rowan's upset in front of Cal, he'll get worked up. She's almost done putting on the flowers."

The door opened behind us, and I expected it'd be Rose ready to pin me. Instead, Chris took one look at his sister and joined us in the hall. "Pop?"

"Rowan's crying because she has to walk down the aisle alone."

He nodded. "I've got this," he said, wrapping his arm around Poppy and walking with her toward the elevator.

I felt a burst of pride. It wasn't the first time the kid had made me proud. I'd trained him for hours before his football tryouts last summer and cheered him on all season. He had real talent and the same love for the game I had at his age. Coaching him and being back in the high school stadium had been the highlight of my year. But it's not like I had anything to do with him taking charge of the current situation. Chris had always been a good brother. It didn't stop the warmth in my chest or the smile on my face.

Good thing too, since Cal looked like a ball of nerves when I reentered the room. He paced between the two beds, his eyes glued to the plastic clock on the nightstand.

"Pin me, Rose," I said, holding my arms wide.

She attached a sprig of greenery to my lapel and gave me an assessing look.

"You're needed upstairs," I said as quietly as I could.

She nodded and plastered on a smile for Cal. "You guys look great," she shouted over her shoulder as she booked it out the door.

"That poor woman," Theo said, taking a seat on one of the beds. "She should have let you hire another florist, Cal. She'll be exhausted before the wedding starts."

Theo wasn't the chatty type. But Cal was. And right now, it looked like he needed to get out of his head. He wanted to marry Rowan. Hell, he needed to marry her if he had any chance at a happy life, but Cal could clamshell tighter than anyone I knew.

"Just like your girlfriend shouldn't have been finishing the cake this morning," Cal said, taking the bait. He took a seat on the other bed across from Theo. "What time did Poppy get up?"

Theo chuckled. "Four. It's like she'd downed five espressos in her sleep."

Cal laughed and then glanced around the room. "Where's Chris?"

"Family picture, upstairs," I said.

"We're that close?" he asked. The nerves Theo had unwound pulled taut again. "I thought that was right before we walked down the aisle?"

"Change of plans. Better get the toast in before the kid gets back," I said because no amount of chit chat was chilling Cal now. I kneeled and opened the cabinet that hid the mini fridge and pulled out two IPAs and a Liquid Death. I passed Theo the sparkling water, Cal a beer, and popped the top on my own.

"To Logan," we said in unison and drank. Theo and Cal's eyes both went a little glassy in the silence that followed, but as usual mine stayed dry.

"I wish he was here," Cal said, setting his can on the nightstand after a sip. He needed to take down more than that if we had any shot of getting through this without his nerves taking over. Until then, I guess we were stuck with chit chat.

I put my drink on the dresser and leaned against it, trying to look as relaxed as possible and searching my brain for something to talk about. "You wouldn't be here if he was," I said, surprising myself. Not that I hadn't thought about it before, but to actually say it out loud?

Theo and Cal both looked at me like I'd lost my mind, which maybe I had. I shrugged, playing the hand I'd dealt myself. Make lemons out of lemonade or some shit, right? "Think about it. You only became a PT because you went through rehab yourself, and you only got with Rowan because she was your patient."

Cal's eyes hardened. "I'd have needed PT even if Logan hadn't died."

I nodded, the usual guilt pressing so hard in my chest I could barely breathe. "If he'd been buckled in, you mean."

Because when it came down to it, Logan's death was my fault. I would have lost my football scholarship and Cal would have needed PT, but Logan would still be alive and Theo wouldn't be a felon if I'd just kept my ass buckled in that car.

Theo stood and walked to me. He set his can down so hard on the dresser the tinny sound echoed in the room. "Not today, man," he said, gripping my shoulders in a hold that almost hurt. "We can hash this out a million times, and I will, whenever you want, but not today."

I nodded because of course he was right. Today was about Cal. I should have said I missed Logan too and told a funny story about him before switching to something lighter. Which was exactly what I planned to do.

"So, you're proposing to Hell Cat," I said. Theo almost smiled. Instead, he shook his head and gave my shoulder a good-natured thump.

"What?" Cal said, standing.

"I was going to tell you after you got back from your honeymoon," Theo said. "This asshole only knows because he walked in on me making the ring last week."

"Hey," I said, giving him a shove. "I was measuring the bedroom for new carpet. You're welcome, by the way. Just be glad I wasn't Poppy."

"Are you serious?" Cal asked. The joy on his face eased what little guilt I had for spilling Theo's secret.

"Yeah, brother," Theo said with a shit-eating grin.

Cal pulled him into a tight hug. "We're going to be actual brothers."

"We already are," Theo said. "Only now it won't be weird that I spend every holiday with you."

Cal laughed and they started talking about the proposal. I smiled and said enough that they wouldn't realize what the conversation did to me.

They were going to be family, their lives twisted tighter than they already were. They'd celebrate every Thanksgiving, Christmas, Easter, and Fourth of July together while I celebrated with my family and Logan's. New ties would bind them. They'd be uncles to each other's children. Then grand-uncles. Their place in each other's lives would deepen and mine would shallow.

As kids, football brought us together. As adults, we'd maintained the bond with our shared guilt and grief. Sometimes I wondered if the three of us would even be friends today if the accident never happened. No question, Theo and Cal would still be joined at the hip. Just like I imagined Logan and I would be, if he was still alive. But would the four of us have remained close after high school?

I knew the answer. Theo and I probably would have drifted apart when he stopped playing football if he weren't Cal's best friend. As QB and wide receiver, Cal's and my friendship would have lasted on some level past high school. No doubt, I'd be at his wedding, Logan too. Whether either of us would be groomsmen was debatable.

But Logan wasn't here. I was the third wheel in our sad trio. For now, at least.

The electronic lock buzzed, and Chris dashed in.

"How'd it go?" Cal asked.

"Um." He glanced at me.

"The kid took pictures with his mom and sisters. He smiled. The photographer clicked. What's there to say?"

"Um, yeah." Chris shrugged and did his best to look like an apathetic teen.

Theo glanced at him and back at me. He knew something had happened, but as expected, he steered the conversation from any landmines by asking Cal a question about dog training. Not that Cal's dog, Skye, had ever been trained. Every visit to Cal's house filled me with terror at some point.

Fucking dogs. I'd hated them ever since a neighbor's mutt chased me and bit my leg. At least Theo's puppy was small, if excitable. Both dogs were unpredictable, which was the only reason Skye wasn't dashing around the hotel room with a flower collar, waiting to be the ring bearer and/or flower girl.

"Everything good?" I whispered to Chris while Cal went on about spray bottles and clickers.

The kid looked at me with pure terror in his eyes. "I'm walking Ann down the aisle. I'm sure Mom would have done it, but I offered before she got there."

I nodded. "Good. They'd have sobbed the entire way if they walked together. At least now the photographer has a chance to get a decent shot before Cal lets out the waterworks. It's game over then."

"What about me?" Cal asked.

"Aiden said you'll cry like a baby when you see my sister."

"Shit, I'll probably cry," Theo said with a laugh.

Chris paled. "You don't think I'll cry in front of everyone, do you?"

I shrugged. "They haven't been conditioned like we have. Plus, who cares? Those cousins of Cal's you were eying up at the rehearsal dinner would melt if you did."

Cal looked torn between protecting his teenaged cousins and putting his future brother-in-law at ease. Theo decided for him.

"No question. Big tough football player getting weepy at his sister's wedding, they'll be putty in your hands."

Some of the color returned to Chris's face. "Guess it's a win-win for me."

"You'll do great, kid," I said, slapping him on the back.

I'd hand him the rest of my beer if I didn't think Cal would throttle me. What seventeen-year-old guy wouldn't need a little liquid courage to walk his sister down the aisle? Instead, I just rolled my eyes to the can on the dresser when Cal and Theo started talking again. Then I stepped in front of

Chris to hide him from view. Being a junior on the football team, it didn't take him long.

He shot me a grateful look and ducked into the bathroom, no doubt to steal some of Cal's mouthwash. I wanted to follow him and ask about Lauren. The fact he hadn't mentioned her meant she must be ok. Unless she wasn't in the bridal suite. A knot formed in my stomach. Everyone would be so focused on Rowan, it'd be easy to miss Lauren getting worse.

I pulled out my phone and texted Cammie.

Does Lauren need a doctor?

Three dots appeared, then disappeared before Cammie texted back.

She's fine

It didn't take three sisters and two honorary ones to know that wasn't good.

Chapter Twelve

Lauren

"DOES IT LOOK LIKE I've been crying?" Rowan asked. "I trust you to tell me the truth."

Her trust cut like a knife. I almost blurted out that I'd lied to her. That I had terrible morning sickness, not food poisoning. That Aiden O'Malley and I drank too much and got frisky on her bachelor/bachelorette trip. That I didn't want to be a mother. That I was terrified.

"Your eyes look brighter, like they always do after you cry, and your makeup is perfect now. Not even a hint of a red nose."

Rowan nodded. "I can live with that. Are you feeling any better? I asked the front desk if they had medicine that might help, and they said they'd bring some up to the room."

The guilt knife twisted in my chest. "I'm fine."

I wasn't. Not even close. I couldn't keep melted ice cubes down, and my head pounded. Cammie hovered near like she expected me to fall over, and honestly, I was glad she kept close.

Rose hurried into the suite with a huge white box. "Oh, Rowan," she said, her eyes getting misty. "You look so beautiful. You all do."

"Thank you, Mrs. Stevens," Cammie said. "Let me help you with that." She took the box from Rowan's mom and set it on the bed.

While Cammie fussed with our bouquets, Rose, Rowan, and Poppy stood together holding hands, their foreheads touching while the photographer snapped a few candids. The bond between the Stevens women was so beautiful. I couldn't help but feel a little jealous before chastising myself. I had them all in my life. I shared brilliant moments like these, as well as the sad ones. I might not be family, but I didn't question my place in theirs.

"We better get downstairs," Rose said, giving Rowan's hand a final squeeze. "Chris is walking me down the aisle first, if that's ok. We'll walk as fast as possible."

"Walk slow. Enjoy it," Rowan said. "It's not like they can start without me."

Cammie handed me a delicate bouquet of roses, peonies, and eucalyptus wrapped in a cream satin ribbon. I immediately gagged at the smell. Poppy, Rowan, and Rose thankfully didn't notice, but Cammie frowned.

"This isn't normal," she hissed in my ear as we walked to the elevator.

"Today has been the worst," I whispered back.

"You should see a doctor, Lauren."

"I just need to lie down. Let me get through the ceremony, pictures, and the bridal party entrance. I'll skip the rest of the reception if I still feel bad. Except when you sing. I can't miss that."

The worry didn't leave her eyes. "Fine, but I'm grabbing Dr. Evers during the reception if you don't start keeping water down."

Dr. Evers had been my GP since middle school. He was the last doctor I wanted to tell about my current condition, but I had to admit, I felt pretty weak.

I nodded and we climbed into the waiting elevator. I held my breath since the combined scent of all our bouquets in such a small space was bound to set me off. The pounding that had started in my head an hour ago intensified. My vision dimmed when the doors slid open on the ground floor. I burst into the lobby and took a few deep breaths.

A woman in a hotel uniform came running toward us with a bottle of pink liquid. Cammie shot toward her and said something to the woman, who smiled at me and turned back toward the front desk.

"Can't risk a spill now," Cammie said, brightly. "Lauren and I will come back before pictures."

"I'm fine," I said, yet again.

This time, everyone looked at me with concern.

"Let's go," I said. "You know Cal will worry if we're late."

That lit a fire under their asses. We headed outside, and the fresh air made my stomach feel a smidge less wobbly.

When we reached the ceremony site, we stood behind an extra tall hedge that hid us from everyone. Soft music filtered through from a string quartet, the perfect, sweet accompaniment for Rowan's moment to shine. Chris joined us to escort Rose. He seemed far more relaxed than when he offered to walk his sister down the aisle. As soon as he returned, Cammie stepped into view of everyone and started down the aisle, which was really just a grassy gap between chairs. Cal and Rowan had tried to keep the wedding intimate with only fifty guests, but it felt like half of Peace Falls was in attendance.

I plastered on a smile when Cammie was halfway down the aisle and begged the universe to let me get through the ceremony without throwing up. Rose had built a beautiful floral arch for Cal and Rowan to stand under and exchange their vows with a glorious mountain view behind them. I set my eyes on the flowers and walked ahead. By the time I took my place beside Cammie, Poppy was halfway down the aisle and already crying.

Cammie sniffed behind me, and I bit my tongue. Crying upset my stomach when I wasn't pregnant. I needed to avoid tears at all costs. I made the mistake of looking across the aisle. Theo's eyes were glassy, and Cal looked close to losing it. Aiden, however, stared right at me, his face void of any emotion. I locked eyes with him and missed the music change that signaled Rowan's entrance.

A collective gasp rose from the audience, and I turned to face my best friend as she floated down the aisle. Rowan was luminous. The setting sun bathed her red hair and creamy skin in a warm glow. I'd never seen anyone look so beautiful or so happy. Chris beamed beside her like he'd walked a hundred brides down the aisle and saved the best for last. I faced the groomsmen when Rowan stepped under the floral arch. Despite the bride's arrival, Aiden's gaze remained on me. The intensity of his stare made my checks flush. I returned my attention to the happy couple and let myself sink into the moment.

After a disastrous first marriage, my bestie had finally found someone to share her life with who actually deserved her. In high school, she'd been too shy to even speak in Cal's presence. Now they held hands, ready to commit their lives to each other. Rowan kept it together until Cal recited his vows. When she started crying, I couldn't stop my own tears. As they promised to love one another for the rest of their days, I felt an unexpected surge of sadness.

I never wanted to get married. In my experience, depending on another person made you half as strong. But seeing Rowan and Cal together led me to the depressing conclusion that marriage could actually work for some people, just not for me.

Cal and Rowan kissed, and I cheered with everyone else as they started down the aisle. Aiden stepped toward me as Poppy and Theo followed the bride and groom, his expression unreadable. I looped my arm in his, just as we'd done during the rehearsal, but he surprised me by laying his left hand over mine. The gesture felt intimate, yet oddly reassuring. I melted toward him as my muscles relaxed.

When we came to the row of hedges that separated us from the audience, I pulled my arm away, but he gripped my hand. "Let me walk you to a chair," he said, concern obvious in his voice.

My stomach dropped. How did he know? Cammie wouldn't have told him, would she? Had he somehow suspected it like she had? The man did have a lot of nieces and nephews and seemed pretty close with his sisters. He'd been around pregnant women his entire adult life.

I opened my mouth to speak but gagged. He pulled a plastic bag from his suit pocket, which I promptly used. Guess the universe took me at my word. When I looked up, Aiden's face had taken on a slightly green color as he stared up at the sky.

He sucked a few breaths in his nose and out his mouth before looking back at me. "Sorry, I have a weak stomach."

"How did you—" Small black dots formed at the edge of my vision and my legs wobbled.

Cammie rushed over and took the bag from me. "Let's get her inside, Aiden," she said, taking hold of my other arm.

"I'm—" I started.

"Don't you say it," Cammie said, shaking her head. "You're paler than Poppy."

They shoved me in a chair as soon as we entered the small room the hotel had set aside for the bridal party while everyone else headed to the cocktail hour.

"Please stop making a big deal," I said weakly. "I don't want Rowan to see."

Cammie pulled up a chair beside me, and Aiden found one as well. "Now we're just three people having a conversation," she said. She gave me a look full of meaning.

I turned to Aiden. "Thank you for helping me."

He nodded.

In the silence that followed, Cammie looked between us and let out a huff. "I'm getting Dr. Evers. Keep an eye on her, Aiden."

I wasn't telling him about the baby during Rowan's wedding. As soon as Cammie took off, I started to stand.

"Sit," Aiden said in a commanding voice.

"I'm not a dog," I said, rising to my feet.

He grabbed my arm and stared up at me with so much concern in his piercing eyes my breath caught. "I know you don't want to take any attention from Rowan and Cal. Passing out is the fastest way to do that."

Aiden kept a firm hold on my arm while I sank back onto the chair. He let go, only to press his fingers to my wrist.

"What are you doing?" I asked and attempted to pull my arm away.

"Checking your pulse. I see dehydration all the time on job sites."

"Oh." I stopped fighting him, and he bent closer and held his fingers to my wrist.

"It's a little fast," he said after a while. His touch lightened, his fingers almost caressing as he pulled them from my arm. He glanced up at me through his thick lashes and pressure built between my thighs. I'd felt so bad earlier, I hadn't noticed how devastatingly handsome he was in a suit.

"How did you know?" I asked in a voice so breathless I should have been embarrassed.

"Poppy told me. It's nothing to be embarrassed about, Lauren. It happens to everyone."

Poppy thought I had food poisoning. Which meant Aiden did too. Part of me was relieved he didn't know about the baby, but I felt every bit of the weight of the secret I kept from him.

He must have seen something in my expression because he reached out and took my hand. "Hey, it's OK. Cal and Rowan are having the time of their lives. They don't have a clue you're not doing well. Look."

Across the room, Cal and Rowan spoke softly with each other, stealing a private moment while surrounded by their best friends.

I let out a relieved breath. "I just need to get through pictures and the reception entrance."

"I'll help you however I can."

"Thanks, Aiden," Cammie said brightly, with Dr. Evers at her side. "We'll take it from here."

He rose reluctantly and crossed the room to where Poppy and Theo stood, but his eyes never left me.

"I filled him in," Cammie whispered.

"Can we go somewhere else?" I asked. Now Poppy and Theo had joined Aiden in staring. Rowan and Cal would break out of their love bubble any moment and notice Dr. Evers.

Cammie and Dr. Evers helped me stand, and the three of us snuck out the door and across the hall to a small conference room. I felt so tired. I wanted to lie down on the ornate carpet and sleep.

Dr. Evers got right to work. "Cammie said you're five weeks pregnant and haven't been able to keep down water."

I nodded. His tone was matter of fact, but he had to have been shocked to learn I was pregnant. Everyone in town knew I was single. Whatever he felt when Cammie told him, he'd pushed it down and was acting like we were in one of his exam rooms, not seated at a hotel conference table mid-wedding.

"When was your last bout of morning sickness before this?"

"I feel sick all the time, but I kept down chicken broth yesterday."

"And before that?"

"Some water and a couple of crackers the day before. It's been like that all week. It usually got better long enough I could keep something down. Until today."

"Are you taking anything for the nausea?

I shook my head. "I didn't think I could."

"Ginger tea. Anything like that?"

"That doesn't seem to help."

"She almost fainted," Cammie added. "Right after the ceremony."

"Any headaches?" the doctor asked.

I nodded.

Dr. Evers sighed. "You're showing clear signs of dehydration, Lauren. You need IV fluids."

"But it's Rowan's wedding," I said. "Just let me take pictures with her. She'll notice if I miss those. Then I'll do whatever you want me to do."

Dr. Evers studied me a moment longer and nodded. "As soon as the pictures are done, I want you in your room resting. A friend of mine has a practice in the area. I'll see if I can get what I need to do the IV here at the hotel. We might even get you back to the reception for a bit after it's done, if you feel up to it. But Lauren, you need to call your OB/GYN first thing Monday morning. Dehydration can become dangerous fast."

I'd been so focused on how I felt, I hadn't stopped to consider what it meant for the baby. Plenty of women get morning sickness. I figured there was nothing to worry about but my own suffering.

"The baby?" I asked, suddenly feeling panicked.

"Will be fine," he said, patting my hand. "If I thought either of you were in danger, I'd be calling an ambulance, wedding or not. After some fluids and rest, you should feel much better."

"Thank you," I said, giving him a weak smile. "You have free lattes for life, doc."

He smiled at me kindly. "Let's get you back before anyone notices."

When we returned to the small room, everyone had left but Aiden. Dr. Evers smiled at him, his eyes sparking liked he'd just guessed his daily Wordle on the first try.

"Dr. Evers is giving me an IV to help with the food poisoning," I blurted. "After the pictures."

"Yes," Dr. Evers said, looking between Aiden and me with obvious disappointment. "I'll be back as soon as I can. Keep an eye on her, young man."

"I got you," Aiden said, taking my hand and giving it a squeeze. "My pockets are full of plastic bags."

I smiled at him, but my eyes burned with tears.

"Everything's going to be all right," he said.

I had to remind myself he didn't know enough to believe that was anything but true.

CHAPTER THIRTEEN

Aiden

I STARED AT THE text and frowned.

"That better not be Carsons delaying the tile again," Sam said.

"Nah." I put my phone in my pocket and focused on the blueprints in front of me. "Are we on schedule for the foundation pour at sites 11 and 12, or do I need to move the cement delivery?"

Sam rubbed his neck. "If you let me grab the new guy from that remodel on Harris Ave, I should be fine."

"Wyatt can't operate an excavator. What good is he to you?"

"Kid's got arms and a good head on his shoulders. I'll put him to work."

I quickly calculated how much time we'd lose on Harris if I pulled Wyatt from the site, but nodded. "Fine. Only until you're back on track for the foundations. Wyatt has carpentry skills, which we need at Harris."

Sam nodded. "I remember. I worked with him last fall on that historic reno on Church. He's good. I'm glad you snatched him from that coffee shop."

My mind instantly went to the text I'd just received from Lauren asking me to swing by and fix a door. Maybe Wyatt had done more around Karma than pour coffee. "I'm headed into town in a few. Any permits you need filed?"

"Surprisingly, no," Sam said, flipping through screens on his tablet.

"Great. I'll swing by the Harris site and pull Wyatt on my way back."

"Thanks, Aiden."

"I'll let you get back to it then."

He nodded and bent over his tablet, fingers flying as he headed out of the office trailer and back to his crew.

I grabbed my keys, waved goodbye to the guys, and climbed into my truck. The entire drive over, I turned Lauren's text over in my mind.

> *I need your help ASAP. The back door won't budge.*

She'd texted me. Not Wyatt, who still worked at Karma part time and could fix a door as well as I could. No question he'd have helped her, but she'd asked me. I tried not to read too much into it. She probably wanted the door fixed right away and knew Wyatt couldn't duck out of a job site like I could.

I parked my truck in front of Karma, pushed through the front door, and right into the end of the line. Cammie was behind the counter working like crazy.

I frowned. She'd been the only person working in the café the two other times I grabbed coffee this week. It was strange enough seeing her at Karma in the middle of a weekday when she usually worked at Cal's PT practice. I guess he'd closed the office while he was on his honeymoon, and Cam was picking up hours here.

I walked around the line and toward the counter, people shooting me death glares the closer I got. "Where's Lauren?" I asked Cammie.

Someone actually huffed at me. Without slowing her frantic pace, Cam shouted, "In the back."

"Excuse me," I said to the lady nearest me in line. "I just need to get through."

"Hope you're here to help," a guy said behind her.

"I'll do what I can," I said, walking around the counter and pushing through the door to the back room.

"Lauren," I yelled.

"Just a minute," she called from her office.

A tailless cat ran over to me, meowing for attention. She started winding around my legs, so I bent to give her a scratch under the chin. She rubbed her furry face on my hand and gave it a lick.

"I thought you hated animals," Lauren said.

"Just dogs," I said, looking up at her. "Had a bad experience with one when I was a kid."

She was leaning against the door frame to her office. I'd seen her the day after the wedding when we'd both helped Poppy move into Theo's house. She'd recovered from the food poisoning, or so I thought. She looked as bad today, if not worse, than she had at the wedding. "Are you OK?"

"Yeah. If you have a minute, I need to talk to you."

I stood and walked to her, my chest tightening. Something was seriously wrong. Despite the dark circle under her eyes, she looked stunning. It was odd. She was clearly unwell, yet somehow even more beautiful, her face soft and flushed.

She walked into the office, which was about the size of a generous broom closet and sank into the chair behind the desk.

"You're worrying me, Lauren," I said, sitting in the only other seat. The flimsy folding chair groaned under my weight.

"There's nothing for you to worry about," she said.

"Bullshit. What's going on?"

She blew out a breath. "This is harder than I thought it'd be."

"Just say it. Whatever it is."

She straightened and looked me in the eyes. "I'm pregnant and it's yours."

I don't know what I was expecting her to say, but it wasn't that. "Wow," I said, grateful for the crappy chair holding my ass. I'm not sure I'd have stayed upright if I was standing. I knew we'd been reckless, but the last time we were together, Lauren mentioned she was on birth control. I'd have gotten around to asking her, if she'd have let me talk to her. "Wow, that's—"

"Unexpected," Lauren said, placing her hands on the desk like I was a Karma employee she was about to reprimand. "But you don't need to worry. I've decided to put the baby up for adoption."

"No," I said, the word firing from my mouth like a bullet.

"I don't want to be a mother," she said.

I tensed at how matter of fact she sounded, like someone saying they didn't want fries with their burger or milk in their coffee. "So? You'll sign over your parental rights to me."

Her eyes softened. "Aiden, you can't raise a baby on your own."

"When are you due?" I asked, choosing to ignore her last statement and the irrational urge to scoop her in my arms and hold her. She was clearly scared and not thinking things through. I wasn't putting my kid up for adoption. Not when I had a family like mine to help me. Not when the thought of my child calling someone else Dad made me want to throw up.

"December 8th."

"So you're about six weeks?"

She nodded. "I would have waited to tell you until after the first trimester—"

"Why?" In case she decided not to carry the baby. My baby. The last time I felt this helpless, I was lying in a hospital bed, my body broken, listening to my parents tell me Logan had died.

"The risk of miscarriage goes down after twelve weeks."

"That wasn't food poisoning at the wedding, was it? Did you know then?"

She nodded.

I sat back, all the air suddenly trapped in my lungs. She'd had considerable time to think about this. Maybe adoption was really what she wanted. It didn't matter. I'd never let that happen. "You should have told me as soon as you found out."

"It was Rowan and Cal's wedding and—"

"You saw me the very next day when we helped Poppy move in with Theo."

"I wasn't ready to tell you."

I thought back to the wedding and how near Cammie had kept to Lauren. She'd almost missed her cue to sing at the reception because she'd been checking on Lauren upstairs. A surge of anger hit me so intense, I wanted to punch a hole in the plywood office wall. "Cammie knows, doesn't she?"

Lauren looked guilty for the first time in the conversation. "She kind of figured it out. I have something called HG."

"Hyperemesis gravidarum," I said. "I know all about it. Ciara had it with her first kid."

"Oh," Lauren said, her eyes widening with surprise. "Well, I have it too. Unfortunately, the smell of coffee does a number on me, so Cammie offered to work here this week while Cal's away."

I blew out a breath and tried to get my anger under control. Lauren was sick. She didn't need me yelling at her on top of feeling like crap. How bad was the HG? Had she needed IV fluids again? Was she on medication? "I'm going to every doctor's appointment with you from now on."

"Absolutely not. It will only make it harder for you later."

"When I take my kid home?" I said. "Doubt it."

She slapped her hand against what little space remained on the desk. "I already told you. I'm putting the baby up for adoption."

"And I already told you no. Look, I don't want to upset you." Or make you consider other options. "I want to help. HG is a bitch."

"I know," she said, narrowing her eyes at me. "But there's nothing you can do."

Want to bet, Princess? I pulled my phone from my pocket and called Wyatt. He picked up right before the call went to voicemail.

"Wyatt," I said, without giving him a chance to say hello. "I need you back at Karma."

Lauren's eyes widened, but I didn't miss the relief on her face.

"Have I done something wrong?" he asked.

"Not at all. You're just needed here."

"Um, OK," he answered.

I figured he had a million questions, but one thing I liked about Wyatt was how willing he was to switch tasks without an explanation. "Head over to Karma now. I'll text Sam and let him know I pulled you." Good thing the Harris site was close to Karma.

"Sure. I'm kind of covered in plaster. Am I needed in the back or the front?"

I rubbed my forehead, shifting through a mental roster of all my employees to figure out what I needed to do to pull Wyatt from both sites. "Take a shower and get your ass over here." After I hung up, I realized I should have asked if he needed a ride to his car. I typed a quick text to Sam, telling him I'd pulled Wyatt for something else and asking him to find the guy a ride if he needed one.

When I looked up from my phone, a tear rolled down Lauren's cheek. Any lingering anger I had evaporated.

"Thank you," she said and grabbed a tissue to blot her eyes. "I haven't been able to replace him."

I was an asshole. First, I'd stolen her employee and left her under-staffed. Then, I got her pregnant. Then I yelled at her for not telling me about it sooner. "He's here as long as you need him," I said. I'd work nights if I had to on the Harris site, so I could send another guy over to the housing development site.

"I'll probably have to tell him I'm pregnant," Lauren said.

I nodded. "You should. You need all the help you can get. Have you told anyone else?"

She shook her head. "I didn't want to take away from Rowan's wedding and honeymoon. Or Poppy's trip."

"Yeah. That's probably smart. Theo's proposing in Greece, but you didn't hear that from me."

She smirked. "No, I heard it from him. I found the ring in his sock drawer when I was helping Poppy move in."

"Why were you in Theo's sock drawer?"

Her face turned a beautiful pink. "I wanted to make sure he wasn't hiding anything. I know he started therapy and that going through someone's sock drawer is a huge invasion of privacy, but I've seen people get creative when they want to self-harm. Finding an engagement ring instead of something he could use to hurt himself was a nice surprise."

She was looking out for him. Something Cal and I should have been doing all along. Yet again, her kindness hit me straight in the chest. Why didn't she want to be a mother? She was already mothering everyone around her. Instead of asking her and risk starting another fight, I smiled and said, "Thank you."

She smiled back and then seemed to remember we weren't friends. "So, um, thanks for Wyatt," she said, shuffling random papers on her desk. "I'd appreciate if you didn't tell Cal or Theo about the baby until I break the news to Rowan and Poppy."

I nodded. "You can tell them I'm fine with the guys hearing about it from them."

"I guess that makes sense. You probably don't want to talk about it."

My anger spiked again. "No, I just don't want Rowan and Poppy to have to keep something like that from the guys. They'd hate it."

Her eyes hardened at my tone. "Got it."

I shoved down all the things I wanted to say and focused on something I could do that wouldn't set off an argument. "I'll take a look at the back door now."

"Oh," she said, her cheeks pinking again. "It's fine. I just needed an excuse to get you here. I didn't think news like this should be texted."

I nodded. "I'm still going to oil that door. It sounds like nails on a chalkboard every time it opens."

"You don't have to."

"But I want to," I said, putting an emphasis on my words, so she understood we were talking about more than a squeaky hinge. "Whatever you need, call me," I said, rising from the plastic chair.

She stood as well and my eyes immediately went to her midsection. It was too early for her to show, but knowing she was carrying my child made my hands ache to touch her. She noticed me staring and wrapped her arms around her waist. "I'm fine, really."

In other words, I don't want your help. OK. But if she wouldn't let me help her, she needed other people on deck. "You should tell Rowan and Poppy as soon as you can. I know you wanted to wait until after the first trimester, but HG changes things. You need help." And I cannot keep this news to myself for another six weeks.

She nodded. "I'll tell them when Poppy gets back from Greece."

So, a little over a week from now. It'd be difficult, but I could manage that.

"When's your next doctor's appointment?"

"Not until the end of May. Unless I get dehydrated like I did at the wedding."

"The twelve-week ultrasound."

"Excuse me?"

"You'll be twelve weeks then, right? That's when they usually do the first ultrasound. I'd like to be there."

Lauren shook her head, and I pressed my lips in a firm line. I had six weeks to change her mind. No sense upsetting her now when she clearly felt like shit. "Let me get to work on that door. Would you like me to tell Wyatt about your HG when he gets here?"

She hesitated a moment but nodded. "Yeah, sure. I better get back to work," she said, dismissing me.

In a daze, I shuffled out to my truck for what I needed, then returned to the back door. The shock of the news wore off as I oiled the hinge. I was going to be a dad. I'd always wanted kids. Four actually. I loved my big family and wanted the same for my own children.

Lauren's pregnancy may not have been planned, but I couldn't stop my face-splitting grin. I'd figured it'd be years before I found someone and settled down. If all went well, I'd be a father before the year ended. At least the baby would have enough cousins to act as siblings if I never had more children.

I hung around in the parking lot behind Karma after I finished oiling the door, waiting for Wyatt to arrive.

"Hey," I said as he walked toward me, his eyes full of questions.

"Hey, Aiden."

I couldn't believe the first person I'd tell the biggest news of my life was a guy who'd just started working for me full time. I swallowed my disappointment and looked Wyatt in the eyes.

"So, Lauren and I are having a baby." But we weren't, were we? Lauren was pregnant with my kid. She wanted nothing to do with the baby or me.

Her womb might as well be a lockbox for how much power I had until she gave birth.

Wyatt's eyes widened, then hardened as he folded his arms across his chest. "I hadn't realized you two were together."

His tone sounded off. Almost challenging.

"We're not. Not that it's any of your business."

"Lauren is my business," he said with a glare.

What the fuck? Wyatt had always been so easygoing. Did he like her? Of course he liked her. Lauren was kind and loving to everyone but me. I'd watched her interact with Wyatt several times at the café and never picked up on an attraction, mutual or one-sided.

"Do you intend to help her?" he asked, stepping closer.

The guy wasn't small, but I could easily take him in a fight. Not to mention, I was his boss. Something in his expression felt familiar. My chest squeezed when it clicked that he reminded me of Logan.

"As much as she'll let me," I answered honestly.

Wyatt nodded and uncrossed his arms, further confirming my suspicion that his feelings for Lauren fell into the brotherly category.

That I could work with. "She's got terrible morning sickness, and she hasn't found your replacement. She needs to rest more, so I'd like you to fill in here until she hires someone."

Wyatt nodded. "I'll work as many hours as she needs me."

"Don't worry about the pay difference. I'll make it up."

Wyatt narrowed his eyes. "If she needs me, I'm here. You don't have to make up the difference."

"But I am," I said.

Wyatt studied me a moment. "I'd rather you just kept me on the company's health plan." He cleared his throat, looking slightly embarrassed. "I'm diabetic and insulin costs a fortune."

He'd never mentioned his health before, but I guess admitting I'd impregnated the woman he cared about enough to go toe to toe with his boss had put us in a different place.

"Deal. Just do whatever you can to make Lauren's life easier."

His face suddenly broke into a huge smile, like he'd been holding it back through our entire conversation until he confirmed I wasn't a deadbeat. "So you're going to be a dad?"

Something sparked through me that felt an awful lot like hope. I couldn't stop the smile on my face. "Yeah, well, it's still really early. You and Cammie are actually the only people who know for now."

Wyatt made a zipper motion across his lips.

I should tell him that Lauren didn't want the baby, but I couldn't bring myself to say the words. "If you could give me updates on how she's doing from time to time, I'd appreciate it."

"I take it she's not updating you herself?" he asked. The edge had gone from his voice. If anything, he sounded sympathetic, which meant he probably understood how closed off Lauren could be.

I shook my head.

"Yeah, sure," he said, and more questions formed in his eyes. Thankfully, he kept them to himself. "I'll check in with you."

"If there's anything I can do to help, let me know."

"Got it. I better get in there," he said, pointing to the door I'd just oiled.

As soon as the door shut behind him, I pulled out my phone and started a text to Cammie.

I reread the text and deleted it. Cammie wasn't an ally I could afford to lose.

I was taking down a wall at the Harris site when my phone buzzed in my pocket.

You have my word

Some of the tension in my shoulders eased. Between Wyatt and Cammie, I'd get a decent picture of how Lauren was doing. Spying on the mother of my child wasn't the greatest thing I'd ever done. But what could I do? Lauren had left me no choice.

Chapter Fourteen

Lauren

"Are you sure I should tell them tonight?"

Cammie looked up from the cheese board she was arranging in my small kitchen and smiled. "Yes."

"Don't you think it'd be rude? Like, 'I'll see your honeymoon and engagement and raise you an accidental pregnancy.'"

The corners of Cammie's lips quirked, but she managed not to laugh. "I think Rowan and Poppy are the type of friends who'd be more upset if you didn't tell them than the type who'd be angry about sharing the spotlight. Shoot, Poppy got engaged less than two weeks after Rowan's wedding. And Rowan is over the moon for her sister and Theo."

"She is," I said, letting out a sigh. Cammie and I were both on the video call with Poppy and Theo when they announced their engagement. Rowan's joyful reaction left zero doubt how pleased she was with the news. Of course, Aiden was on the call as well. He appeared to keep his focus on the happy couple, but he was quieter than usual. It'd been over a week since I'd told him about the pregnancy and, apart from a few texts asking how I felt and his usual coffee runs, he'd left me alone.

Now that Poppy was back from her trip to Greece, I'd invited her and Rowan to my apartment, presumably to hear all about their respective trips. I'd worn my favorite boho dress for a boost of confidence and to avoid the strong elastic squeeze of leggings against my tender stomach. Desdemona and Medusa had figured out something was up and were both curled in my lap, coating my dress with cat hair. Dido had somehow climbed to the top of the fridge, knocking off a few cereal boxes before she found the perfect spot to crouch down and stare at me. Of all people, she had to like Aiden. Ever since she met him, I swear her hisses had become louder, her glares more judgmental.

Cammie asked Wyatt to pull an extended shift, so she could be with me when I told the Stevens sisters my news. She said it was to support me, but I suspect she wanted to ensure I actually told them.

"All the cheese is pasteurized, by the way, so you can eat it," Cammie said, artfully draping a bunch of grapes on the board.

"Thanks," I said. "You really didn't need to go to all this trouble."

"Please, any excuse to eat cheese is a win for me. And you, my friend, need some calories. When was the last time you ate?"

"I had some crackers this morning."

A flash of concern crossed Cammie's face. "Well, I have plenty of those too, if that's all you can stomach."

"I'm fine."

Cammie glared at me. I'd lost at least ten pounds since the morning sickness began, and I swear she could somehow measure my weight loss to the ounce. Luckily, Rowan and Poppy thundered up the stairs and knocked on the door before Cammie could chew me out.

"Come in," I yelled from Grandpa's old recliner. Both cats lifted their heads, but quickly snuggled back into the worn leather, a smell I not only tolerated but enjoyed. I found myself sitting in the chair more than usual and falling asleep at random times of the day.

Rowan and Poppy burst through my apartment door wearing huge smiles. Rowan had a bottle of prosecco, which she held up in greeting, and Poppy had a plate of assorted cupcakes. Rowan walked straight to the drawer in my kitchen and got to work popping the cork. Since I didn't own champagne flutes, Poppy handed Cammie the cupcakes and grabbed four wine glasses from my cabinet. Cammie shot me a worried look when she put the cheeseboard and cupcakes on my small coffee table.

Well, so much for easing into the subject.

Rowan handed me a glass and took a seat on my two-seater couch. Poppy settled in beside her, and Cammie perched on the sofa arm closest to me.

"To love and friendship," Rowan said, lifting her glass.

I clinked glasses with her, then Poppy and Cammie. I held the glass while they all took a sip, hoping no one noticed I wasn't drinking. I'd gotten away with it at the wedding because of my "food poisoning" but abstaining from a toast wasn't something I'd ever do. Unless I couldn't drink.

Poppy reached for a piece of cheddar, completely oblivious, but Rowan studied me intently.

"Are you OK, Lauren?" she asked. "You look tired."

"Don't tell her that," Poppy said, making a neat stack of alternating crackers and cheese in her palm. "No one wants to hear they look like shit."

Rowan let out a sigh only a big sister could give a little one. "I didn't say she looked like shit. I said she looked tired. We both know Lauren has a habit of working too hard."

"True," Poppy said, ignoring her snack to study me herself. "Wow, you do look like shit, Lauren."

"Poppy!" Rowan said, smacking her sister's arm.

I took a deep breath and set my wineglass on the coffee table. "It's OK. I'd wanted to wait until after you told us about your trips, but I guess I better get this out of the way."

Cammie nodded, urging me on.

Rowan and Poppy both straightened their spines like they were bracing for bad news.

"I'm pregnant."

Despite their different styles and personalities, their shocked expressions looked so similar I almost smiled. They glanced at each other as if to confirm they'd heard the same thing, then back at me.

"There's more," Cammie said.

"I plan to give the baby up for adoption."

"I don't understand," Rowan said.

Poppy let out a huff. "She's having the baby, but she doesn't want to raise it."

"She doesn't think she can raise it," Cammie amended.

"Well, that's—" Rowan started.

"Bullshit," Poppy finished.

They all nodded in agreement.

I shook my head. "People with childhoods like mine have a way of repeating their parents' mistakes with their own kids."

You took the best of my looks and gave me all my problems.

I could have been something if it wasn't for you.

You're worthless.

I let out a sigh, hoping to push my mother's words from my mind. "I won't do that to an innocent child. Trust me, I'd be a terrible mother."

Rowan reached over and grabbed my hand. "For what it's worth, I believe you're someone who learns from mistakes instead of repeating them."

I gave her hand a squeeze and dropped it. "I guess I'm not willing to take that chance. Not with something this important."

"Tell them the rest," Cammie pushed.

"It's Aiden's."

"Wow," Rowan said, collapsing back onto the sofa. "I might need a minute. That's a lot to process."

"She neglected to tell you she's been extremely sick," Cammie added, taking a sip of her sparkling wine. "Like, needing IV fluids during your wedding sick. Aiden sent Wyatt back to work at Karma because the smell of coffee makes her puke."

"Sometimes," I said.

"Most times," Cammie said, reaching for a slice of Havarti.

"Are you seeing a doctor?" Rowan asked, all surprise pushed aside, her face etched with worry.

I nodded.

"How far along are you?" Poppy asked, finally closing her mouth.

"I'll be eight weeks on Thursday."

"What does Aiden think?" Rowan asked quietly.

I laughed, the sound as hollow and sad as a beautiful chocolate crumbling into air on the first bite. "He thinks he can raise the baby on his own."

Poppy set down her wineglass on the coffee table with a clang. "Why couldn't he? Women raise kids alone all the time. Our mom is a prime example."

"I'm not saying a man can't be a single dad," I said. "I'm saying Aiden can't."

"And you're basing this on?" Poppy asked.

I narrowed my eyes at her. "He's an immature asshole with a temper, which is why I already started researching adoption agencies."

Poppy's eyes blazed. She opened her mouth, but Rowan laid a gentle hand on her sister's knee. "If Aiden wants to be a father, why would you put the baby up for adoption?"

"Because," I said, my eyes burning, "he doesn't really want a baby. He just wants to use it against me. He's already trying to control my life. He wants to go to all my doctor's appointments. Can you believe that?"

Mom had a super controlling boyfriend once. Frank. He liked to set limits on how much we could eat or sleep or even speak, and he'd get irate if we didn't follow his demands exactly. Part of me wondered if Mom stayed with him as long as she did because she needed his financial help to support me, which was yet another reason why I didn't want to be a mother. I was never putting myself in a position like that again.

"Yes," Poppy snapped. "Aiden's a guy who shows up." To my surprise, Rowan didn't try to calm her down. "He's not trying to control you. He wants to be involved. You just don't like it since, for whatever reason, you two can't seem to get along."

"Unless you're naked," Cammie interjected, then buried her face in her wineglass.

OK, Aiden wasn't Frank, but he was demanding and resolve-crushingly hot while he demanded.

"It doesn't surprise me he wants to raise his kid," Poppy continued. "Honestly, I'm surprised you don't, but I respect your decision. What I don't understand is why *you* not wanting to be a mom means *Aiden* can't be a dad. This kid could be the most amazing thing to happen in his entire life. Preventing him is cruel, Lauren. I'm shocked, honestly. Not that you're pregnant, and not that Aiden is the father, but that you'd do something so hurtful."

I crossed my arms over my chest. "I don't want him at my doctor's appointments."

"And why is that?" Rowan asked gently.

I threw my hands up in the air. All three cats startled and stared at me, including Medusa, who couldn't see a thing. "I don't even want to go to my doctor's appointments. Next time they're doing an ultrasound, and I'll have to see the baby. Do you know how much harder that will make giving it up? Trust me, he'll change his mind. I know he will."

"He might," Rowan said. "But if he doesn't, that's the kind of wronged that's hard to forgive. Tell me this, if you found the perfect couple to adopt the baby, and they wanted to go to the ultrasound, would you let them?"

I didn't answer. Because I knew, and she knew, that I would gladly let the baby's adoptive parents join me at doctor visits. I'd encourage the bond as much as I could.

"Figured," Poppy said. "So you have more respect for a fictitious couple than the father of your baby? Got it."

"Dial it back, Poppy," Cammie said, her voice devoid of its usual warmth.

Poppy deflated a little, but when she looked at me, she had actual tears in her eyes. It was unlike Poppy to be so emotional or protective. She reserved both for people she genuinely cared for, which apparently now included Aiden. "I don't know what happened between you two," she said. "I agree he's rough around the edges, and maybe he's an asshole to you, but he's a good man. Better than most people even know."

"What's that supposed to mean?" I asked.

Poppy shrugged. "The asshole act is just that, an act. I know it. Theo knows it. And I suspect you might know it too."

"So you're saying he pretends to be an asshole?" I asked. Because I couldn't agree with her. That would expose too much of the night Aiden and I shared years ago. Underneath all that cocky attitude was a sweet guy who'd done his best with the curveball life threw his way.

"Yes," she said, narrowing her eyes. "Just like you pretend to be nice."

"OK, woah, Poppy," Rowan said. "She didn't mean that. Did you?"

"Guess not," Poppy said with a shrug.

She meant it. And what's worse, I agreed with her.

"Fine," I said. "Tell Aiden he can come to the ultrasound as long as he doesn't talk to me."

Poppy nodded. "That's a decent compromise."

Rowan handed me a red velvet cupcake, my favorite, and practically shoved a salted caramel one in her sister's mouth. "Now," she said with a bright smile. "How can Poppy and I help?"

"I'm fine," I said, placing the cupcake on the table next to my wine glass. My stomach was in knots from the conversation. No way was I consuming something with food coloring so I could puke red.

"She's not," Cammie said, peeling back the wrapper on a toasted coconut cupcake. "She needs help at Karma, and we're having a hard time finding it."

"I can cover mornings," Rowan said.

I shook my head. "It's wedding season. You got married in April because you knew how busy you'd be."

"And you're my best friend," Rowan said, breaking off the bottom of her chocolate cupcake and smashing it into the raspberry frosting. "We'll make it work."

Poppy swallowed her mouthful of cupcake and sighed. "I can work noon until Cammie's done at Cal's office."

"You hated working at Karma," I said.

"I hate feeling like a bitch more," she said, glaring at me. "If I don't help you, I'll play this conversation on repeat in my head."

"She will," Rowan said, taking a delicate bite from her cupcake sandwich.

"I promise not to yell at the customers, but as soon as you feel better, I'm out. I only have so much patience." Poppy picked up her wineglass and guzzled half as if bracing herself for the peopling in her future.

"Thank you," I said, looking at each of them. "I don't know how I'd get through this without y'all."

Poppy pressed her lips in a hard line, but I knew her well enough to guess what she wanted to say: I could let Aiden help me.

"You could let Aiden help you," Rowan said.

"You could," Cammie added.

I picked up the red velvet cupcake and shoved it in my mouth. I might regret it later, but I needed something sweet to pull me from my bitter thoughts.

Chapter Fifteen

Aiden

Cal

I don't know what to say

That's on brand

Theo

We're here for you, A

Thanks. I got to go

Cal

Don't shut us out

I'm not. I'm texting you in front of Everly's office. I'm late to meet her

Theo

You can go to the ultrasound as long as you don't talk to Lauren

How?

Theo

Poppy

I smiled and shoved my phone in my pocket. Hell Cat had used her claws for me. As much as I wanted to know what she'd done to get me an invite to the ultrasound, I really was late to meet Everly.

I grabbed the drink carrier from my passenger seat and headed toward the law firm with a bounce in my step. If Lauren gave into Poppy, maybe she'd listen to me and ditch her stupid adoption plan. The receptionist smiled when I entered the lobby. "You can go right back, Aiden."

"Thanks, Hattie," I said, handing her a chai latte.

She wrapped her fingers around it and sighed. "You're the best. It's been a week."

"It's been a month," I said with a wave before I tromped down the hallway to Everly's office. I probably should have changed out of my dirty boots, but I'd been so strapped for time, things like looking presentable in a lawyer's office had fallen away.

I still made my tri-weekly trips to Karma. As soon as I saw Rowan behind the counter this morning, I knew Lauren had filled her in. The texts from the guys confirmed it. I'd called Everly while I was in line at the café and asked to see her ASAP. By the time I got to the counter, I had an appointment and her drink order.

The door to Everly's office was open, but I gave it a knock, so I didn't startle her. Like Logan, Everly hyper focused when she worked. I'd lost track of the times I'd scared the shit out of Logan just by saying his name when he was studying. His reaction was so intense, it became my favorite prank to sneak into his house when I knew he'd be doing homework. As funny as it was to make a 220-pound linebacker squeal like a girl, I stopped doing it after I unintentionally gave Everly a jump scare as well, and she kicked me in the nuts.

Everly looked up from her computer and scanned my face. "Come in," she said, her expression blank.

I set the coffee holder on her desk and closed the door behind me. When I turned back to face her, I almost laughed. "Breathe, Ev. I'm not in trouble."

She reached for her drink but stopped when I added. "Well, not really."

"That doesn't sound good," she said, pulling her flat white from the carrier.

I grabbed my coffee and settled in the seat across the desk from her. "This isn't about work," I said, hoping to prepare her a little for what I was about to say.

She nodded. I'd known her long enough to know she'd already shifted her mind from property line disputes and zoning variances to the unexpected.

"No one in the family knows this yet."

"You're in my office, Aiden. Anything you say here is confidential."

"I know," I said, smiling at her irritated tone. "But what I'm about to tell you changes everything for me."

She nodded, keeping her expression stoic.

"I'm going to be a dad. At least, I hope I am."

"OK," she said, fighting to keep the calm on her face. Her eyes lit with joy, but she kept the rest of her expression neutral. "Who's the mom?"

"Lauren Arnauld."

"You knocked up Lauren at Karma?" she shrieked, but then remembered we were meeting in a professional capacity. "Sorry."

I waved my hand. "I get it. Shocked the hell out of me too. I'm scared, Ev."

Her eyes softened. "You'll be an amazing dad."

"Yeah, I hope so," I said, blowing out a breath. "But first, I have to convince Lauren to let me raise the kid. She wants to put the baby up for adoption."

Everly morphed into lawyer mode and grabbed a notepad. "You're sure you're the father?"

"We're not together or anything, but she seemed certain."

Everly nodded and scribbled something on the notepad. "We can easily confirm that."

"No need. I trust her. If for no other reason than it'd be easier for her if I wasn't the dad. Plus, the dates add up."

"How far along is she?"

"Almost eight weeks."

Everly looked up from the notepad. "You need to be careful."

"I know. I'm doing everything I can to make things easier for her while trying not to annoy her. She's got HG like Ciara had, and I'm worried she'll—"

I couldn't bring myself to say it, but Everly nodded. "There's nothing you can do to prevent that, Aiden."

I rubbed my forehead. "I know. I think she's committed to the adoption route, but I can't let that happen either."

"It won't," she said with so much conviction the knot in my stomach that'd been keeping me company for the past week and a half eased. "Virginia has a Birth Father Registry. Basically, you add your name as the presumptive father, and you'll be notified if she puts the baby up for adoption, so you can assert your rights."

"Will she know when I add my name?"

Everly shook her head. "Not unless she requests to check the registry or you claim your rights. We have until ten days after the baby is born to file."

"Fuck that," I said, hitting her desk. "I don't want some other family taking my kid home from the hospital."

Everly reached across the desk and put her hand on my fist. "We'll file after 27 weeks. Once you're in the registry, the child typically can't be adopted without your consent."

"Typically?"

"You'll be notified if she signs adoption papers, which can only happen after the birth, but it could get messy. She could argue you're unfit, and you'd have to prove your ability to care for the child."

"No judge in the state would find me unfit. I'm financially stable and have three sisters willing to testify they'd trust me to raise their kids."

"I agree," she said. "But as your lawyer and your friend, I'm advising you to do everything you can to convince Lauren to relinquish her parental rights to you."

"I couldn't even convince her to let me go to the twelve-week ultrasound."

"You have no right to attend her doctor's appointments."

"I know. Lucky for me, Poppy went into attack mode. I can go as long as I don't talk."

Everly blew out a breath. "I'd advise against doing that again. I get you want to be part of the pregnancy but keep your eye on the long game."

"So, you're saying I shouldn't go to the ultrasound?" I asked, the disappointment slamming into my chest like a brick.

"No, go. Just be on your best behavior and don't pressure her for anything else." She looked at the to-go cup in her hand and frowned. "Maybe cut back on the Karma trips. Send one of your guys if you're using them as an excuse to see how she's doing."

"I have people for that."

"I don't want to know," she said, trying not to laugh. "But for real, don't do anything that could be considered antagonistic. If she's granted a restraining order against you, it would really help her case to deny your paternal rights."

"Seriously, Ev?"

She nodded. "Seriously, Aiden. It's my job to think of the worst-case scenario. It's your job to prevent it."

"OK"

"Now, can I talk to you as a friend?"

"Sure."

Her face broke into a huge smile. "I'm so freaking excited!" She ran around the desk and wrapped her arms around me.

I laughed and returned the hug. "I like your friend reaction a hell of a lot better than your lawyer one."

"I promise to only bring out lawyer me when necessary," she said standing. "When are you telling everyone?"

"I'm not sure. Normally I'd wait until after the ultrasound, but she needed to tell people because she's been so sick."

"Your mom is going to flip out."

"Mom is going to tell me to make an honest woman out of Lauren."

Everly frowned. "You're right. You need to explain the situation."

"Or you could," I said, tugging a napkin from the drink holder and tearing it. "They'll have a hard time understanding why Lauren doesn't want the baby. When they find out she doesn't want me to have it—"

"They'll make Poppy look like a kitten."

"Yeah," I said, gathering the pieces of napkin and shoving them in the drink holder.

"Let's wait a bit and tell them together. I'll explain what you're up against and why they have to be on their best behavior."

"Thanks, Everly. I hate to drop this bomb on you and run, but I got three crews working at different sites and they're all behind."

"Of course," she said as I stood. She wrapped her arms around my middle and gave me another squeeze. "It'll be ok, Aiden."

I hugged her back but didn't say anything. On my way to the truck, I texted Poppy.

> *Thank you*

I should tell Poppy to stop fighting for me, but if I had to keep my distance from Lauren, I wanted someone near her who had my back.

> May 27th *2pm Dr. Phillips. Don't be an asshole.*

> *I won't say a word*

Chapter Sixteen

Lauren

When I arrived at my OB/GYN's office, Aiden was already seated in the waiting room in a chair facing the door. He looked up from his phone and nodded at me before casting his eyes down again. OK, so he really wasn't going to talk to me.

I hadn't heard a peep from him in six weeks. Not a single text to check how I was doing. He hadn't even come into Karma to buy coffee. I'd hoped he'd come to the same conclusion I had and accepted that the baby was better off with other parents. Probably not, since he was here now.

I signed in at the front desk and debated whether I should sit with Aiden or across the room from him. It would seem odd when the nurse called us back if we weren't sitting together. I should have called ahead and explained our situation. Rather than point it out in front of everyone else in the waiting room, I took a seat in the empty chair beside him.

His entire body tensed, but he kept his eyes on his phone. Half the waiting room snuck glances at him with obvious appreciation. I understood the lust-filled stares. Aiden was looking far too sexy for my own good. He even smelled sexier than usual. Now that I only threw up once or twice a day, a few new pregnancy symptoms had emerged. I'd gone up a cup size and my libido spiked to match. Mother Nature had a sick sense of humor. I was already pregnant. What need did I have for sex, biologically speaking?

Too bad my body thought otherwise. I needed to set up something with one of my friends with benefits. Someone whose orgasm skills were reliable and willingness to keep things casual established. I just had to get through the ultrasound with Mr. Pheromones first.

"Ms. Arnauld," a nurse called from the doorway.

Aiden and I both stood. He kept a solid six feet between us as he followed me into the back. "Dad can have a seat there," the nurse said, pointing to a chair on one side of the exam table. "Let me grab your weight before you lie down, Mom."

No one had called me Mom before. The word felt like a punch.

"I'm Aiden," I heard him say. "And this is Lauren."

I couldn't see him, but the nurse's reaction told me he'd somehow signaled for her to stop addressing me as Mom. "Ah, yes, Lauren," she said, scanning through my file on the laptop she'd carried into the room. "Hop up on the scale."

The nurse fussed with the scale and smiled at me. "You've maintained your weight since your last visit. That's great. I didn't see any hospitalization or ER visits in your chart. Have you needed intravenous fluids again?"

I shook my head. "I've been trying to take it easy, and that's really helped with the nausea. I'm only sick a couple times a day now."

The nurse nodded and typed into my chart. "Hopefully it will lessen even more in your second trimester. The ultrasound tech will be here soon. Go ahead and lie down on the exam table."

I stretched out on the crinkly paper and was hit with the smell of Aiden's cologne again. Damn, he smelled good. Like springtime and sawdust and toe-curling sex. OK, he didn't smell like sex, but his scent always reminded me of the night we shared. I wanted to bury my face in his neck and sniff.

Instead, I turned my head away and watched the nurse gently close the door after she stepped into the hallway.

Aiden settled back into his vow of silence. I heard him shift on the plastic seat, then clear his throat. That ultrasound tech better hurry up. The tension in the room was already making my head hurt. Another great side effect of pregnancy.

We waited in complete silence for a good five minutes while I stared at the door. I couldn't even hear him breathing. When the ultrasound tech finally arrived, Aiden and I both let out a sigh of relief.

"Let's get started," the tech said without so much as a greeting. I wondered if the nurse had given her a heads-up that ours would be an awkward appointment. "If you could just pull up your shirt and move your skirt down a little. I'm going to put some gel on your abdomen."

I'd thought ahead enough to wear a simple black tank top and a loose maroon skirt with an elastic band that I could fold down. I pushed my shirt up to my bra and flipped the elastic band on my skirt. The tech squirted a blob of warm goo on my skin. "We warm the gel, but the ultrasound wand is cold. Sorry about that," she said, using the wand to rub the gel across my stomach. "There you are," she said, pointing to the screen beside her.

Aiden sucked in a breath.

I'd told myself I wouldn't look. I'd stare at the ceiling or close my eyes, but that single breath broke me. I glanced at the screen and my heart skipped a beat at the white and gray image set against a perfect black oval. A tiny head. A curved little body. Buds where the arms and legs would lengthen and grow.

The tech hit a couple of buttons on either side of the image. "Gestational age puts your due date at December 8th. Would you like to hear the heartbeat?"

Aiden leaned closer to the screen, the awe on his face obvious.

The tech smiled at him, waiting for an answer.

"Yes," I said before I could change my mind.

He tore his attention from the screen and watched me as the tech hit a button and a staccato whoosh filled the room. I closed my eyes and listened.

"Can I have a picture?" Aiden asked in a broken voice.

My eyes snapped open in time to see him wipe at his face.

"Of course," the tech said, hitting another button. An image of the screen shot out of the machine on flimsy paper. "I'll get a few from different angles."

"Is it healthy? Big enough?" I asked.

The tech smiled. "The doctor will go over everything and call you if there's an issue, but between us, the heart rate is strong and the fetus is measuring the size of a lime, which is right where it should be. I can't tell the gender yet, but if you want to know, we should be able to tell you at the twenty-week scan."

My eyes filled with unexpected tears. "I was so worried. I haven't been able to eat much with the HG."

She nodded. "That's understandable." She moved the wand away from the little peanut and stared intently at the screen.

"What are you doing now?" I asked.

"Just double checking there aren't multiples. HG is common with those."

"Oh," I said, my stomach doing a dangerous flip. I glanced at Aiden, but he was focused on the screen. I spotted a nearby trashcan just in case and tried to breathe.

"Just the one," the tech said, moving back to the baby.

Something strange crossed Aiden's face. Something an awful lot like disappointment.

The tech snapped several more images before handing the ribbon of printouts to Aiden. She hit a button, and the same images reprinted on another length of flimsy paper. She tore it off and laid it on the top of the machine. "In case you each want a copy."

Clearly this tech had seen some shit.

"Thank you," Aiden said with genuine warmth. He stared at the strip of paper in his hands with a goofy smile on his face. I knew in that moment he wanted this baby, not to piss me off or for some weird ego trip, but because he already loved it.

I didn't know my dad, but I knew my mom. In all my time living with her, I never saw the powerful look of love on her face that Aiden gave that piece of paper. For the first time, the thought of him wearing an infant around town didn't feel absurd. "You really want this baby?"

He looked up from the pictures and nodded.

"You can talk, Aiden," I said as I rubbed the gel from my stomach with the paper towel the tech had handed me before she left. "You honestly think you can raise a child on your own?"

"I wouldn't be alone," he said.

"I told you. I don't want to be a mother."

"I just meant that I have a huge family. They'll love this baby and help me however I need."

I hadn't even had a decent mom. I couldn't imagine what it'd be like to have aunts and uncles and cousins in my life. Living with my grandfather had given me stability, but his affection was measured. I always felt like he gave me a home because it was the right thing to do, not because he wanted me. The only extended conversations we ever had were about books.

But Aiden wanted this child. Truly wanted it. He'd raise it in Peace Falls with his family, and I'd have to see them walking hand-in-hand to the ice cream parlor or playing in the park. Part of me was relieved I'd at least get to watch them from afar, but the selfish side, the side that had helped me survive my childhood no matter the cost, didn't want to know that pain.

To be always on the outside looking in. It was easier to think of the baby in some other place with some other family.

"I better get back to Karma," I said, rolling my shirt down and swinging my legs off the exam table.

"I'll walk out with you," he said, opening the door for me. We walked through the waiting room together, and I couldn't help but notice when he shortened the distance between us to about three feet.

"I guess I'll see you around," I said, heading toward Karma.

"Wait."

"Yes, you can come to the twenty-week scan."

"Great, but that isn't what I wanted to ask you."

"What, Aiden?" I said, turning around to glare at him. "Want to know if I'm drinking enough water? Or maybe you want to know if I'm still considering adoption after what we just saw in there?"

His eyes softened. "I want to know how you're doing. Maybe not down to how much water you've had, but I'd like to know you have everything you need."

"Right now, I need you to leave me alone, so I can get ready for my date."

"Date?" he asked, stepping so close I could smell his cologne again.

"More like a booty call," I said. Best way to lie: Throw in a little truth. If I had a date planned, it would have been more like a booty call. "But we'll probably order dinner in at some point."

"No," he said in the same tone he'd used when I told him I planned to put the baby up for adoption: commanding, resolute, and strangely hot.

"Excuse me? What makes you think you have any control over what I do with my body?"

He closed his eyes and blew out a breath. When he opened them again, all the anger had morphed into something more dangerous. "When I said everything you need, I meant it. You got an itch you need scratched, Princess? I can do that."

My stomach swooped. Aiden's ability to give orgasms was unparalleled, but our situation was complicated enough without adding sex.

"Go away," I said, shoving his hard chest. He grabbed my fingers and lifted them to his lush mouth, placing a gentle kiss on each sensitive tip. "If all you need is to get off, you know I can deliver."

"You don't want to sleep with me," I said, hating how breathless I sounded. "You just don't want me sleeping with anyone else while I'm carrying your baby."

"I *never* want you sleeping with anyone else," he said, eyes blazing.

My stomach dipped, but I straightened my spine and stared into his intoxicating eyes. "Remind me again why I'd care what you think?"

He snaked his arm around my back, pulled me close, and slammed his lips to mine.

Chapter Seventeen

Aiden

Holy shit, what was I doing? I'd given Lauren everything she needed to file a restraining order against me. And yet, she hadn't pulled away.

I ran my tongue across her lips, and she opened for me. Fuck, she wanted this too. Our tongues collided and I yanked her closer, letting her feel exactly what she did to me. She let out a whimper, and I rocked into her. I didn't care that we were on the sidewalk, in the middle of downtown, but she did.

"Stop," she said.

I dropped my hands from her waist and took a step back. Everly was going to kill me.

"I'm not yours to claim like that. Got it?"

"Claim?"

She held up her hand to stop me. "If we do this, no one knows."

I shrugged, trying my best to look like I didn't give a shit. She was carrying my kid for fuck's sake, but she didn't want to be seen with me.

"And you can't talk."

"Isn't that implied with not telling anyone?"

"During," she said, her eyes narrow. "You can't talk to me at all."

"Fine, but you can't either."

That seemed to surprise her, but she nodded. We looked at each other a beat before I started toward Karma. She ran a little past me, so I had to follow her. Fine by me. Her ass was the best view in town.

She turned down the side street that intersected Main a block down from Karma, and I followed her into the narrow alley that ran behind the storefronts. The employee parking lot and back entrance sat on the corner by the next side street. No one would see us enter the building, and because I'd greased the door, no one would hear us either.

While Lauren fumbled in her purse for her keys, I took the opportunity to mess with her. I pressed my body against her ass and ran my tongue down the smooth column of her neck. She tasted exactly as I remembered, salty with a hint of sweetness. I sucked the sensitive spot just below her ear. Learning all her fun buttons was a challenge I couldn't wait to master. She let out a soft sigh and dropped her purse. I did my best not to laugh while I grabbed it and handed it back. I didn't need to take control yet. I just needed her to know I could.

She unlocked the door and motioned me ahead to the staircase that led to her apartment above the café. I crept up the stairs on my toes like a damn robber, and she followed soundlessly behind.

I waited on the small landing at the top for her to unlock the door to her apartment, but she waved me on. I glared at her. How many people had a key to the back door? Not just the ones she knew of, but the people her grandpa had entrusted. The lock was older than Lauren. No telling how many keys were floating around Peace Falls.

She pushed past me to open the door. I followed her into the apartment and all the air rushed from my lungs.

It looked exactly the same as it had the night we spent together. She'd done so many renovations downstairs, I'd assumed the upstairs would be different. Blissfully unfamiliar. It wasn't.

I couldn't move my damn feet. I placed my hand on the sofa where we'd talked for hours. I'd laid my heart out on the musty old couch, and the sight of it pulled me right back to that night. I'd told her things I'd never told anyone, not my family, not my best friends. Things I barely admitted to myself. Like how lost I felt without Logan. How angry I was that my dream of playing pro ball had been taken from me. How guilty I felt for caring about a game when Logan would have done more important things with his life.

And she'd opened up too. She'd told me about her childhood. About bouncing from foster home to foster home. Never feeling like anyone had her back. She confessed she didn't think anyone would like her if she wasn't perfect all the time. That she rarely trusted anyone.

Lauren hadn't paused on her way to the bedroom, but she must have sensed I hadn't followed. She turned and I yanked my hand from the sofa before eating up the distance between us.

I placed my hands on her hips and pushed her gently toward the bedroom.

Thankfully, she'd redecorated the room. The bed looked new. Which, considering the old one's springs had poked my ass, was a needed improvement.

Lauren didn't give me time to look for other changes. She ripped off her tank top and kicked off her flats before shimmying out of her skirt.

I wished she'd have let me undress her. I loved peeling a woman out of her clothes. It felt like unwrapping a present. I always took my time like I did with any gift. But Lauren was already down to her mismatched underwear. Her body had changed in the best ways. Her breasts were more than a handful now, her hips rounder.

I kicked off my shoes and pulled my shirt over my head. She sucked in a breath. I stared at her as I dropped my shirt on the floor and unbuckled my belt. Her cheeks reddened and her breath became labored, which made the color in her cheeks deepen. She wanted me, but she didn't want to want me.

Fine. I could live with that.

Before I shucked my jeans, I pulled out my wallet to grab a condom since I always wore protection when I hooked up with anyone—minus one drunken encounter in St. John. She crossed the room and knocked it from my hands. OK. We'd obviously had unprotected sex before, and I knew I was clean. I knew her well enough to know she wouldn't put anyone in danger if she had something. She wanted me bare, and that's what she'd get.

I dropped my pants, and she reached around and popped open her bra. Her breasts were fuller, softer looking. I wanted to bury my face in them.

She dropped her panties and stood before me completely naked. I yanked off my boxers, my dick fully ready to join the party, but when I reached for her, she placed both hands on my chest and shoved me onto the bed.

I'd barely landed, my feet still dangling off the side, when she straddled me and rubbed my cock against her slick folds. I leaned forward to kiss her, but she shoved me flat on the bed with one hand while guiding me into her entrance with the other.

We both groaned as she lowered herself onto me. She leaned forward, placing her hands on my chest and lifted herself off me before slamming back down. She started a pace guaranteed to race us both to the finish.

Usually, I loved when women took their pleasure, but this was Lauren. I didn't want to be her real-life dildo, even if that's what I'd signed up to be.

I wrapped my arms around her waist and stood. She let out a gasp and frowned at me. I turned and placed her flat on the bed. A flash of fear shot across her face. Maybe she was worried I'd crush the baby. I knew I wouldn't, especially this early, but I figured it was better to change positions to put her at ease.

I pulled out and climbed onto the bed beside her. Now she looked pissed and confused. This would be a hell of a lot easier if I could just tell her to kneel and grab the headboard. Instead, I had to position her body like some blow-up fuck doll, which she apparently found funny. All the mirth drained from her face when I lifted her arms and pinned them to the headboard.

That's right, Princess. I was taking control. I used my torso to bend her forward, so her ass lifted for me. Then, keeping her hands pinned with one of mine, I used the other to guide myself back into her tight heat.

I ran my free hand across her breast and rolled her stiff nipple in my fingers. She let out a moan and squeezed my cock, her breath coming in pants. I knew Lauren was responsive, but this was next level. She wiggled her ass, trying to get more friction, her legs shaking with need.

I started to fuck her with languid strokes. I wanted this to last, but I also wanted to give her what she needed. Multiple times. I slid my hand from her breast to her clit and gave her the speed she wanted. Fast, firm. Unrelenting. She shattered in moments, crying out so loud I wondered if people could hear her in the café below.

I hoped they could. Her body sagged against the headboard, completely drained. Shit. She looked exhausted. As much as I wanted to keep pounding into her, she needed to rest. I pulled out again and she turned to look at me over her shoulder, her eyes questioning.

I climbed off the bed, my cock painfully hard and straining for her. When I reached for my pants, she scooted off the bed and placed my hand on her breast. Thank fuck. She wasn't done either. I started to lay her down on the bed like before and the same look of fear crossed her face.

I stopped, unsure what to do next. Did she want me to fuck her? Did she want me to leave? My confusion must have been clear on my face because she smirked.

You want to smirk at me, Princess? Fine. I'll fuck the smirk right off that beautiful face. I just needed to know what positions were off limits.

She pointed at me and pointed to the mattress. I let out a frustrated huff and stretched out on the bed, placing my hands under my head. I guess I could be her fuck toy. This time.

My eyes rolled back when she sank onto me. Instead of the frantic pace she'd set before, she moved her hips in achingly slow circles. Every muscle in my body tightened. I fought to keep still, to keep from taking her like I wanted. Hard. Punishing. Unforgettable.

Instead, I watched her ride me. The sight of her, head thrown back, hands gripping my chest as her breasts bounced above me, made my balls tighten. Fuck, she was gorgeous. I wasn't going to last long enough for her to come again. As if she could read my mind and wanted to test me, she quickened her pace. I was about to place my hands on her hips to slow her down when she suddenly found her release.

"Aiden," she cried, her nails digging into my skin.

My name on her lips sent me over the edge. I came and came until my vision darkened. I reminded myself to breathe as she climbed off me and laid on her back panting. When I reached for her, she curled onto her side, putting as much space between us as possible.

It hurt, even though I'd expected her to pull away. She'd made it clear she didn't like me, that at best she'd ride my dick instead of someone else's to get off and then go back to pretending I didn't exist. But she'd said my name when she came. And, fine, I can admit I like holding a woman after being inside her, the comfort of her skin on mine while we're both relaxed and sated.

I laid my hand on her hip, testing. She didn't tense, but she didn't move closer. I swallowed my pride and inched closer to her. She still didn't move. I wrapped my body around hers and placed my hand on her stomach. She snuggled into me and let out a soft snore. I fought the urge to laugh. She'd fallen asleep. Deeply asleep.

I should leave and let her rest, but what if she woke up and thought I'd ditched her? I could leave her a note but scribbling *Text me when you need my cock again* on a piece of scrap paper didn't sit well.

I should leave because I had a million and one things that needed my attention at three different job sites. But fuck it, I had Lauren Arnauld in my arms, my hand resting on her body where the child we'd made together was healthy and safe. I'd been so preoccupied with the baby's heartbeat earlier, I hadn't realized how emotional I'd gotten until I tried to speak. It felt strange to cry, even stranger because I was so damn happy.

I might never get an opportunity to hold them both again. I'd learned the hard way to take what I could get from Lauren. I'd thought our incredible night together was the start of something amazing. You don't share your deepest fears and biggest dreams with a one-night stand. You share body fluids and a good time. But that night wasn't just about getting off. Not for me, and I suspect not for her either.

I curled my body closer to Lauren's, savoring the earthy smell of her shampoo, the softness of her skin, before slipping into the most peaceful sleep I'd ever known.

Chapter Eighteen

Lauren

THERE WAS ALWAYS A moment of panic on the rare occasions I woke in someone's arms. In the place between sleep and waking, my mind sometimes forgot the life I'd made for myself and recalled only those clandestine fumblings when I woke terrified, my body someone else's plaything. I reminded myself that my body was now my own before remembering it wasn't. Not completely. Surprisingly, the thought filled me with warmth instead of fear.

When I opened my eyes, night had turned my windows black. Thankfully, all the lights were off, or anyone on Main Street would have been able to see inside my bedroom. Aiden's arm rested over my waist, his large hand splayed across my stomach. He held me so close his head shared a pillow with mine. The warmth of being surrounded by another person was both soothing and suffocating. I didn't cuddle. Ever. It felt too intimate, too reckless. At least for someone like me.

I should elbow him and push his arm off, but for the first time since I saw the positive pregnancy test, the fear clawing inside my chest had quieted. I lay still, enjoying his heated skin on mine, until his arm tightened, and his thumb brushed my stomach with gentle strokes.

I turned in his arms and his eyes fluttered opened. His hair was an adorable mess in the weak light from the streetlamp. He gave me a small smile and my chest squeezed. Yep, reckless.

"We fell asleep," I said, stating the obvious.

He nodded.

"I need to get downstairs and help close."

He tightened his arms around me and kissed the spot just beneath my earlobe that drove me wild. An ache formed between my thighs and deepened when I felt him harden against me. He lowered his hand between us and let out a groan when he found me soaked. Pregnancy was doing things to my lady parts and my brain. Sleeping with Aiden was the worst thing I could do, again, but as he slipped a finger inside me, I gave up any pretense of stopping him.

I'd always enjoyed sex, perhaps in some twisted way because of what I experienced in foster care, perhaps in spite of it. I found power in owning my pleasure. Only now, I was desperate for release, the urge overriding any sense of control. I didn't want foreplay. I wanted him inside me. I gripped his thick cock and gave it a solid pump before throwing my leg over his. He pulled his hand away, and I guided him exactly where I needed him. He rocked into me, the fullness so exquisite my eyes burned. Or maybe it was the way he held my face in his hands. It was too much.

"I can't," I said, my voice strained.

He rolled onto his back, pulling me on top of him. I closed my eyes and rode him hard, fast, my orgasm exploding at embarrassing speed. I knew he wasn't anywhere near finishing, so I kept my eyes closed and continued moving as I fell back down. To my surprise, the ache built again, deeper this time. I'd always been a one and done woman with everyone else, everyone but Aiden. As I grew impossibly tight around him, I had to fight to take all his length. He panted beneath me, bucking his hips at a frantic tempo. Still, he didn't come, no doubt waiting for me.

He reached up and rolled both of my nipples in his rough fingers, and I cried out, pleasure unlike anything I'd ever known shooting through my body. My release kept going on and on, so intense I screamed his name until my throat ached.

He let out a deep groan that rumbled up my core as he came, setting me off again. I collapsed on top of him, our bodies still connected, and tried to catch my breath. He rubbed slow circles on my back until I could finally draw in a lungful of air. I'd tried to prevent this feeling by avoiding eye contact. It wasn't the first time sex with Aiden had been so intense I'd almost blacked out. But it should be the last.

I climbed off him and hurried into the bathroom, slamming the door behind me.

"You OK?" he asked from just outside the door. "Are you sick?"

"No talking," I yelled. I flipped on the light and gripped the edge of the sink. "Stop being an idiot," I told myself in the mirror. "Sex is just physical. It means nothing."

"If I can't talk to you, you can't talk to yourself."

Had he heard what I said? I decided he hadn't, otherwise he'd have kept quiet and continued eavesdropping on my mirror pep talk.

I turned on the faucet and splashed cold water on my face, which immediately woke my bladder. Once I'd taken care of business, I pulled my silky pink robe from the hook on the back of the door and tied it around me.

"Everything all right?" Aiden asked when I opened the door. He was standing in my bedroom completely naked with the blinds still open, the light from the bathroom and shadows enhancing every contour of his toned body. I quickly reached back into the bathroom and flipped the switch.

"Fine." I hurried to the windows and yanked down the shades, pulling darkness around us. "I need to get downstairs. You can show yourself out."

I groped my way to the wall and flicked on the overhead light before fumbling around on the floor for the clothes I'd ripped off before we fell into bed. My cheeks warmed at how desperate I must have seemed to him, both then and just now.

"Sure," he said, "but since we're talking, I just want to reiterate that if you need anything, call me."

"We aren't in a relationship, Aiden," I said, sliding my bra straps over my shoulders. "I won't be calling you for anything."

His eyes narrowed. He still hadn't bothered to reach for his clothes, and the fact he had the confidence or composure or cajónes to fight me while buck naked was sexy as hell. "I know we're not together, Lauren, but you're carrying my child. I'll do anything for that little lime. If that means pipping you down on occasion, so be it."

Little lime. The tiny human growing inside me this very minute. "You can't control who I sleep with."

He nodded. "I know. I also know no one makes you come as hard as I do."

"You sure about that?" I yanked on my skirt and waited.

He stepped into my space, so close I could smell the cedar of his cologne, my own perfume on his skin, the primal scent of our sex. "Positive."

My breath left my lungs in a whoosh and that stupid ache started again. I needed to invest in some better toys or something.

He smiled and his entire face brightened. "I'm happy to use those on you too."

My mouth fell open. "I did not say that out loud."

He let out a short laugh. "You didn't have to. You looked at your nightstand, and if I remember correctly, that's where you keep all your sex toys."

"You haven't been here in years."

He walked over to my nightstand, opened the drawer, and pulled out my favorite vibrator. "Did you want me to use this on your now?" he asked, turning it on.

My idiotic vagina clenched in anticipation, but I yanked the toy from his hand and turned it off. "So you can get me off. Big deal. In case you didn't notice, my orgasm is on a hair trigger these days."

His eyes heated and a slow smile spread across his face. "I noticed. I wonder how many times I could make you come before you begged me to stop."

My clit throbbed, but I finally ignored it. "However many times I came today," I said, grabbing my shirt and tossing it on. "This was a mistake. I'm begging you to stop now."

He looked pained but nodded.

My chest ached. I'd hurt him. Again. I tried to be a nice person. I tried really hard, but with Aiden, I couldn't stop saying and doing the wrong things.

"Thank you," he said as I started to leave. "It meant the world to me to see the baby today and hear its heartbeat."

I stared at my bare feet. I couldn't look at him. His sincerity would crush me. "You're welcome. But I really need to get to work."

"Would it be OK if I came by Karma once in a while? I just want to see with my own eyes that everything's good."

Of course, he wanted to check up on me. Make sure I was doing exactly what he wanted. I glared at him. "I'd tell you if anything was wrong with the baby."

He nodded and pressed his lips together, like there was something he wanted to say, but decided against it. "I'll show myself out."

I hurried through my apartment, only stopping to slip my feet into my flats, and went downstairs. It wasn't until I was in the back that I realized I had no clue what time it was since I'd left my phone in my purse, which

I'd tossed on my sofa as I led Aiden into the apartment. According to the clock over the industrial dishwasher, Karma didn't close for a couple hours. Based on the noise beyond the door, we had a full house.

The moment I stepped into the front, Cammie rushed me.

"Thank the stars," she said, wrapping her arms around me while holding a mug in one hand. "Is everything OK? When I got here, Poppy said you hadn't been back since your scan. Then you didn't answer anyone's texts. Is the baby OK? Your face is flushed. Have you been crying?"

Aiden chose that moment to stick his big head out the swinging door. "I'm getting you a new lock for the back. Don't argue with me."

Cammie's eyes widened as she took in his disheveled hair, his misbuttoned shirt, the boots in his hands. She looked at me again and smirked.

"I don't need a new lock," I said. "The back is keyed the same as the front."

"Then I'll change the front too," Aiden said. "With locks that old, no telling how many people have keys. Hi, Cammie."

She wiggled her fingers at him, and he bent over and started putting on his boots for everyone in the packed café to see.

"I don't need new locks." But shit, I probably did. Grandpa was kind of a loner, but chances were he'd given keys to someone at some point. I should have changed them years ago.

"Come on, Lauren," Cammie said, pulling me into a side hug. "Let the man give you a key for your lock."

Aiden threw his head back and laughed. Dido yowled and booked it across the café toward him, startling more than one patron.

"I hate you both," I said.

"Well, look at that," Cammie said as Dido sat on Aiden's boots mewing. "That cat doesn't like anyone."

Aiden stepped completely through the door, crowding me in the small space behind the counter and bent to give the cat a scratch.

"We don't let animals in this area," I said, shooting him a glare. Bullshit, since the cats pushed in and out of the swinging door all day to get to my apartment. Still, I pointed to the bookshop.

"Ah, a rebel," Aiden said, scooping up Dido and lifting her to his shoulder. "I always did like a rule breaker." He winked at me and walked around the counter toward the bookshelves.

Cammie smiled and filled the coffee mug in her hand with dark roast.

"I don't want to talk about it," I said as Aiden pushed out the front door, stopping briefly to examine the lock. Dido shot through the café. She stood at the glass door, meowing frantically as she watched him walk away.

Suddenly ravenous, I grabbed a double fudge brownie from the display case and shoved half of it in my mouth. After Cammie handed the mug to the teenaged girl who'd been waiting patiently, she poured a glass of water and set it on the counter in front of me. She didn't say a word.

Damn her and her understanding silence. Of all my friends, her past was most like mine. She respected my boundaries and was firm with her own. Oddly, knowing she wouldn't press me made me want to tell her about what had happened today.

"He cried during the ultrasound," I heard myself say. "He was so happy."

Cammie nodded like that didn't surprise her. "He'll be a great dad."

"How could you know?" I asked. "What makes someone a great dad anyway?"

"That's easy," Cammie said with a sad smile. "A good dad loves his kids more than himself. A great dad does the work to give them the best he can."

"I know he'll be a good provider." Even I could admit Aiden was a hard worker. He'd just started his company the first time we got together, and as the years passed, I couldn't help noticing the projects he took on around town and the growing number of people he employed. Wyatt wasn't the first to tell me Aiden was a good boss, generous and fair.

"It's more than that," Cammie said, drumming her fingers on the glass counter. "A great dad works on himself, so he's the best person he can be for his kids. That's where a lot of parents fail. At least that's where mine did. I'm guessing yours too."

"Mine didn't get past your 'good' definition," I said with a bitter laugh.

Cammie nodded, not pressing for more. "I've watched Aiden for a while now, the way he's helped Theo and Cal become better men. He's the one who made them finally work through Logan's death and everything that came after. I'm not sure where he is on that journey himself, but I know he's started it. I'm just saying, of all the guys who could have gotten you pregnant, you lucked out. Karma was kind to you."

"Karma's a bitch," I said, shoving the rest of the brownie in my mouth. "How many men would lean into this situation? Most would have let me put the baby up for adoption without a fight," I added around a mouthful of gooey chocolate.

"And why exactly are you fighting him?" she asked in a soft voice.

I swallowed the last of the brownie past the lump forming in my throat. "Can you imagine what it will be like if Aiden gets his way? The poor child will have to grow up in this tiny town where everyone knows everyone's business, seeing me and knowing I didn't want to be his or her mother. Aiden hasn't thought this through, at least not as far as the baby and I are concerned. He needs to stop fighting me."

She gripped my shoulders. "When are you going to realize he's not?"

"Excuse me, have you not seen the two of us snarl at each other like feral dogs?"

"You're fighting yourself, Lauren. From where I'm standing, he's been fighting for you, for the woman he knows you could be."

"That's ridiculous."

She shrugged. "Let him win once in a while and see what happens."

I guzzled the water while giving Cammie my best don't-fuck-with-me stare. It'd saved my ass in more than one foster home.

She just wrapped me in another hug. "I know, hon. I know."

And that's how I ended up crying my eyes out in front of the entire SAT-prep club, including Rowan's brother Chris, and the local writers' group. Based on the sympathetic looks beamed my way, the entire town either thought I'd lost my mind or figured out I was pregnant. Probably both.

Chapter Nineteen

Aiden

Five days and not a word from Lauren. I'd had the usual updates from everyone around her. Wyatt confirmed the morning sickness remained, but Lauren had been able to eat small meals. Rowan sent me detailed accounts of everything Lauren consumed and the number of times she ran out of the cafe, presumably to be sick. I didn't ask for that level of detail, but I had to admit, it helped quantify Wyatt's vaguer insights. What's an OK day? What's a bad one? Rowan's texts were like a cheat sheet for Wyatt's. Poppy refused to spy for me because "she'd done enough already and wasn't a creep." Cammie didn't text often, but when she did, she reported more about Lauren's headspace than her physical wellbeing. Cammie's the one who told me to give Lauren time before coming into Karma again. I took her advice until I couldn't anymore.

A steady rain beat against my windshield as I sat in my truck a block from the café, trying to decide if I'd make the situation worse by showing my face. It'd been somewhat easy to keep away while I worked my ass off, but the remodel on Harris Street wrapped up yesterday, and the two housing development sites were shut down because of the rain. My phone buzzed in my pocket. I ignored it.

Theo and Cal had been trying to see me since they found out the news. We hadn't gone this long without getting together since Theo's incarceration and Cal's college days. I'd told them I was busy, which wasn't a lie, but I'd also been avoiding them.

I responded to their texts often enough that they hadn't searched me out. I'd even stopped by Red Blossoms Bakery yesterday to install more shelving. Unlike Theo and Cal, Poppy had let the elephant in the room stretch out and take a nap while I worked. Then she'd shoved a to-go box of my favorite apple streusel at me and told me to stop being a wuss and talk to Theo before I gave him a panic attack.

I never wanted to trigger one of those, but I still couldn't bring myself to give more than single word replies to my friends. Why? Because they were already too involved. I relied on their women, and to some extent, them, to maintain a connection with Lauren. I couldn't vent to Theo and Cal about how much it hurt to be shut out by the mother of my child because they'd tell Rowan and Poppy and then Lauren would know the terrible truth: I wanted her. Not just because she was pregnant, though feeling the slight changes in her body and her hyperresponsiveness had blown my mind, but because I'd never stopped wanting her.

I'd tried. Fuck, I'd tried. I'd avoided her as much as anyone could in a small town until Cal started dating Rowan. At first, I'd been too humiliated to say anything to Lauren. But her obvious disdain for me made it easy to act like the stupid asshole she thought I was. I gave back as good as I got, savoring every time I made her angry because then I knew she felt something for me—even if it was hate. It had to mean something.

So instead of keeping my distance, like Cammie advised, I hopped out of my truck and ran through the torrential rain into Karma. I'd timed my visit between the early morning rush and lunch break coffee grabs, hoping Lauren might have time to talk. Rowan smiled at me from behind the counter when I walked in and wiped my boots on the rubber mat by the door.

"Hey," she said as I made my way inside. "Are you here for Lauren?"

"I am, but I didn't tell her I was coming. Do you think now's a good time?"

"Should be. Things were so quiet, Lauren went to change the litter box."

"She what?" I must have yelled because Rowan took a startled step back.

"Sorry," I said, working to push the anger from my voice. "Are you sure?"

"Um, that's what she told me and then she headed to the closet in the back of the bookstore where she keeps the litter box."

I knew which door with the cat-sized cutout she meant and stormed through the bookshelves without another word to Rowan. When I got to the closet, it was open, and Lauren was on her knees inside.

"Stop," I yelled so loud an old guy who I vaguely recognized as a Karma regular spit his coffee down the front of his shirt. He glared and kept his beady eyes focused on me as Lauren grabbed the door frame and pull herself up.

"What's your problem?" she huffed.

"Go wash your hands."

"Excuse me?"

"Damn it, woman. For once in your life, just listen to me."

The old geezer rose from the leather sofa and shuffled toward us. "Is there a problem?"

"Oh, Mr. Fitzwilliam," Lauren said, staring at his soaked shirt. "Are you OK? Are you burned?"

My brain fired at the name. Mr. Fitzwilliam. Brandi's father-in-law.

"I'm fine, sweetheart. I put so much milk in my coffee it's tepid at best. Are you all right? Is this man giving you trouble?"

"Just ignore him. I do."

"She's pregnant and changing cat litter," I blurted out to Mr. Fitzwilliam because if anyone in this town was going to help me right now, it'd be him.

Lauren shot me a death glare that made my balls shrivel, but Mr. Fitzwilliam grabbed her elbow and marched her straight to the small bathroom by the coffee bar. "Make sure you use soap and sing happy birthday twice," he said, crossing his arms over his wet shirt while he waited for her to follow his directions.

"I don't understand," she said, standing in front of the sink but making no effort to wash her hands.

"For fuck's sake, Lauren, wash your damn hands."

Mr. Fitzwilliam shook his head. "You need to learn some finesse, young man."

We stood outside the door while Lauren thoroughly washed her hands and dried them on a paper towel. By the time she'd finished, Rowan had abandoned the counter and the customers she'd been helping to stand with us.

"What's going on?" she asked, clasping her hands together.

"Pregnant women can't change cat litter," Mr. Fitzwilliam said calmly. "There's a parasite in cat poop that can cause birth defects. Didn't your doctor tell you?"

Lauren paled. "Maybe. I was so sick at the first visit, I'm not sure I remember everything. It was probably in the packet he gave me."

"Damn it, Lauren," I said, fisting my hands at my side. "What else have you been doing? Drinking coffee? Eating sushi?"

"Aiden," Rowan said, placing a firm hand on my arm. "I didn't know about the cat litter either."

"Well, you know now," I said, raising my voice. Cal was going to try to kick my ass later for sure. "Someone other than Lauren needs to change the litter every day. Got it?"

Rowan nodded.

"Fuck that, I'll do it myself," I said, heading back to the closet.

As I passed through the café and bookshop, I realized everyone had stopped whatever they were doing to stare at me. Great. By this afternoon, the entire town would know about Lauren's pregnancy and, given my outburst, make the understandable assumption I was the father.

I squeezed myself into the narrow closet and started flicking cat turds into a plastic bag with a scoop.

"You didn't have to yell at me," Lauren sniffed behind me. "Now everyone knows."

Part of me felt like a complete asshole for making her cry, but I wasn't sorry. "You put my kid at risk. What did you think was going to happen?"

"I didn't know," she said, quietly.

"Clearly or you wouldn't be standing there. Toxoplasmosis can be airborne. Back up."

"How do you know all this?" she shouted from further away.

"Because I've been through ten pregnancies before yours," I said, leaving out what had happened to Brandi and Max. There was nothing more I could do now.

I tied off the bag and carried it straight to the dumpster after yelling for Rowan to open the door, getting good and soaked in the process. Lauren stood outside the tiny bathroom while I washed my hands like I'd been handling an Ebola-infected monkey brain and started to calm down.

"I drove to my sisters' houses every time one of their husbands had a work trip during their pregnancies to change the litter," I said calmly. "Let me help you. I'm not doing it for you. I'm doing it for the baby."

And for her. But she didn't want to hear that, especially from me. Because I didn't want her to know the guilt I'd seen in Brandi's eyes every time Max struggled.

"I'm sorry," she said again. I finally looked at her and my heart ached. She hadn't stopped crying and both Rowan and Mr. Fitzwilliam looked like they wanted to kick me in the junk. I half wished they would. "But you have to get control of your temper," she said, narrowing her eyes at me. "People make mistakes. Kids make mistakes. Are you going to be the kind of father who screams at his kids? Because if you are—"

"You'll do what? Have an abortion? Yes, Lauren, I understand I have no fucking control over what you do with your body, but I can't stand by and watch you do something so stupid."

She paled, and Rowan rushed to her side. "You need to leave, Aiden," Rowan said.

The front door flung open and Cal and Theo thundered inside, not even wiping the water from their shoes before gripping my arms and dragging me out into the rainstorm.

"What the fuck?" I asked as they pulled me toward Cal's car. His dog, Skye, barked at me from the backseat, and I fought against them for the first time since they'd laid hands on me. "I'm not getting in there with the dog."

"Fine," Cal said, turning us around and dragging me toward my truck. "I'm driving though. Theo, get his keys for me, then take my car and Skye back to your place. I'll take Aiden to mine."

Theo shoved his hand in my jean's pocket and started rooting around like a cop about to start a pat down. "They're in my jacket," I gritted out. He grabbed my keys, then smacked me on the back of the head for good measure before shoving me into the passenger seat of my truck.

"Not a word," Cal said, starting the ignition and following behind Theo. "Not one word until we're at my house."

We rode in tense silence to Sullivan Street. I took my time climbing from the truck while Cal went ahead of me to unlock his front door. At least the dog wouldn't be here.

"I didn't mean to scare Rowan," I said, dripping on his welcome mat.

"Take off your shoes," Cal said, throwing me a towel. "You're not going anywhere for a while. I'll grab you a change of clothes once Theo gets here."

"Afraid I'll ditch as soon as you leave the room?"

"Yes," he said, without a hint of humor in his voice. "And what do you mean you scared Rowan? All she did was text that you were at Karma. Theo and I figured it might be the only chance we got to talk to you since you keep blowing us off."

"Where are his keys?" Theo asked, coming in the front door without knocking and kicking off his boots.

Cal tossed my keys to Theo, and he shoved them in his pocket. Cal was in great shape, but Theo had scrapped his way through a year of state prison. No way in hell would I be attempting to take those keys from him.

"What do you mean you scared Rowan?" Cal asked again, crossing his arms over his chest.

I pointed to Theo. "Keep him off me."

He nodded and I took a step back from Cal to give myself a chance to block a swing. "I lost my shit because Lauren was changing the cat litter. I yelled at Rowan. Or rather, I yelled, and she was the one standing in front of me."

"Why can't Lauren change cat litter?" Theo asked.

"Toxoplasmosis," Cal said, frowning.

"Exactly," I said, throwing up my arms.

"Am I supposed to know what the fuck that is?" Theo asked.

"No," Cal said, shaking his head. "But Lauren should."

"Like I said, I lost my shit. I'll apologize to Rowan."

"I don't think she's the one you need to worry about," Cal said, sinking onto his couch in his wet clothes.

"Yeah, I know. I'll apologize to Lauren too."

Cal narrowed his eyes. "That's a given, but I meant Theo and me, asshole."

Theo nodded and took a seat next to Cal on the couch. Cal pointed to the armchair where I usually sat whenever I came over to watch games. I flopped down and waited, my wet jeans chafing me and my shirt sticking to my chest like shrink wrap.

"First, I had to hear you're going to be a father from my wife," Cal said, holding up a finger, his middle one. "And then you refused to talk to us for six weeks," he added, holding up the middle finger on his other hand.

Double salute. This wasn't good. "You just got married. And you," I said, pointing to Theo, "just got engaged. You have enough going on without worrying about me."

"Unbelievable," Theo said, fidgeting with one of the gauges in his ear. In the past, I'd say he was pulling on it to hurt himself, but he seemed lost in thought rather than anxious. "The jerk hands us our asses any time we're slightly off base, but he's not man enough to come to us when he needs help."

"I don't need help."

They both burst out laughing.

"I don't."

"Keep telling yourself that, brother," Theo said.

My chest ached. "What did you call me?"

Theo glanced at Cal, confused. Cal shrugged.

"You called me brother," I said.

"Yeah," Theo said, tilting his head to the side. "What's the problem?"

"You don't call me that. Ever. That's what you and Cal call each other. You call me man or A or asshole."

Theo scrubbed his hand down his face. "Shit. Why didn't you say something before?"

Cal looked between Theo and me and shook his head. "I'm confused."

Theo blew out a breath. "I should have realized when you told me I had to be Cal's best man because he calls me brother."

"Seriously, can someone please explain what's going on?" Cal asked.

"He thinks he's a second-tier friend," Theo said. "That you and me are closer than he is with either of us."

"Because you are," I said, surprised by how hurt I sounded. "You always have been. Just like Logan and I were."

"Oh shit," Cal said, as though the thought had never crossed his mind. "It's not like that."

"Well, it kind of is," Theo said with a shrug. "Less so now than when Logan was alive. But, Aiden, the brother title doesn't mean what you think it does. Cal and I never had siblings to call us brother like you and Logan did. It started as a joke because we were jealous."

"Jealous?"

"Yeah," Cal said. "Your older sisters doted on you, still do. And Logan's sisters looked up to him like he hung the moon. I always wanted a sibling, so did Theo, so we just kind of decided one day to be each other's."

"Bullshit," I said, getting angry. "Theo's your best friend. Just like Logan was mine."

"So you're saying we're second-tier friends," Cal said, leaning forward to put his elbows on his knees. "Got it."

"I'm not sure how this has anything to do with him ghosting us after finding out he's going to be a father," Theo said.

Cal put his hand on Theo's shoulder. "Like I said, we're second-tier friends."

"For fuck's sake," I said, standing. "I've been avoiding you because I'm terrified, OK. I'm scared I'll never stop remodeling and demoing my house every few months because I'm still pissed Logan died, and I had to stop playing ball, and I hate myself for even thinking about football when my best friend is dead because of me. And yes, I'm scared the two of you will become even more of a family than you already are and realize you only hang out with me because we're trauma bonded. And I'll be left alone in my half-demolished house, talking to Logan like a lunatic while Lauren gives up my child for adoption or worse. Oh, and just so everything's on the table, I'm scared I'll never find a woman I like more than her, so I'll die alone since she hates me."

Cal and Theo stared at me with their mouths hanging open.

"Well," I said, slapping my hands on my wet jeans. "Say something or give me my damn keys."

"That's a lot to process, brother," Cal said.

"Fuck," I said, rubbing my forehead. "Now you're doing it too?"

"Yeah," Cal said, standing. "I'm calling you brother from now on, asshole, because that's what you are to me. I figured you'd want to reserve the title for your sisters, but hey, who am I to judge?"

Theo still hadn't moved, which I guess was better than having a panic attack. Finally, he looked up at me and smiled. "Does this mean we finally get to see the inside of your house?"

I shoved his shoulder and he stood up, pulling me into a hug. "Thank you," he said, taking a step back. "I know it wasn't easy sharing all that with us."

Cal nodded. "Now that we know what we're working with, we might be able to help you."

"Good," I said, gripping each of them on the shoulder. "Cause I'm going to need all the help I can get to convince that woman we can raise our kid together."

CHAPTER TWENTY

Lauren

As soon as the door shut behind Aiden, Mr. Fitzwilliam gently took my arm and walked me to the closest chair. "Move," he told the young man at the bistro table, who was clearly on a first date with the woman across from him. The guy jumped up from his chair and the young woman quickly left her seat as well. They both grabbed their drinks and scurried to the back of the store. If they became a couple and got married, one day they'd be telling their children about their crazy first date at Karma.

Mr. Fitzwilliam took a seat across from me. "I didn't know," I said again.

"Here," Rowan said, shoving a glass of water at me.

"I'm fine." It would have sounded more convincing if my voice hadn't cracked on the second word. I took a sip of water and tried to center myself. "I'm fine," I said with more conviction. "Can you please help the people in line? They've been waiting."

Rowan's eyes widened like she'd completely forgotten about the customers staring at us. "Of course," she called out as she ran back to the counter.

Mr. Fitzwilliam reached across the table and wrapped his weathered hand around mine. "Brandi didn't know either."

"Max?"

He nodded and my stomach dropped. For a terrible moment, I thought I might throw up the small sip of water I'd drunk onto him.

"I'm not telling you to make you worry, but to explain why that young man got so heated. I'm assuming he knows Brandi and Max?"

"He does," I said, thinking back to all the times he slid her a twenty when she waited on our group at the bar where she worked. "Now that I think about it, Brandi probably went to school with one of his sisters. His name is Aiden O'Malley."

"Ah, yes," Mr. Fitzwilliam said. "That explains it. Kayleigh is my daughter-in-law's best friend. She's one of the only people outside our family Brandi trusts to babysit Max."

"Should I call my doctor?" I asked as an overwhelming panic made my breath come in spurts.

"If it'd make you feel better, why not? There's no sense making yourself sick with worry." He squeezed my hand. "Congenital toxoplasmosis is rare, and Max's case is more severe than most. The Karma cats stay indoors, so that lowers the chances quite a bit. But you should listen to Aiden and have someone else handle the litter for you."

I pulled my hand from Mr. Fitzwilliam and forced a smile on my face. "Thank you. I think I might go upstairs and lie down now."

He shoved back from the table at the same time I did. I could feel his eyes on me as I walked past the line, which had thankfully shortened during our brief conversation. "I'm going to lie down," I told Rowan. She nodded and continued adding whipped cream to a drink in a to-go cup.

Desdemona meowed the second I stepped into the back and hopped toward me on her three legs. I froze. Could I still pet my cats? "Sorry. I need to check first," I said, rushing past her into my office. I shut the door, one of the only ones in the entire building without a cat entrance and woke up my computer.

After reading enough about toxoplasmosis that I had to heave into the wastebasket under my desk, I came to two conclusions:

First, I could do everything I usually did for my cats except change their litter.

Second, the universe had confirmed I was never meant to be a mother.

The doctor gave me that packet of information for a reason, and I was too clueless or selfish to learn what I needed to know to protect the baby. A good mother would have taken the time to read a few sheets of paper.

After a quick call to my doctor's office, who did their best to calm me down, I exited out of all the terrifying toxoplasmosis articles and searched for adoption agencies in Virginia. I clicked through the different sites, my stomach knotting. I knew Aiden had rights. However, just because he was eager to be a dad didn't mean he was ready. Yes, he apparently knew more about pregnancy than I did. Yes, he had a large family to support him. But Aiden didn't have it all together. I knew it. And I think deep down, he knew it too. Losing Logan and his dreams had scarred Aiden for life. He was quick-tempered and brash, two qualities that could terrify a child.

I should know. Mom had dated a couple of hotheads like Aiden. One had tossed me across the room into a wall because I hid the remote right before the Super Bowl. Another shouted to the entire neighborhood that I'd wet my bed again and asked if anyone had diapers for ten-year-olds. I knew comparing Aiden to either of these men wasn't fair, but parenthood had a way of widening the cracks in someone's personality.

He wasn't a bad person. Which was why I might have a chance to convince him to do the best thing for our child. I clicked around until I found an agency I liked and created an account. Once I logged into the private portion of the site, I had access to video clips of prospective parents.

There was so much hope in everyone's videos, so much love waiting to be shared. I stopped wiping the tears from my face and allowed myself to cry freely as I clicked and watched, clicked and watched. And then I found them. The perfect family.

They had already adopted one child and wanted another to give their son a sibling. Some people might think it'd be wrong to give parents another baby when so many childless couples were waiting for their first. Perhaps that was true, but it also meant they'd already proven themselves as parents. The joy on their son's face confirmed it. The way they interacted with him in the video made my heart ache. They were the exact type of parents I'd watched with envy my entire life. Kind, connected, and stable, the love between the three of them blazingly obvious. Not to mention they lived in Northern Virginia and had asked for a closed adoption. I'd never have to see the baby again.

I placed my hand on my stomach. What I'd told Cammie was true. I'd experienced the pain of seeing a parent I couldn't live with. The few times I'd visited Mom while in foster care had been some of the most hurtful and confusing hours of my life. And selfishly, I knew I couldn't bear to see my child being raised by someone else. Which was why I absolutely had to convince Aiden to place the baby up for a closed adoption.

Chapter Twenty-One

Aiden

I sent Lauren an apology text right after I left Cal's. She shocked the hell out of me by apologizing back for being careless. It didn't sound like Lauren. At least not the version of herself she reserved for me. My Lauren would have handed me my balls on a platter for behaving the way I did, in the middle of her business, no less. I didn't like it. The text was too forgiving, too polite, too Citizen of the Year Lauren. I'd messed up. Big time.

Instead of trying to get a rise out of her via text message, I laid low a few days until Sunday afternoon, when I knew both Cammie and Wyatt would be working at Karma. I had the locksets I'd picked up and an excuse to be there while I installed them. And yes, I know, installing new locks at a café during weekend hours was a stupid idea, which was exactly why I chose it. The tables were filled, and Wyatt and Cammie were both hustling behind the counter.

Cammie glared at me, but Wyatt gave me a respectful chin dip and went right back to work. I ignored them both and walked into the back with my toolbox. I had everything spread out on a drop cloth by the back door when

Lauren came running down her apartment stairs in an oversized Peace Falls High t-shirt, purple fuzzy slippers, and nothing else.

She was without question the most beautiful woman I'd ever seen. Her long, toned legs went for miles, ending under her shirt, which I'd bet my tools she'd thrown over her naked body. Her chestnut hair was in the usual side braid, but pieces had fallen out, framing her face. Her eyes looked heavy, liked she'd bolted out of a deep sleep to race down the stairs and stop me. I felt a prick of guilt for waking her since I assumed with the hours she kept at the café she didn't get enough sleep for a regular woman, let alone a pregnant one barely in her second trimester.

"I told you, I don't need new locks," she said, crossing her arms over her chest. Either in annoyance or to hide her pert nipples, probably both.

"Spare me," I said, turning on my drill. She only got real with me when I acted like an asshole, and I was more than willing to oblige.

She kept talking, but when I didn't respond, she shoved my shoulder. I switched off the drill and smiled up at her like a jackass. "What's that, Princess?"

She let out a huff at the nickname and the tension in my shoulders eased. Perfect Lauren had left the building. The riled-up woman before me was exactly who I'd hoped to see.

"Stop making all that racket," she yelled. "Why would you come here on a Sunday afternoon? You know we're always packed, and you can't change the front locks without stopping foot traffic into Karma."

I narrowed my eyes, doing my best to look pissed even though her reasonable reaction was exactly what I wanted. "Because I work the other days. This is the time I have for this little project. Unless you want me switching the locks at 4:00 am."

She nibbled her bottom lip, and I stayed quiet while she went through whatever tornado of thoughts swirled in her beautiful head. "We close at five today. Can't you do it then?"

I smiled. Not only had I gotten her to agree to installing the locks, she'd given me a couple of hours to kill, and I knew exactly what I wanted to do with them.

"I guess I could do that, but I'll need to borrow you until then."

"Borrow me? Really, Aiden? We're not having sex again."

I shrugged like her brush off didn't hurt like hell because as much as I wanted a repeat of what we did the day of the ultrasound, I had other plans. "You know I'm down for that whenever you change your mind, but that wasn't what I wanted."

"What else could you possibly want with me?"

Everything. "Your opinion."

She snorted. "Like you've ever cared about that."

I stood and walked close enough to make my chest ache. Fuck, I wanted to touch her. But there was something I wanted more: her trust. Falling into bed wasn't the way to get it. "I want your opinion on the remodel I'm doing at my house."

She shook her head. "Bullshit. You flip homes for a living. There's no way you need my advice. You're just trying to lure me into your sex den and tickle me with feathers until I beg you to fuck me."

A genuine laugh burst from my chest. "What the hell, Lauren? Do you honestly think I have a sex den?"

She shrugged, her cheeks pinking. I couldn't tell if she was embarrassed or turned on, and the ambiguity sent a rush of blood to my cock. I shifted, hoping she couldn't see the semi she'd just brought on.

She fiddled with the hem on her short shirt, which only made the situation in my jeans worse. "Rowan and Poppy said you never let anyone in your house, not even Cal or Theo. I figured if you're inviting me, it's because you do something kinky there and mistakenly assumed I'd want to play with you."

Yeah, Princess, I want you to play with me. I shook my head, desperate to clear the images of Lauren in a windowless playground of sex toys. "I never let anyone into the house because I've been remodeling the kitchen and bathrooms then demoing them after. I've done it over and over again for the last two years."

Her brows scrunched in confusion. I couldn't blame her. I'd just waved my crazy flag right in her face. "Why? Are you that bad at making design choices?"

"I wish," I said, sticking my hands in my pockets. This conversation was happening exactly as I'd planned, but actually getting the words out was like walking through wet cement. Theo and Cal seemed to get it without further explanation, or rather they didn't need an explanation to accept my weird because they had plenty of their own. "You said I have anger issues."

She nodded.

"I guess anger is my default, so I don't feel other things."

"Like fear," she said, her eyes widening.

"Yeah," I said, dropping my eyes to my boots. "Or grief. Disappointment. You name it."

She shocked the hell out of me by hugging me around my waist and resting her head against my chest. "You do all the work to make something wonderful and then destroy it because of what happened to you and your friends."

I bent and rested my head on her shoulder so she could feel me nod before I pulled my hands from my pockets and wrapped her in my arms.

"What can I do to help?" she asked gently.

This. Everyday. Let me hold you when I fall asleep and wake up with you in my arms. Let your warmth fill the rooms of my house instead of my regret and one-sided conversations. "Help me make the final design choices," I said instead. Because anything else I told her would send her scurrying. "I think if someone knows my plan, I'll be less likely to tear it up after I finish."

She dropped her arms, and I let her step away from me, even though every cell in my body wanted to cling to her. "Why me?"

I shrugged. "You have the lowest opinion of me of anyone I know, so I figure you're the safest bet to keep me accountable."

Several emotions crossed her face at once: shock, sadness, anger, before she erased them all. "OK, let me get dressed," she said, turning and running back up the stairs to her apartment, flashing me a glorious view of her bare ass.

I got to work packing up my tools and pushing down the shock that she'd agreed to come with me. A few minutes later, she returned in a short flowery sundress that showed way too much skin for my self-control and a pair of flip flops.

"Do you have sneakers or boots? I do my best to clean up, but there could be nails."

"Oh," she said, glancing at her feet. Her toenails were painted a deep red like a ripe berry. I'd always been more of a tits and ass man than a foot guy, but every inch of this woman turned me on. "I have rain boots. Would those work?"

"Sure," I said, pulling my eye from her toes. She came back down wearing a pair of navy plastic boots covered in cats. Cats preening. Cats sleeping. Cats chasing balls of yarn. Fucking adorable.

"You like them?" she asked with a smirk.

"Hell, yeah," I said, bending to get a closer look. "Where'd you buy them? I'm getting pairs for my nieces, so I can see them all the time." I pictured the girls all lined up in matching boots. Maybe I could find raincoats to go with them. I'd have to get my nephews something too. Frogs maybe. Anything but fucking dogs.

When I stood back up, Lauren was staring at me with a strange look on her face. "Do you, um, do that sort of thing often?"

"Like someone's rain boots?" I asked. I honestly didn't have a clue what she was asking.

"Get things for your nieces and nephews. When it's not their birthday or Christmas or something."

"Yeah, I'd buy them stuff more often, but my sisters would have my ass if I spoiled them too much. Rain gear is practical. Anything like that, I can usually get away with. I got them all swimsuits last summer for our Fourth of July party and rented a water slide and splash pad."

"That's nice," she said in a small voice.

I wanted to press her, to understand how rain boots could shift her mood so quickly. I reminded myself she was pregnant and pregnant women changed moods faster than Usain Bolt. "After you," I said, holding open the back door.

She walked ahead of me into the parking lot and toward her beat-up sedan.

"I can give you a ride."

She looked over her shoulder and flashed me a dimpled smile, and I swear my stupid heart skipped a beat. "No, thank you. I want my car in case you were lying about that sex den. Are you parked on Main?"

"Yeah," I said, walking backward down the alley toward my truck. I didn't like the idea of her driving that rust bucket anywhere, but my relationship or situationship or whatever you wanted to call it with Lauren had always included some give and take. "I'm parked at the corner."

"Great," she said, opening her car door with a key. The car was so old, it didn't even have a key fob, but at least she'd locked it.

In my truck, I wrapped my sweaty palms around my steering wheel and paid more attention to my rearview mirror than the road ahead. By the time we both started down the dirt road leading to my farmhouse, my stomach hurt.

"Wow," Lauren said, climbing from her car. "There's so much space out here."

"I love it," I said, taking her arm as if we were back at Cal and Rowan's wedding. "The ground's a little bumpy. I don't want you to fall."

"Oh my gosh, you're as bad as Cal with Rowan," she said. The smile slid from her face, and she wrapped her arm in mine. "He must be so worried."

I honestly hadn't given Cal a thought lately, but the tone of her voice raised the hair on my arm. "What's wrong?" Shit, I'd been a bad friend. I'd been avoiding Cal for so long, who knew what fresh hell could have dropped into his life. I figured if something terrible happened, Theo would have filled me in.

"Rowan's surgery," she said like I was the biggest idiot on the planet, which right now I might be. "Wouldn't you be worried if someone you loved was having an operation on their spine?"

I'd forgotten about Rowan's surgery. I knew it was scheduled for some time in June, but I couldn't remember if it was the beginning or the end. If it was in the beginning, it could be as early as tomorrow. "Yeah, of course, I'd be worried sick," I said, making a mental note to text Theo later and get all the details.

We walked through the yard and up the porch steps without talking. I dropped her arm while I unlocked my door because even out here in the middle of nowhere, I wasn't making it easy for anyone to wander in. I motioned her ahead of me and enjoyed how her dress's thin straps framed her delicate shoulders from behind.

"This is incredible," she said, standing in the center hall.

I'd bought the house because it was next door to the barn, but I fell in love with it because of the entrance. The detailed woodworking on the walls and the staircase was unexpected and masterful, far grander than you'd expect in a farmhouse. "I did a little digging and found out a furniture maker built the house for his daughter and son-in-law."

She ran her hand over the ornately carved chair rail. "There's a lot of love in this. You can feel it."

Sometimes Lauren's new-age hippie tendencies drove me crazy, but I had to agree with her in this case. Now that I thought about it, maybe I should ask her to sage the house. But I had a feeling the only bad vibes here were mine, which I'd dump right back the moment she finished waving a sage stick around.

"I'm not touching this room," I said. "Other than to give the walls a fresh coat of paint and make sure the light fixtures are wired to code."

She nodded, still admiring the details in the trim work. As much as I appreciated the talent that went into making it, I didn't want to spend all our time in the front hall.

"The kitchen is through the dining room here," I said. "Watch your step."

The room was large enough to hold a table for ten, which covered all the adults in my family, plus an extra chair on the off-chance I ever found someone I wanted as much as I wanted Lauren.

"I'll warn you," I said as we walked through the empty dining room. "It's a mess." I slid the pocket doors into the walls and her eyes widened at the destruction beyond.

"Right now, this is the only way in here, but I'm taking down a wall on the other side of the house to connect the kitchen with the living room and give the first floor an open concept feel."

"You have a lot of space to work with," she said, not commenting on the various holes in the walls that could only come from someone going apeshit with a hammer. "In all your remodeling, did you ever come across things you liked more than others?"

"Light wood cabinets," I said. "Like scrubbed pine with brushed nickel finishes. Maybe white with brushed copper."

She smiled at me. "So am I here to pick between those two?"

"Or suggest something better. What would you put in here?"

"I like white cabinets. Definitely a light countertop too, so you can see if it's clean."

"How about light gray marble?"

"Fancy," she said. "If you go with copper finishes, you could add pops of dark blue."

"That could work. I thought about adding a breakfast table with bench seating there," I said, pointing to a corner by the large bay window. "I could make that a slate blue or colonial blue to bring in color."

She shook her head and laughed.

"What?"

"You clearly don't need me for this. Why don't you just show me the rest of the house, so I can picture it in my head, and then you can tell me what you decide to do. I'll hold you accountable."

Because I want to know what your perfect home would look like. Because I don't give a shit if it's white cabinets or scrubbed pine. I just want to drink my morning coffee with you. "Sure. I'll show you around."

I quickly showed her the rest of the downstairs before motioning for her to climb the steps ahead of me.

"I swear if you slap my ass, I will punch you in the throat," she said, gripping the railing.

Her ass was very smackable, but I wouldn't risk her falling down the stairs for a cheap feel. "I promise to keep my hands to myself."

She still glanced behind her several times before we got to the top of the staircase and looked relieved when I started walking beside her. I gave her a brief tour of my room and my latest bathroom remodel.

"Don't change a thing," she said, admiring the steam shower. "This is perfect."

"Thanks," I said, opening a drawer in the vanity to demonstrate the soft close.

"It reminds me of the bathroom we shared in St. John."

"Yeah, I might have stolen some inspiration from there."

She poked her finger in my chest. "If you tear this bathroom apart, I'm telling the entire town you have a furry fetish."

I threw my head back and laughed, the sound echoing off the tile.

"Great acoustics for singing."

I caught a glimpse of my burning cheeks in the mirror before I led her out into the hallway again. "I'm thinking of turning this room into a second primary by combining it with the room next to it. I can add an en suite like the one in my room."

"Why would you do that?" she asked, peeking into both rooms, which at the moment were empty and decorated with '90s floral wallpaper.

"There's currently five bedrooms," I said, answering her question and not answering it at the same time. "I'll either turn this one into a home office or a guest room, maybe a combo space," I said, pointing to the room closest to the stairs. "And this," I said, walking ahead of her into the final room. "Will be the nursery."

She froze in the hallway.

"I was waiting to paint and decorate after the twenty-week scan, assuming you want to find out if it's a boy or a girl. If you'd rather be surprised, I can go with neutrals. I mean, I can do that either way if conforming to gender stereotypes isn't your thing."

"You have furniture," she said, her eyes wide.

"Yeah, my oldest sister is done having kids, or so she says, so she passed along her crib and changing table. I'll need to get a dresser and maybe one of those glider chairs. There's wood flooring under the carpet, which I'll rip up and then we can get a rug—"

"We," she said, feet still planted in the hallway.

I shoved my hands in my pockets as my nerves made them shake. "Yeah, I um, thought maybe, if you wanted, you could move in here with me, so we can coparent better. The second primary would be yours."

I'd wracked my brain for all the reasons a person as nurturing as Lauren didn't want to be a mother and settled on two: lack of housing and help. I knew there were countless reasons more, but those two seemed the biggest I could easily eliminate.

The look of horror on her face was enough to suck every ounce of confidence from my body. OK, I know I'd dropped a lot on her, but did she have to look like I was the Beast about to lock her away in my house? And yes, I know my fairytale references. Any stellar uncle would.

"You want me to live with you?" she said, her feet finally moving. Backward. Toward the stairs.

"It's just a thought," I said, holding up my hands like I was trying to settle a wild horse. Definitely time to pull back. Did I want her to move in? Absolutely. But more than that, I wanted her to trust she could depend on me. "I could get your apartment ready for the baby instead, if you want. That second bedroom at the back would make a better nursery since it overlooks the alley. It'd be quieter than your room facing Main. Hell, I can fix up your apartment and put in a second primary here. Then you won't have to choose right away."

Her eyes filled with tears. "I never had rain boots when I was a kid."

OK, not what I was expecting.

"I didn't even have pajamas. I used to envy the kids who had them. I called them pajama rich, like that's even a thing. And living somewhere like this," she said, motioning to the upstairs at large. "Wasn't something I could even imagine."

I took a cautious step toward her, watching carefully for signs she was about to bolt as I shrank the distance between us. Lauren had given me another peek into her past. I'd be a fool not to attempt to learn more. "That must have been hard," I said, walking close enough to watch her pulse jump in her throat.

She nodded and her eyes went glassy. "It's why I have so many clothes and shoes now. I don't spend money on anything else because I'm always worried—"

Her voice dropped off, but for once I knew exactly what to say. "You're worried something will happen and you won't have enough to get by."

She nodded and everything clicked into place. The beat-up car. The dingy apartment. The small staff at Karma despite the obvious success of the business.

"I didn't have a lot growing up," I said gently. "But I always had what I needed."

"You had so much more than that," she said, the tears falling freely now.

I nodded. "And so will our child. Our little lime will have so much love and will never want for anything. I promise you that. And if you'd let me, I promise the same for you."

She turned and started walking down the hall. My heart shattered, but before I could call after her, she turned into my bedroom, leaving the door open for me.

Chapter Twenty-Two

Lauren

I SHOULD HAVE LEFT. I should have gotten in my car and driven back to Karma. My stomach felt settled, so I could have worked behind the coffee bar for the first time in weeks. My mind knew this, but my feet turned into Aiden's bedroom instead of walking down the stairs.

The rest of the house was either a construction zone or rooms with little to no furniture, but the primary suite looked like something out of a home design magazine. The space gave masculine vibes without being cold. Warm greens, rich woods. Homey. The man had throw pillows. Multiple. Sure, he didn't have them on the bed, but they were stacked on a long window seat that looked comfy enough to sleep on.

Aiden called my name from the doorway. I wanted him to give me space. I wanted him to come to me. I wanted to wind back time and erase all the shit in my childhood that made me an indecisive mess.

I closed my eyes and imagined the rest of the house remodeled to the same level of perfection as his bedroom. What would it be like to grow up in a house like this? With a man like Aiden? With a family like his? Cousins to play with, aunts and uncles to step into the parent role when needed, grandparents who hugged. I didn't know for sure if Aiden's parents were huggers, but he was so tactile, I had to think they were.

"Lauren," he said again, this time closer.

"You brought me here to show me the home you can give the baby." My voice sounded frayed, heartbroken.

"Yes," he answered without hesitation.

My eyes snapped open. I knew in that moment he'd never agree to put the baby up for adoption. I started shaking, the tremors began in my hands and rocked through my body until my legs weakened. A pair of strong arms steadied me from behind and guided me toward the king-sized bed, which was even softer than it looked.

Aiden sat beside me on the fluffy green comforter and took one of my unsteady hands. "Talk to me, Princess."

"That's the stupidest nickname you could have picked for me," I said, but I gripped his hand tighter as though it was the only thing tethering me to this side of sanity.

With his other hand, he brushed a loose piece of hair from my face. "I don't know. I think you look pretty regal, especially when you let your hair down."

"I hardly ever wear it down."

"I know." He let go of my hand, slid the elastic from my braid, and undid each strand with his fingers so gently I wanted to cry.

He wrapped a section around his finger and rubbed it with his thumb. "Definitely princess material. I love how soft it is and how long you keep it."

I sucked in a breath. He didn't know I wore it cropped before I came to Peace Falls. Have your hair yanked enough times and it became a weakness, not something to be admired, cherished.

"Bullshit," I said weakly. "You chose the name because you enjoy pissing me off."

"Nah, that's a bonus. I called you Princess in my head long before I ever said it out loud. If it makes you feel better, you can give me a nickname."

"Oh, I already have one, but I'll never say it out loud." I can't believe I just told him that. Pregnancy brain must be real.

"That bad, huh," he said with a huge smile. I hoped the baby inherited his smile. Life would be easier for anyone with his warm grin. "Come on. Let me hear it."

Telling him could change everything. But hadn't it already changed? I could no longer pretend we hadn't been together, that I didn't know what it felt like to be in his arms. I placed my hand on my stomach and cleared my throat. "What If."

"What if what?"

"That's it. What If."

He nodded. "It fits. I think that way more often than I should. What if Logan never died? What if I had a chance to play college ball? Would I have gone pro?"

I shook my head. "What if I hadn't pushed you away years ago? What if I hadn't been too scared to let you in?"

He dropped his eyes to his hands, which he'd balled into fists on his lap. "Don't say shit like that to me, Lauren." His voice was low, each word pushed out with precision.

Fear flooded my body. When did I become so stupid? The girl I was would never have put herself in this position, alone in a large man's house in the middle of nowhere and, to top it off, make him so angry he had his hands in fists. "I'm sorry. Please don't be mad."

His gaze shot up to meet mine, and he sucked in a breath. "I'm not angry," he said gently. "I'm trying to keep my hands to myself. I want to peel that dress off you and worship every inch of your body, but I know that's not what you want."

"It's not that I don't want you to. I'm afraid of what will happen if I let you."

He gave me a confident smirk. "I'll blow your mind, Princess. Like I have every other time we've been together."

"You're so annoying," I said, glaring at him. "Never mind."

I stood and he gripped my hand. "I'm scared too, but if losing Logan taught me anything, it's that nothing hurts more than regret."

I sat back on the bed, my brown eyes searching his blue, our hands clasped tight. "I don't know how to do this."

"Simple," he said, placing his palm on my face and brushing his thumb across my cheekbone. "We just stop fighting it."

My fingers shook as I placed my hand on his chest and leaned toward him. His heart pounded beneath my fingertips, but he didn't erase the inches between us. He kept his hand on my face, his touch gentle, waiting for me to decide.

I slid my hand up his chest to the back of his neck and pulled him toward me. Our mouths met in a kiss so gentle I almost pulled back. That kiss was the start of something more than sex. I ignored the warning bells clanging in my head and allowed Aiden to lower me on the bed.

He hovered over me, keeping his weight on his forearms as he trailed kisses down my neck. Any thoughts I had of leaving vanished as he slid down the straps of my dress with his teeth and traced the curve of my shoulder with his tongue. I grabbed the fabric of his shirt and tried to yank it over his head. He chuckled and lifted to pull it off. I traced the ridges of his abs, every peak, every valley, with the same painstaking attention he'd given my neck and shoulders. His breathing became rapid, his muscles contracting with every pass of my fingertips.

He grabbed my hands and I looked up at his face again. His pupils had blown so large only a hint of blue remained. He kissed the pad of each finger before pinning them over my head.

"Don't move them until I tell you." He sounded pained. I wanted to ignore him, to slide my hand inside his jeans and along the erection he was trying so hard to keep from pressing against me. But then his eyes softened, and he looked at me with so much warmth my chest ached and lip trembled.

This was too much. I was about to lower my hands and take us to a more familiar place when he kissed me, hard. His tongue slipped past my lips and danced with mine as he slowly undid the long line of buttons on the front of my dress. He sucked in a breath when he placed his hand on my breast and found it bare. His other hand immediately slid over the gentle swell of my stomach to the skin below. He groaned when he realized I hadn't been wearing underwear either, and I couldn't help laughing against his mouth.

The chuckle turned into a gasp when he slid his hand lower and started drawing slow circles on my throbbing clit. He ran his fingers along my slit and whispered, "Good girl," when he found me soaked, his voice deep and full of need.

My arousal dripped down my thighs, the ache between them so intense I rocked against his hand, searching for release. He rolled my nipple in one hand at the same time he thrust two fingers inside me, leaving his thumb to caress my clit. I moaned into his mouth and he let out a frustrated huff. He broke our kiss but kept moving his talented fingers as he worked his way down my body, stopping briefly to suck and lick each breast before he lowered his head and replaced his thumb with his tongue.

He devoured me like a man starved. Within moments, waves of intense pleasure rolled from my toes to the top of my head as I came. He sucked my clit into his mouth, drawing out my climax until I begged him to stop when it became too much.

He pulled his fingers from inside me and placed a gentle kiss on both my thighs before smiling up at me. He stood and pulled the boots I'd forgotten about from my feet and kicked off his own shoes. He kissed his way back up my body before locking his lips with mine. I could taste myself on his tongue and the ache that he'd just quieted with it roared back.

I rubbed myself against the roughness of his jeans, no doubt soaking them as well, and whimpered. Despite the earth-shattering climax he'd just delivered, I'd never wanted anyone more. My fingers shook so badly as I yanked at his belt, it took me a lifetime to unbuckle. His eyes blazed as I pushed his pants and boxers down his body and ran my fingers along his hard length. When I wrapped my hand around him, he threw his head back, thrusting once, twice, before gently placing my hands over my head and positioning himself at my entrance.

We both sighed as he sank into me. He held still as he brought his hands to mine and stared deeply into my eyes, then began with a languid pace, pulling out nearly all the way before slowly thrusting into me until I was so full of him my heart ached. He made love to me until his need took over and his thrusts became erratic, desperate. I clung to him as my body exploded with pleasure again, sending him over the edge with my name on his lips.

He smiled and kissed me, our bodies still moving together, gently now, as we drew every ounce of pleasure from each other. Eventually, he rolled over, pulling me with him. I nestled into his embrace and something unfamiliar spread through my body. It took me a moment to realize I felt completely safe in his arms.

Chapter Twenty-Three

Aiden

"I should go," Lauren said, rolling away from me not even two minutes after we came together.

I looped my arm around her waist and pulled her back to me. "Ten more minutes. Then, we'll both go back to Karma, and I'll help however you need. I promise we'll make up any time you missed there."

She sighed like I was the biggest pain in her ass, but her body relaxed against mine. "I've never been a cuddler."

I ran my hand along her arm and kept my mouth shut. Asking questions never got me anywhere with Lauren. Silence did. Not the tense, awkward void we'd inhabited for years, but in the peaceful quiet after we shared our bodies that one night, she'd told me things she'd kept locked from everyone else. Or at least, that's what I told myself. Maybe everyone in Peace Falls knew the details of Lauren Arnauld's tragic childhood, and I was last on the list. Doubtful. The hesitant way she spoke during cuddle time suggested every word was precious.

"My mom and grandpa weren't affectionate people, at least not with me."

"Their loss," I said, nuzzling my face into her hair. She smelled like coffee and rosemary today. She must rotate her shampoos because last time she smelled like oranges and coffee.

"Are your parents?" she asked quietly. "Affectionate."

"Yeah. And my sisters."

She placed her hand on her stomach, and I let the silence sink around us again before I placed my hand over hers. I kissed her shoulder and goose bumps erupted on her skin.

When she spoke again, her words were so soft, I almost didn't hear her. "I meant what I said before. You scare me. More than anyone I've ever known."

Shit. Maybe she didn't mean emotionally. I had gone off on her about the stupid cat litter, which wasn't stupid, but my handling of the situation was. She'd been terrified earlier when I balled my fists. Fuck, maybe I made her feel unsafe. I was built solid from lifting weights and doing manual labor for a living, and she knew I tore up my remodels to let off steam. I opened my mouth to apologize for making her uncomfortable, but instead, the absolute truth poured out. "You terrify me."

She rolled in my arms to face me, her warm brown eyes filled with pain. It hurt to look at her. I wanted a list of every person who'd treated her wrong, so I could track them down and beat them to a pulp.

"You're right to be scared," she said, placing a hand on my chest. "As hard as I try, I'm not a good person. I will disappoint you, hurt you. It's only a matter of time."

She sounded so sincere, so certain, my stomach rolled. I'm a firm believer of the whole "when people tell you who they are, listen" advice. But not with Lauren. Sure, it didn't feel great to hear her say she'd break my heart if I stuck around, but what upset me more was the terrible view she had of herself. "You're a good person."

"The moment a man gets too close, I cut him loose. You of all people should know that."

I cupped her face in my hands. "That doesn't make you a bad person, Princess. Just because you can't trust someone else with your heart doesn't mean you don't have one." But damn, I hoped she'd let herself trust me. "You're the kindest, most generous person I know. You're always thinking of ways to help and encourage everyone around you. If that's not a good person, I don't know what is."

"I do it for the karma. To pay back the universe for all the shitty things I did as a kid, not because I'm nice." She dropped her eyes from mine and started tracing something on my chest. "I stole from people, Aiden. Stores. My friends. Their parents. I lied all the time. And when I was in foster care, I got into fights. Bad ones. I hurt people. I broke a girl's arm."

I wanted to throw up. I knew without a doubt everything that weighed on Lauren's conscious she'd done to survive. No kid should have to live that way. The fact she'd become an amazing woman, despite an awful start in life, should make her feel proud, not guilty. "I'd bet my company you broke that girl's arm to protect yourself."

She nodded but refused to look me in the eyes.

I gripped her chin and forced her gaze to mine. "Whatever you did back then, it wasn't your fault. You were just a kid taking care of herself. You don't need to pay back the universe for any of it. And deep down, I think you know that. You are kind. You are good. I'm not scared that you'll hurt me when I fall for you. When, not if, Lauren. I'm scared you'll push me away before I have a chance to make you fall for me."

Her eyes welled with tears and she nodded. "It's been twelve minutes. We should go."

And that's a wrap for this conversation. The vault of Lauren had closed. At least she said we. I placed a kiss on her forehead and she wrapped her arms around my neck and gave me a squeeze before climbing out of bed.

"I have a request," I said while she buttoned the front of her dress.

"I'm not giving you a blow job. This is the first day in weeks I haven't barfed. The last thing I want to do is choke on your cock."

I did my best to ignore the instant hard on that gave me and shook my head. "As much as I love bjs, and if memory serves, yours in particular, my request isn't sexual."

She grabbed her rain boots and took a seat on the bed. "This ought to be good."

I ran my hand through my hair, suddenly nervous. This woman put me so far off my game, I might as well be a thirteen-year-old asking his crush to the eighth-grade dance. "Give me another nickname."

She laughed.

OK, not the response I'd hoped for, but I could work with it. I smiled at her despite the ache in my chest. If she wanted jokester instead of sincere, I'd deliver. I just didn't want her to think of me as a hypothetical. I wanted all in.

She tapped her chin like she was giving the request serious thought, and a smile spread across her gorgeous face. A pair of deep dimples flashed on her cheeks, and this time the smile on my face wasn't forced. I'd missed having those dimples aimed in my direction.

"Since you're the only person Dido likes, how about Cat Man?" She raised her eyebrows, waiting for my response.

"I do love all kinds of pussy."

She rolled her eyes. "Nope. Definitely not that."

"I wouldn't rule it out. It has a nice ring to it and goes with the Stud Man nickname Poppy gave me."

"Forget I ever suggested it. I'll think of something."

"OK," I said, getting out of bed. I didn't care what she called me as long as it wasn't "What If." The appreciative look she gave my body made me want to tackle her onto the mattress. Her eyes darkened and her cheeks flushed before she turned her back to me. For the first time in my life, I fucking loved pregnancy hormones.

And just to prove I wasn't a total neanderthal who only thought about getting himself off, I got completely dressed before I sank to my knees and made Lauren my afternoon snack.

Chapter Twenty-Four

Lauren

Wyatt beamed at me when I joined him behind the coffee bar the next morning. "You look like you're feeling better."

It'd been weeks since I'd worked with him. He handled the opening shift with Rowan since that's when my HG hit the hardest, but today I woke up feeling half human and texted her to take the morning off.

"I'm just not hurling. Yet." I tied my Karma apron around my waist and tossed my long braid over my shoulder.

Wyatt bumped my hip. "You look good, Lauren. Accept the compliment."

"Thanks." I crossed to the other side of the coffee bar and peeked in the fridge to do a quick count for my weekly milk run. Halfway through the oat milk, Wyatt cleared his throat. I was onto the macadamia milk when he cleared it again. It was a tick he had sometimes when his blood sugar dropped. I looked up from the notepad where I'd been keeping a tally and found him leaning against the counter with his arms crossed, staring at me.

"Do you need to eat? You're doing that throat thing."

"I was just trying to get your attention," he said quietly.

His intent expression suggested he wasn't about to ask me to add more coconut whipped cream to the list. "What's up," I said, rising.

"Are we good?" he asked, uncrossing his arms to motion between us.

"Why wouldn't we be?"

He blew out a breath. "Look, I'm sorry I cut back when I did. I never would have if I'd known how sick you were going to be. I've been really worried about you."

I swatted him with the notepad. "I wasn't pregnant when you ditched me. You have nothing to feel guilty about."

He nodded, but the worried look didn't leave his face. "I'm glad you're feeling better."

"Don't jinx it. I'm going to place the grocery order before the rush starts. Yell into the back if you need me."

Wyatt gave me a look I couldn't decipher but nodded and went back to stacking coffee mugs. His shoulders looked tense. He probably wanted to ask when he could go back to Aiden's crew now that I wasn't running to the bathroom as often. I added up the final milk count and pushed through the door into the back.

"Hey, Princess."

I let out a yelp and jumped. Aiden was standing in the small commercial kitchen with his own notepad and measuring tape.

"What are you doing here? And how did you get in?"

"I wanted to measure, and I used my key."

"Your key?"

He shrugged. "Made myself a copy when I made ones for Cammie and Wyatt."

"That's creepy." I held out my hand for the key, and he placed it in my palm.

"Noted," he said, leaning in to place a gentle kiss on my cheek.

Once again, my traitorous vagina ignored every signal from my brain. I fought the urge to wrap myself around him and took a few steps back for good measure. "What do you need to measure?"

Aiden flashed me a mischievous smile. "Your kitchen and bathroom in the apartment."

"You're not remodeling upstairs. It's fine."

"Let's not bullshit. It sucks. Even if I can't convince you to stay at my house, I want to make the apartment comfortable for you and the baby. That way you could work during naps or run up for feedings if someone babysat. Not that you have to breastfeed, but it would be easier to do if you and the baby were close together. The paint probably has lead in it, but I'm not touching that while you're living there. I want to measure for a dishwasher today and get that in to make things a little easier for you now."

I could love this man. The thought came out of nowhere and with it my mother's smoker voice, slurring the only advice of hers I'd ever chosen to follow: *Never fall in love. It ruins you.*

Dark spots hovered at the edge of my vision.

"I noticed you didn't have a window unit in the back bedroom," Aiden continued. "So I figured I could do that today. I want to make sure you're comfortable this summer and adding another unit should make it easier for the ones in your bedroom and living room to keep up with the heat. Ideally, I'll add an HVAC for upstairs later or tap into the downstairs unit."

The darkness crept from all sides until only Aiden's face remained. His eyes widened and he rushed forward to catch me as I pitched backward. My feet left the floor, but instead of crashing down, my body became weightless as Aiden put his arms under my legs and pressed me against his chest.

He yelled my name, and the dots receded back until his terrified eyes came into view. The door beside us flew open and Wyatt appeared.

"Open the door to her apartment," Aiden said.

My stomach lurched. "Sink," I said weakly.

He carried me there just in time. As soon as I finished emptying my stomach, Aiden lowered his head into the sink and did the same.

Wyatt stared at us. "Is there a carbon monoxide leak or something?"

"Nah," Aiden said, spitting into the sink and flipping it on with his elbow. "I have a sensitive stomach."

Wyatt laughed. "Good luck being a dad."

Aiden chuckled. "I'd puke a hundred times for my kid."

My stomach twisted again. Aiden shot me a worried look and switched off the sink. "Your stomach settled enough for me to carry you upstairs, Princess?"

I nodded and buried my face against his chest to hide the tears stinging my eyes.

"Mind walking behind me, Wyatt?" Aiden asked, the worry clear in his voice. "In case I trip or something."

By the time he'd carried me carefully upstairs and laid me on my bed, I was shaking.

"Should I call a doctor?" Wyatt asked from the doorway of my bedroom. "She was fine a few minutes ago."

I shook my head. "Go back downstairs. I'll be OK."

"I'll stay with her," Aiden said without taking his eyes off me. "Are you cold?"

"No." I was terrified.

Aiden ran his fingers across my forehead. I wanted him to crack a joke or say something obnoxious, but he just kept touching me with tender strokes.

"I'm sorry," he said after the silence between us stretched uncomfortably. "I should have asked for a key, and I should have asked if you wanted to change your apartment." He cleared his throat. "The truth is, I'm excited.

And I haven't felt this way in years, not since before Logan died, if I'm being honest."

"You really want this baby?"

He tilted his head like I'd spoken in a foreign language he didn't understand. Of course, he wanted the baby. He'd made that clear from the moment I'd told him I was pregnant. He smiled, his eyes soft. "I've never wanted something more. But it's not just the baby. I want you too, in whatever way works for you."

"What does that mean?"

"I'll take whatever you're willing to give me, Lauren. But I want us to be a family."

And sweet karma, I wanted that too. A family is all I'd ever wanted. But I couldn't have both, Aiden and the baby. He'd grow to hate me because I'd never be the mother his child deserved. And by then, it'd be too late. I'd have a taste of his love, and it'd ruin me. Worse than my mother, who fell into a deeper hole of depression with each failed relationship because, unlike the assholes Mom dated, Aiden O'Malley was a good man. Maybe even a great one. Which was why I knew he'd never stop fighting for his perfect dream family. He'd fix my apartment and his house. He'd improve my life every chance he had. He wouldn't stop until I fell in love with him. The only way I could stop it from happening was to make him hate me.

Chapter Twenty-Five

Aiden

To say Lauren scared the hell out of me two days ago would be an understatement. I'd seen her dizzy, I'd seen her throw up, but I'd never seen her shake so hard. I could tell she was scared too. However, she'd played it off, and within ten minutes of getting to her apartment, she'd called Rowan to help Wyatt downstairs and insisted I go to work.

I wanted to stay with her, but the housing development project was behind again. I made Lauren promise to text me throughout the day and sent Rowan and Wyatt texts asking them to check on her. Lauren didn't send updates, but she responded to all my texts with a thumbs up emoji. Thankfully, Wyatt and Rowan came through with enough reassurances that I didn't drive back to Karma.

Instead, I gave her space. I'd have to be twice as emotionally inept as Cal not to see that I'd made her panic. I should have known better than to make myself a key. I had copies to all my sisters' houses, not to mention Cal's and Theo's. Once Everly and Maddie moved into places they owned, I'm sure I'd have their keys too, so I could dip in and fix things when I had time. I figured if Wyatt had a copy of the new key, Lauren wouldn't care if I did, especially after she let me make love to her. Still, I should have asked.

I knew better. If someone had made a key to one of my sisters' places without asking, I'd have punched them. Then, I'd gone and made things worse by suggesting all those changes to her apartment. It wasn't until after I'd left her curled in her bed that I considered the possibility she didn't want anything to change. I assumed, based on the crumbs of her past she'd shared with me, the apartment was the most stable home Lauren ever had.

Hence the space I gave her and the burning in my gut. I was halfway to an ulcer when she texted me this morning and asked if I could stop by after work.

I assumed she meant mine since Karma stayed opened until 8:00 pm on weekdays. I stopped by Peppers on the way and grabbed a plain cheese pie. Normally, I'd have gone for half pepperoni and green peppers, but I didn't know which smells might make her queasy. I figured the plainer the better. When I arrived at the café, Cammie and Lauren were both behind the counter.

"Hey, Aiden," Cammie said from the register.

"You can head upstairs," Lauren called without looking up from the drink she was making. "I'll be there in a minute."

All the tension I'd been carrying in my shoulders for the past two days released. She'd invited me into her home. Not to take a seat at one of the café tables or in the closet she called her office. I wanted to stop and kiss Lauren, but I waved to Cammie and kept walking into the back room and up the stairs to the apartment.

The whole place smelled like lemons. The tiny kitchen sparkled as much as a forty-year-old kitchen could. Every throw pillow and blanket had been placed meticulously. Yep. I screwed up. She loved this place exactly like it was. I could test the paint for lead and probably convince her to add central air conditioning, but I wouldn't discuss any other updates unless she brought them up. I placed the pizza box on the small table shoved against the wall and snooped around in the cabinets until I found two plates. I thought sparkling water might help Lauren's stomach, so I'd grabbed two cans at Peppers and shoved them in the pockets of my cargo pants. I rinsed off the can lids at the sink because no telling what kind of dust could have gotten on me today.

I'd just set the cans on the table and taken a seat when Lauren opened the apartment door. She looked at the plates, the pizza, the sparkling water, and sucked in a breath. OK. I tried to remind myself she was pregnant and pregnant women got emotional about stupid shit but that little inhale freaked me out.

"Have you eaten?" I asked, like my heart wasn't slamming against my chest.

She shook her head and took a seat in the chair across from me but kept her hands clasped tightly on her lap. I opened the box, separated out a slice, and plated it for her.

"Thank you," she said, looking at the pizza like she'd never seen anything like it before.

I tore myself off a slice and took a bite, even though I felt like throwing up. She watched me the entire time instead of reaching for her food. After I forced a lump of pizza down my tight throat, I took a sip of water and decided I couldn't pretend to eat anymore. "How are you feeling?"

"Good," she said, plastering a smile on her face that looked faker than an orange spray tan. "I wanted to show you something."

She moved the pizza box and our full plates to the counter before going to her bedroom. She returned a moment later with a stack of papers and a pen.

"Try to keep an open mind," she said.

"Are those design ideas?" I asked like a hopeful prick. Because fuck me, I'd never hoped for remodel renderings more in my entire life.

She shook her head and had the decency to drop the plastic smile. She slid the first page across the table facedown, and I picked it up. It was a printed-out snapshot of a man with his arm around a woman who had a cute little boy on her hip. They were standing under several large airplanes suspended from a ceiling.

I stared at the picture, grasping for a reason why she'd show it to me. "You want to go to the Air and Space Museum in D.C.? Or is this an idea for the nursery?"

She shook her head, tears filling her eyes. "This is the family I'd like to adopt our baby."

I didn't say anything. This time I wasn't silent because I wanted to hear more. I knew if I opened my mouth, I'd scream things I could never take back.

"The little boy is adopted as well, and they'd like to give him a sibling," she said, still clutching the rest of the papers.

I stared at the papers until she got the hint and slid them across the table to me. It was a registration form for an adoption agency with my name and hers already filled out. She'd even stuck a little flag to mark where I needed to sign my consent.

"I can't be a mother, Aiden," she said softly. "I know you think you can be a dad. But do you honestly believe you're ready to raise a child on your own?"

I dropped the papers on the table and folded my hands over them. "Absolutely. Family is everything to me."

"Sometimes the best thing a parent can do for their child is give them to someone who can better care for them."

I didn't even recognize my voice when I spoke. I'd never sounded so cold, so firm. "No judge in this state or any other would let a child be adopted when its biological father is willing and able, fuck eager, to be a parent. If you submit this application behind my back and contact this family, you'll only disappointment them. Don't be cruel."

"There's another reason you might consider," she said softly.

"Let's hear it," I said, crossing my arms over my chest. Not that anything she said would change my mind, but it might give me a clue where her head was at.

"I can't be a mother. But I'm willing to try a relationship with you."

I couldn't believe my ears. "You want me to give up my child, so I can have a chance with you?"

She nodded.

"Wow," I said, scrubbing my face. "You don't mean that."

"I do."

"You honestly expect me to choose you over my kid?"

She shrugged. "My mom did."

My heart cracked for the little girl whose mom had chosen wrong and for what I had to do next. "When people tell you who they are, listen."

She nodded, her face blank. I didn't know this emotionless woman. I doubt she knew herself. She'd locked away the person I wanted to build a life with, and fighting this version of Lauren would get me nowhere. Still, I wasn't giving her the satisfaction of breaking up with her.

"I want to be a dad. You know this, so let's not bullshit around with your offer to date me if I sign away my rights. You want us to be done? Fine. But don't pretend like you aren't the one ending things. I should have listened when you said you didn't want to be a mother. For that, I'm sorry."

"Can't," she said, straightening her spine. "I can't be a mother."

I nodded. "I believe you now."

She dropped her eyes to her clasped hands. "I know you said you wanted to support me however I needed while I'm pregnant, but I think it's best if we don't see each other again."

This was really happening. She was cutting me out of her life, and if I wasn't careful, she still had options that would kill me. I pushed back from the table and stood.

She started sobbing before I reached the door. It took everything in me, all the anger at the people in her past, the disappointment in the choices she'd made for both of us, and the love I had for the child inside her, to continue down the stairs and out of her life.

Chapter Twenty-Six

Aiden

WHEN THE DOORBELL RANG, I'm not sure how long I'd been frozen in my bathroom, gripping the sledgehammer. I'd sped home, hellbent on tearing the room apart, but something kept me from slamming the hammer into the mirror or ripping out the tiles with the crowbar I'd put on the counter. Maybe it was because I wouldn't have a working toilet if I destroyed the one in here.

Throughout my remodel redoes, I hadn't touched the primary suite. The bathroom had pink everything and a mirror so chipped and flaking, I'd had to stand at an exact spot to see enough of my face to shave. My bedroom wasn't much better. The walls were a dingy white. The curtains a sun-faded brown. The only thing decent was my furniture, which I'd brought with me from my one-bedroom apartment.

After Lauren told me about the baby, I had an urge to fix up the primary and went with it. I plopped the pink commode and sink in the bathroom down the hall, where I'd torn up my latest remodel after Lauren ignored me for a week, and showered at the gym. The materials I chose were the best I'd ever bought for my projects: marble tiles, top-of-the line faucets, and radiant flooring. I'd even had Sam help me install a custom-built steam shower. He'd given me shit about not leaving a working full bathroom while I remodeled but accepted the lie that I'd done it to force myself to focus on my own project instead of all the others in the pipeline.

The finished bathroom was beautiful. The kind of work I'd snap pictures of for the company's social channels. Seeing Lauren's appreciation of the work only made it better.

But damn it, I needed to get rid of this feeling in my chest. It differed from the anger that usually led to my moments of destruction. My chest ached. No, it hurt. A slicing, breath-stealing pain that would make me think I was having a heart attack, if I hadn't just had my heart broken.

The doorbell rang again. I ignored it again. I should definitely take a picture of the bathroom for our socials. At least then it wouldn't be an entire waste.

"Aiden," Cal yelled as my front door swung open. My locked door, which only had one key. And yes, I realize the hypocrisy of having keys to all my friends' and family's houses and not giving anyone mine.

"Where are you?" Theo yelled.

I leaned the sledgehammer against the vanity and walked to the top of the stairs.

My best friends were scurrying through the first floor like a two-person SWAT team, an ineffective one since it took them a full minute to look up and notice me.

Cal skidded to a stop in the front hall when he finally saw me, and Theo smashed into his back. "Why didn't you answer us?"

Because it hurt too much to breathe, let alone speak. Time to pull it together before Cal and Theo had a fit. I forced in a breath and shrugged. "Didn't want to interrupt your self-guided tour since you went through the trouble of committing a B&E to take it."

"You weren't answering the doorbell," Cal said, climbing the steps. He gave my shoulder a good-natured thump and walked past me.

Theo pulled me into a two-armed hug when he reached me, which was one arm too many for any guy who wasn't my dad. "You learn how to pick locks in prison?" I asked him with my face smashed against the shoulder of his leather jacket.

He stepped back and smirked. "Just because I'm a felon doesn't mean I'm a complete degenerate."

"I picked it," Cal said from down the hall where he was looking into the baby's room. Of course, he'd go straight to it. For all his lack of insight, the man had killer instincts.

"Dr. Cardoso," I said in mock surprise.

"Don't pretend you weren't the one who taught me," Cal said, walking into the nursery. "You should thank me for respecting your boundaries this long since I could have popped that lock years ago."

I rubbed my forehead. "So, why did you do it now?"

"Cammie called Cal," Theo said, heading toward the nursery as well. He came to an abrupt stop in the doorway and turned to face me with shiny eyes.

"Don't start," I said, shoving past him into the baby's room. The man might look like an extra on *Breaking Bad*, but he was a gooey marshmallow on the inside.

Cal looked up from his staring contest with the crib when he heard me enter the room. "What happened with Lauren?"

I shoved my hands in my pockets. "I don't want to talk about it."

Theo grabbed the paint samples I'd spread across the changing table and started flipping through them. "That was well established with the twenty text messages and five calls you ignored. Have you considered a muted green?"

"Focus, Theo," Cal said, taking the little paper strips from Theo and returning them to the changing table. "We aren't here to give decorating advice."

Theo let out a long-suffering sigh and gave me a look that had my lips quirking up despite how terrible I felt. "Aiden doesn't want to talk about his feelings, so I'm asking him practical questions in line with the subject we're here to discuss until he loosens up."

"I hadn't considered green," I said. "What do you mean by muted? Like sea foam?"

Theo wrinkled his nose. "No, something like sage with warm undertones."

"I might as well go home," Cal said.

Sage. I could see how it would work well as a neutral shade, but could I pick a color that would remind me of Lauren every time I stepped into the nursery? Like the baby wouldn't be a reminder, dumbass.

"You can't leave," Theo said, leaning against the wall. "I might need you if Aiden goes apeshit and starts demoing something he'll regret tearing down."

"I had enough time to destroy half the house before you two got here," I said. They gave each other worried looks, and I blew out a breath. "But it might be a good idea if you took my sledgehammer and crowbar for a couple days."

"We can do that, brother," Cal said.

"For fuck's sake, you don't have to call me that."

"OK, Big Daddy," Theo said with a smirk.

Cal threw his head back and laughed. If I didn't think Theo would pin me to the ground in five seconds, I'd take a swing at him.

"Fine. You can call me brother. My tools are this way."

"I don't know," Cal said, following me out of the nursery and down the hall to my room. "Big Daddy has a nice ring to it."

"Don't test me," I said without turning. "I've had a day."

They didn't say another word until I led them to the bathroom and grabbed the sledgehammer from the floor.

"This is incredible," Cal said quietly. He held out his hand, and I handed him the hammer. Theo grabbed the crowbar from the counter and walked deeper into the room. Truth was, I had plenty of other tools that could wreck anything I wanted, but knowing my friends had seen the completed bathroom gave me some much-needed restraint.

Theo opened the shower door and peeked at the tile work. "You came up here to tear this room apart, but you stopped yourself."

"Yeah, can we not do this here?" I asked. "We've already had one bathroom intervention for you, Theo. Our friendship is weird enough." And I still had the urge to rip the light fixtures from the wall over the sink.

"Of course," Cal said, backing out of the room. "We can sit on the stairs since you don't have a couch, and that window seat doesn't look sturdy enough to hold more than one of us."

"Speaking of which," Theo said, following him, "I don't want any more shit about how long it took me to furnish my place."

"I have a couch. It's just not here."

Cal sat on a step halfway down the staircase and frowned up at me. "You're paying for a storage unit with all this space? Half the rooms are empty."

"It's in the tree house."

"Fuck," Theo said, paling. He slid down the wall and plopped onto a step a few above Cal before laying the crowbar across his lap. "I didn't know you'd built it."

Technically, the tree house wouldn't be finished until August. I could have completed the project months ago, but I'd held off so it'd all come together around the time of the accident. I wanted something to keep me busy in the weeks leading up to the anniversary. Plus, Theo and Poppy needed time to finish the memorial statue. But all the structural elements of the tree house were done. My entire crew had volunteered to help me put up the floor, roof, and walls during the off season. The day before I finished my bathroom, I'd gotten Sam and a couple of my guys to help me move my couch from the living room to the tree house.

"When I found out about the baby, I knew I had to stop wrecking the house. So, whenever I felt angry, I went there until I cooled down."

"I can go with you now, if you want," Cal said, sending a worried look at Theo, who was doing the weird-ass breathing exercises he'd learned to center himself.

I squeezed onto the same step beside Theo and gripped his shoulder. "Not now."

"I'm sorry," Theo said, his breaths labored. "Just ignore me. We're here for you, A."

"Nah," I said, giving him a shove. "I like knowing I'm not the only damaged one in this group."

Cal narrowed his eyes at me. "Did you try to give him a panic attack?"

"Of course not. They scare me as much as they do you. I wasn't thinking."

"Or you were thinking about whatever happened at Karma," Theo said, the color slowly returning to his face.

My heart thudded in my chest. Instead of walking out the back door, I'd stormed through the café so I could yell at Cammie to check on Lauren if she didn't come down in a few minutes. What if she hadn't checked on her? What if she'd just texted Cal and told him I was pissed? What if Lauren had fainted when she was trying to come down the stairs? "You don't know?"

Cal shook his head. "Cam just said you left Karma looking pissed, and Lauren was crying so hard she was afraid to leave her. Cammie asked Rowan to come to Karma."

"Poppy too," Theo said. "She said Lauren hasn't told them anything, so they've just been taking turns staying with her and working downstairs."

I nodded. She didn't want her friends to know that she'd shown the worst version of herself to me. I wasn't an idiot. I knew she'd broken my heart to protect herself, that the sweet woman I loved was still there, hiding behind a cold exterior she hadn't shown anyone else. The tears confirmed it, which made the entire situation so much worse. She cared, deeply. Just not enough.

"Did something happen to the baby?" Theo asked, gently.

"No," I said. Both of them visibly relaxed. "Shit, text that to your women." Rowan, Poppy, and Cammie must be beside themselves by now if Lauren hadn't at least told them the baby was OK.

Cal and Theo pulled out their phones and typed.

"So I'm assuming something happened between you and Lauren?" Theo said after he'd sent his text.

I nodded.

"You aren't going to tell us, are you?" Cal asked.

I started to shake my head, but decided they needed to know the gist if I had any chance of making it through the rest of Lauren's pregnancy with my sanity. "Lauren might be the love of my life, but that baby is the best thing that's ever happened to me. I would do anything for my child. Even if it means letting go of any chance with Lauren."

Cal and Theo stared at me, then each other. "Love of his life?" Cal asked Theo. "Did you hear that too?"

Theo nodded.

"And you're just as surprised as I am, right?"

Theo nodded again, and I realized he was speechless.

"I thought you and Lauren got plastered and had hate sex that one time," Cal said.

I shrugged. "That's a fair assumption."

Cal rubbed his forehead. "I'm still confused. So she's upset because you two were together without any of your friends knowing, and now you're not?"

"I wouldn't say we were together."

"But she's the love of your life?" Theo asked, finally speaking.

"You of all people should know you can love someone without being with them."

Theo nodded.

Cal sat up straighter. "Right. So, what do you need us to do?"

"I told you. Just keep my tools awhile."

"Besides that," Cal said.

"Make sure Lauren has everything she needs."

"Guarantee she doesn't," Theo said, studying the crowbar in his hands. "But not everyone can accept what they need."

"Well, that's depressing," Cal said, standing with the sledgehammer. "Want to go pick up green paint samples? Maybe grab tiny jars of different colors, so we can paint squares of each on the wall tonight. That way you'll be able to see how the colors look in different light before you decide."

Theo beamed at Cal like he was one of the old farts in the community center art classes who'd finally figured out how to mix watercolors. "That's a great idea."

Despite my world falling apart, I smiled. I might not have gotten to play in the NFL or found a woman who loved me back, but I had great friends and a baby on the way who deserved a kick-ass room. "Hell Cat taught you that, didn't she?" I asked Cal. "She did the same thing at the bakery."

Cal grinned.

"Yeah, let's do it," I said.

Theo stood, still gripping the crowbar. "While we're at the store, maybe we should look at kitchen stuff too. I noticed yours was gutted. You'll probably need one with a baby."

"Yeah, maybe we should start there instead. Lauren could still—"

Cal shook his head. "Paint samples. That's all we're getting. After we paint the nursery, we can move on to the kitchen."

"Who made you foreman of this project?" I asked.

"Logan."

My breath caught and Theo's mouth dropped opened. Guy was definitely having a panic attack before the night ended.

Cal's eyes widened. "I have no idea why I said that. I was going to say that I needed something to distract me because I'm worried about Rowan's surgery, but his name just came out."

I shrugged. "I've been talking to the guy ever since I moved in. Guess he finally said something back." More likely, Cal had a momentary lapse between his mind and his mouth, but I kind of liked the idea of Logan butting into the conversation. He had always been the one to know exactly what each of us needed.

"Our friendship really is weird, isn't it?" Theo asked.

"Yeah, but it works, brother," I said, slapping him on the back.

CHAPTER TWENTY-SEVEN

Lauren

I FROWNED AT MY reflection in the tiny mirror above the bathroom sink.

I could barely open my swollen eyes, and the tiny slits of white that showed were bloodshot. My nose throbbed red despite layers of concealer and foundation. I didn't even try to cover the dark circles under my eyes. "Pull it together. You don't deserve anyone's sympathy."

If I walked downstairs looking like this, every regular would fuss and worry while I made their morning beverage. And ask questions. I reached for my phone to text Rowan but stopped. She'd dashed over yesterday to help. She had her own business to run, and I couldn't take advantage of her kindness. Plus, for the first time in our friendship, I didn't want to see her.

Somehow, I'd made it through several hours of crying without telling anyone why. I heard Poppy tell everyone the baby was fine or at least was before I lost my shit. That made me panic for a good thirty minutes until Rose arrived with Dr. Evers. He took my blood pressure and checked the baby with a portable ultrasound machine. Rose demanded I settle down like I was a tired toddler throwing a fit before naptime. She sent everyone else from the room, and I cried myself to sleep soon after while she rubbed my back. In the morning, Rose was gone, but I found Poppy asleep on the couch.

I dabbed a layer of powder on my nose, slapped some blush on my pale cheeks, and switched off the bathroom light. Poppy didn't move at all when I walked past her and out the door. Dido hissed at me from the top of a stack of boxes in the back room, which was already lit despite it being a quarter to five in the morning.

"I deserved that," I told her, pushing through the door to the café.

Cammie and Wyatt were leaning together, whispering.

"Morning."

They both spun around with matching shocked expressions.

"What are you doing up?" Cammie said, hurrying to me. "Get back in bed."

I was about to tell her I was fine, but one look at me confirmed what a crock that was. "I want to be busy."

Cammie frowned. "Cal gave me the OK to work here until ten since Rowan needed to finish some baking. Between her, Wyatt, Poppy, and me, we have the entire schedule covered today."

"If you want to help, fine. But you're leaving before eight, so you don't mess up Cal's day, and I don't want to see you back until after his office closes. I don't want to see Rowan here at all. She's done too much for me already. Poppy too. I'm sending her home as soon as she wakes up."

Cammie let out a huff. "You're not backing down, are you?"

"Nope," I said, reaching for an apron.

Cammie and Wyatt had a silent conversation with their eyes, which would have made my morning if I didn't know it was about me. He dipped his chin once, and she rubbed his arm. He blushed and cleared his throat before walking around the counter to flip the chairs from the tables.

"What was that?" I asked Cammie while she refilled the napkin holders.

She snapped the holder in her hands closed and reached for another. "I'll tell you if you tell me what happened yesterday."

"You don't know?"

I assumed one evening was more than enough time for the news of my cold-hearted bitch move to spread through our friend group.

"Why would I?" Cammie asked, tilting her head.

"I figured Aiden told Cal and he told you."

Cammie's hand stilled over the pile of napkins. "I told Cal to check on Aiden. He said Aiden was OK."

"Thank you." My eyes burned. At least I could stop worrying about Aiden and focus on getting through today without breaking down in front of customers.

Cammie looked away and fumbled with the napkins. We were both sympathetic criers and had set each other off more times than I could count. I grabbed the milk thermoses for the self-serve station and began filling them. I nearly dropped the two percent when I realized what Cammie hadn't said. "Aiden didn't tell Cal what I did?"

Cammie shook her head, but didn't ask me to explain. We both had secrets and treated our closest friends with a wariness that can only be learned from terrible experience. She wouldn't pry. Unlike Rowan and Poppy, who had only seen the best of me and wouldn't understand the dark pieces I hid from them. Cammie put all the napkin holders on a tray and joined Wyatt at the tables. I pulled out my phone and texted Rowan that I didn't need her help today.

She responded immediately with a thumbs up and a question.

Are you OK?

Yes

And because I couldn't face her after again what I'd done to Aiden, I sent a text I knew would hurt her.

> *I want space to process. I'll text you if I need you. Please give me time*

> *OK. Love you*

Even through a text message, Rowan could bring me to tears. Instead of answering that I loved her back, I shoved my phone in my apron pocket, wiped the moisture from my eyes, and got to work.

But no matter how many lattes I made or books I sold, I couldn't push Aiden from my thoughts. As much as I loved the idea of the baby completing the picture-perfect family I'd found, I knew, with a certainty unlike any I'd ever felt, that Aiden and our child would make an incredible family.

He'd seen the ridiculous choice I'd offered him for what it was: a test, one he'd passed with ease. Aiden wasn't my mom. He would put our child first, always. But what I couldn't understand was why, despite everything, he was protecting me. He had every right to tell our friends what a terrible person I really was, but he hadn't.

Each time my thoughts threatened to send me to sob town again, I found something to do. I inventoried every book in the self-help section. I drafted my newsletter and scheduled a month's worth of social media posts. I made cappuccinos with leaf designs in the foam, dessert lattes with towers of whipped cream in artful swirls, and shot after shot of espresso. By the time story hour rolled around, I could barely drag myself to the rocking chair with a handful of books.

I'd grabbed a few beloved classics since my brain felt too full to snoop the shelves for the latest and greatest releases. I smiled and pushed as much cheer into my voice as possible, but the kids fidgeted and squirmed more than usual. When I ended a book early, no one complained.

Max stayed at my feet, petting Medusa while the other children scampered off to their adult. "Ms. Lauren," he said, looking up at me with those huge blue eyes, only made bigger by his glasses.

"Yes, Max."

"I'm sorry you're sad."

"I'm fine," I said, smiling at him. "Why do you think I'm sad?"

He frowned. "I can hear it in your voice. It's OK. Everyone gets sad sometimes. Even my mommy."

I glanced over his head to Brandi, who had just come up behind him. She stood completely still like she wanted to hear what he was about to say, so I pretended not to notice her.

"You're right. Everyone gets sad sometimes."

Max nodded and gave me a serious look. It felt like I was staring into the face of a wise old man, not a preschooler. "I'm sorry you're sad, Ms. Lauren. But I'm happy you're you."

And I lost it.

Brandi swooped over and let me sob on her shoulder for a good five minutes. No questions asked. She really was the jackpot of moms. I hoped Aiden found someone like her for the baby. Thinking of another woman taking my place in Aiden's bed and our child's life made me cry harder because deep down I hoped Aiden would be as celibate as a monk, even if it meant the baby never had a mother. Which basically confirmed what a terrible one I'd be.

"I'm so sorry, Brandi," I said, wiping my tears and probably snot from the poor woman's shoulder. Of course, she had on a sleeveless top, so I'd snotted all over her bare skin.

"Mom doesn't mind," Max said, still sitting calmly at my feet, petting my blind cat.

"I don't," Brandi said.

"You're an amazing mom," I blurted out. "And I'm not just saying that because you let me cry on you. You're patient and attentive but not overprotective. You're generous with your praise and purposeful with your corrections. You're like the best mom I've ever seen."

"Thank you," Brandi said with a small smile that didn't touch her eyes. She didn't believe me. Or maybe she did, but the guilt of what happened to Max outweighed any compliments tossed her way by a random barista in the middle of a breakdown.

I took a breath to get myself under control. She needed to understand how serious I was. "You're an amazing mom," I said, this time slower.

"My mommy is the best and the prettiest," Max said, grinning up at her.

Brandi laughed and bent over to kiss Max on the top of the head. She studied me a moment while Max told Medusa goodbye. "I have a feeling you'll be amazing too," she said before taking Max's hand and leading him outside.

The sobfest had left me so drained, I leaned against the counter and took orders at the register while Wyatt filled them. We hit the usual pre-lunch lull, and I decided to take a break.

"I'll be back in fifteen."

"Before you go," Wyatt said, shifting from one foot to the other. "Cammie said you hadn't interviewed anyone in a while."

So this was the conversation Cammie was having with Wyatt. I'd hoped he finally convinced her to go on a date with him. Wishful thinking. Of course, they were just worried about shift coverage.

I shrugged. "I've been too sick. But you're right, I'll post an ad online."

"I noticed you haven't put a help wanted sign in the window or added a listing to the job board in the career center. I could do that if you want. Cammie was a regular before she worked here, right?"

"She was, but I asked her directly. I don't want to turn down a regular customer if they're a bad fit for the job."

He nodded, grabbed a towel, and started wiping the counter. The muscles in his jaw ticked like he was fighting to keep his mouth closed.

"Whatever you're thinking, just say it."

He spoke without turning to face me, his hands gripping the counter. "I know what a privilege it was to be someone you trusted. Even more so because you didn't know me before you hired me. I almost didn't take Aiden's job offer. Not because I didn't enjoy the work or need the insurance, but because I worried you'd hate me for leaving. Cut me out of your life. And my instincts were spot on. If you didn't need me so much, I doubt you'd still speak to me at all. And now it's like you're afraid to hire someone else because of how much trust you lost with me."

"Hey," I said, placing my hand on his shoulder. "What makes you think I wouldn't have spoken to you again?"

He turned to face me, and the hurt in his eyes made my chest ache. He pulled his phone from his pocket, unlocked it, and handed it to me with the text thread between us open.

There were the usual exchanges about shift times and updates from him about how the café was doing when I was too sick to work. "I don't understand."

"Scroll back," he said, softly. "To before I gave my notice."

I did as he asked, and my stomach knotted. I'd texted him more in the two days prior to him quitting than I had in all the days after. Gone were the witty exchanges about his crush on Cammie or the Karma cats' antics. I scrolled back down to the more recent texts and saw that he'd tried to start similar conversations that I'd ignored. "Don't read anything into it," I said, handing his phone back. "You know how sick I've been."

He nodded and shoved his phone in his pocket, but I could tell he didn't believe me.

"I'm going to take a break before the lunch rush," I said. "Let me know when you need me up front."

"Yeah, sure," he said, wiping the counter he'd already cleaned.

I hurried back to my office, scaring Dido on the way. She hissed at me and resumed licking herself. I yanked my phone from my pocket and opened one text thread after another. I had been sick. So sick. Of course I wasn't sending funny videos and interesting news articles at the same rate as before. But I was texting everyone, except Wyatt.

He was right. He'd gone from someone I treated like family to someone who barely warranted a reply. What's worse, I hadn't even noticed.

I shuffled around the desk and looked at the time sheets I'd forced Rowan and Poppy to fill out. Not only had I avoided texting Wyatt, I'd avoided working with him. Rowan, Poppy, or Cammie had covered nearly every shift he worked. I'd seen him as little as possible since he gave his notice because it hurt. Plain and simple. If I couldn't handle seeing Wyatt, how would I ever manage seeing Aiden and the baby around town?

I wouldn't.

I sat with the thought, letting the brutal truth seep in. I had to leave Peace Falls. But even as I started a list of everything I needed to do, I knew I'd be leaving my heart in this small mountain town.

Chapter Twenty-Eight

Aiden

It'd been over a week since I'd seen Lauren. I'd avoided Karma and town in general. I spent my evenings working on the house, sometimes with Cal or Theo, sometimes with both, sometimes alone. It took a lot to get those two to give me the solitude I craved, but as days passed without me tearing apart my bathroom, they slowly gave me space.

Space I needed to talk with Logan. Crazy as it sounds, he was the only person I wanted to know how heartbroken I was. And fuck was I heartbroken. My chest ached. My stomach hurt. I couldn't even sleep in my bed because it reminded me too much of her, so I'd camped out in the tree house every night, talking to Logan. Which really meant talking out the situation to myself, hoping he could somehow hear me. And every time I pondered ways to keep Lauren and the baby in my life, I came to the same conclusion: Nothing I said or did would ever be enough. Which made me so pissed I would have torn my house apart by now, if I didn't think Cal and Theo would be on my ass 24/7 after, or worse, tell my sisters.

I tried to focus on the baby and forget the woman who carried it and my heart. I might have slipped and told Cal and Theo that Lauren was the love of my life, but anytime they tried to talk about her, I changed the subject until they finally gave up. I still received regular texts from Cammie and Wyatt, but only about the pregnancy. Rowan had been strangely quiet, but I'd chalked it up to her loyalty to her best friend, until Cal told me otherwise.

"Lauren is avoiding Rowan," he said, as he helped me fit a piece of drywall. He'd purposefully waited until we were crammed in the upstairs half bath together with a literal wall preventing my escape. "Any idea why?"

"I'm the last person who'd know," I said, driving in the first screw. I wanted the board secured as fast as possible if Cal planned to stay on the subject.

"It's odd," he said. "Especially with Rowan's surgery coming up."

"How's she doing?" I asked, both because I wanted to know and figured it was the fastest exit from the current topic.

"She's scared," he said, his voice tense. "She won't admit it, but she hasn't been sleeping well. And she's been baking like crazy. More than what she needs for Red Blossoms. She's delivered cookies and brownies to everyone on our street, and she's baking cupcakes for Theo's neighbors now. We're both ready for the surgery to be over."

I wanted to tell him it would be fine, but what did I know? "The surgery still scheduled for Tuesday morning?"

He nodded.

"I'll be there," I said before driving in another screw.

"I know I should tell you not to come since you've got enough on your plate, but thanks, A. I'm already a wreck just thinking about it."

"Understandable," I said.

We finished securing the board and went into the hallway to grab the next. I glanced in the nursery and nudged Cal to look inside. Theo stood in the middle of the room, staring at a blank wall.

"Thought you were working in the kitchen with the other guys?" Cal said.

Theo turned, looking slightly dazed. "I want to paint a mural there," he said, pointing to the wall.

Theo was an incredible artist, so I had no problem giving him any wall he wanted in my house. "That'd be great."

"Are you going to find out what you're having?" he asked, turning back to the wall.

"Probably not," I said, trying to keep the disappointment from my voice. I doubt Lauren would want to find out at the twenty-week ultrasound, and even if she did, it wasn't likely she'd tell me.

"Doesn't matter, really," Theo said. "I was thinking of a jungle theme."

"Like lions and monkeys," Cal said.

Theo shook his head. "No, like in St. John."

"The view from the house?" I asked, my stomach sinking. I didn't think I could handle having that on my wall, but Theo seemed really invested in whatever he was imagining.

"The Bay Reef Trail."

The trail I didn't hike with them. The one part of the island that wouldn't remind me of Lauren. Sure, it would remind me of Logan, but I didn't mind. I wanted my kid to know about him.

"That sounds amazing," I said.

Theo smiled at me. "I hate to leave your guys down a man, but I want to get this idea on paper. It flashed in my head while I was carrying a sink, of all things."

"Cal and I can help them."

Theo took off down the stairs. I knew he kept a sketch pad and pencils in his truck for moments like these.

Cal chuckled. "That baby is going to have an epic room."

"Good," I said, leading the way downstairs. I planned to go a little overboard wherever I could. Not that murals or luxury bath fixtures could make up for not having a mother. But my kid would know each and every day how much they're wanted and loved.

"Checking up on us, Boss?" Sam asked when we entered the kitchen.

The guys had made impressive progress in one morning. Sam was a perfectionist, so I knew every tile had been laid with precision, every cabinet hung exactly. My entire crew had volunteered again to help me on our day off. I had them working six days a week, from sunup to sundown. They needed the rest, but everyone showed up at my house this morning ready to work—for free. Like I'd ever let that happen. They were all getting fat bonuses in their next paycheck.

"These are nice," Cal said, looking at the cabinets. "They aren't what I'd expect from you, but I like them."

That's because they were a blend of what Lauren and I liked. White-washed beechwood cabinets. A little rough, a little sophisticated, combined to make something warm and inviting.

I'd chosen white granite with the most subtle gray veins I could find. Antique copper fixtures that looked time-worn. I'd incorporated a few blue and copper tiles in the otherwise plain backsplash. It'd required the guys to hand lay each tile, but it looked fantastic.

"We definitely need to add this one to the website," Sam said, gripping my shoulder.

"It looks better than I imagined," I said.

"Wow," a woman exclaimed behind me.

We all turned, and I didn't miss the appreciative look Sam shot Everly. She was in a pair of cut-off jean shorts, a tank top, and my extra work boots. "Theo made me put these on before I came inside," she said, pointing to her feet.

I elbowed Sam in the stomach. "Eyes on her face."

Sam winked at Everly before returning his attention to the backsplash. Guy had some balls.

"Hey, Everly," Cal said. "You here to work too?"

"Oh no," she said, holding up her hands. "I just need to talk to Aiden a minute."

"Back in five, guys," I said before blocking Sam's view of Everly's ass as she turned and headed for the dining room.

Everly ran her hand along my new table and smiled. "Everything is really coming together. I can't wait for that dinner invite."

"Just because I have a table and half a working kitchen doesn't mean I can cook."

She shrugged. "You'll learn. You always could when you put your mind to something."

Shit. I'd given Everly the perfect opening to bust my balls, and she'd gone sweet instead of sassy. "What's up, Ev?"

We stepped aside as two of my guys walked through carrying wood for the built-in bench in the kitchen. Hammers thudded throughout the house where other projects were being done.

"Is there somewhere quiet we can go?"

The knot in my stomach tightened. "Not in here. We can go outside."

She glanced out the window and frowned. "You might want some privacy for this."

Fuck that wasn't good. I wasn't fighting any town ordinances at the moment, which meant she probably had something to tell me about Lauren and the baby. "Follow me."

I led her outside, past two more of my guys cutting a board with a table saw, and across the dirt road separating my yard from Old Man Crawford's place, which was technically my yard now too. The grass was high on either side of the path that I'd mowed through the field to the tree house. In a couple of weeks, a woman who ran a rescue farm for horses would bring a baler to make hay. She got free food for her animals. I got free mowing.

I kept an eye on Everly as we neared the tree house. We could have sat in my truck or her car if we wanted no one to hear us, but for some reason, I felt pulled to bring her here.

"Oh, Aiden," she said, placing her hand on her chest when the tree house came into view. "It's perfect."

"You think he'd like it?" I asked, suddenly nervous that I hadn't honored Logan the way he'd have wanted. "It's not too childish?"

Everly straight-up punched my arm. "You know he would have loved it. Why are you doubting yourself?"

I rubbed my bicep, more for effect than to ease any damage she'd caused. "I guess my ego has taken a couple hits lately."

"Is it safe to go inside?"

Yep. She knew something about Lauren and the baby. Otherwise, Everly would have taken my statement as an invitation to talk about my feelings, something I gave into occasionally with my sisters, adopted or otherwise. "Solid as a rock. Or as solid as any tree house can be."

She rushed to the ladder and scaled it to the deck above. I had a flash of her doing the same thing when she was little, Logan following her closely so he could catch her if her foot slipped.

I climbed up slowly, giving Everly a few moments alone. She'd already taken a seat on the couch, a look of awe on her face. Thank God she wasn't bawling her eyes out. I was anxious to know what she had to tell me, but no way would I have rushed her if she'd gotten overwhelmed.

"What do you think?" I asked, taking a seat beside her.

"It's amazing," she said, smiling at me. "You're going to have so much fun here with your nieces and nephews and your own children."

Her face grew serious and my heart stopped. "You're killing me, Ev."

"It's not bad," she said, taking my hand. "Actually, it's the best-case scenario for you, legally."

"Spit it out, Everly, before I hurl off the deck."

"Lauren called this morning. She asked me to put together whatever paperwork we need to relinquish her parental rights to you."

I nodded.

She blew out a breath and let go of my hand. "I was afraid you didn't know about it, and I had to drop the bomb on you."

"I didn't know she called you, but I knew she didn't want to be a mom."

"I told her there wasn't anything we could file or sign before the baby was born except a Voluntary Acknowledgement of Paternity. We could file it at the hospital, but doing it ahead of time ensures your name is on the birth certificate."

"I'll sign anything you need."

She nodded and narrowed her eyes at me. "The entire family is pissed, by the way, that you haven't officially told them. Your mom heard about the baby in the cereal aisle of the grocery store."

"She never called and asked me."

"Because she figured there was a reason you hadn't told her."

"Can you blame me?"

Everly bit her bottom lip and shook her head. "But you might want to stop by this afternoon so we can explain the situation with Lauren. The longer you let them stew, the worse it'll be."

I could only imagine what my sisters would say the next time they went to Karma if they knew the whole story. "I can't. They'll hate Lauren."

Everly shrugged. "Let them. Better than them being pissed at you."

"I'll think of a way to tell them that doesn't make her look bad and talk to them next week."

"You care about her," Everly said, softly.

"You know what an idiot I can be." Because only a fool would pine for a woman who didn't want to be loved.

Everly gripped her knees and looked out the window facing the old barn. Was she thinking about Logan, like I did every time I saw the rotting wood?

Probably not. She hadn't been at the party where Logan spent his last hours partying with me, Theo, and Cal. He didn't die here, so to Everly, this place was just the spot where I'd built her brother's memorial.

I wanted to smack my forehead. Of course, she was thinking of Logan. We were sitting in his memorial tree house.

"Can I be honest?" she asked after a few moments.

"Are you ever not?" I said, nudging her shoulder.

She pressed her lips in a line and turned to me. "Are you sure you're ready to—"

"What the hell, Ev." Anger boiled in my chest, making my vision narrow. "I can't believe you'd ask me that. Yes, I'm ready to be a dad. It scares the shit out of me how much I love that kid already. I'd cut off my arm for the little lime."

She looked near tears. "I never doubted it. You'll be an amazing father."

"You're not making any sense."

She blew out a breath but didn't call me on the fact I'd interrupted her before she could explain herself. "Are you sure you're ready to let Lauren go? Because even if she doesn't want to be a mom, I don't see how she could stay in Peace Falls while you're raising the baby here."

My heart ached so bad, I rubbed my thumb across my chest. Deep down, I knew Everly was right. I loved Lauren, and the thought of never holding her again, never seeing her again, made me so angry I wanted to burn my life to the ground. But I couldn't. Because if all went well, she'd give me someone I could love unconditionally, a life-changing love. So it didn't matter what I felt for her, or whatever decisions she made after the baby was born, I had to move on. "I can't make her want me. Or the baby. I don't have a choice but to let her go."

She nodded. "And you think you can do that?"

"Like I said, I don't have a choice."

She started picking at a loose string on the cushion beside her. "You didn't have a choice with Logan either, but you're still holding onto him, to the grief, the guilt. You've helped Cal and Theo let go of the past enough to move forward, but you haven't been able to do the same."

"I'm trying," I said, rubbing my forehead. "All that work in the house. That's me trying to build the life I know Logan would want me to have, the home my child deserves."

She pulled her legs into her chest and wrapped her arms around them. "You're still angry," she said, staring at the barn again. "Angry he's gone. Angry at yourself for the role you think you played in his death. I can feel it."

"Yes," I answered honestly. "Logan would be alive today if it wasn't for me. That's something I'll carry the rest of my life."

"He'd hate that," she said, looking back at me, her eyes blazing. She resembled Logan so much it sometimes took my breath away.

"Logan wasn't capable of hating anything."

She shook her head. "Logan wasn't a saint, Aiden. He was as beautifully flawed as the rest of us. He got impatient in traffic, made fun of sappy movies, and lost his shit on anything and anyone who hurt the people he loved. How many times did he get into fights on the field because someone fouled you or Cal? He'd have hated what his death has done to Cal, Theo, and especially you."

I scrubbed my hand down my face. "I don't know what you want me to tell you, Everly. Logan and Lauren aren't the same. I can let her go because that's what she wants. Logan didn't have a choice. He was taken from us, and I don't know if I'll ever be able to get over it. But I can promise you, nothing and no one will get in the way of me being the best father I can."

"OK," she said with a small smile. "I'll tell your sisters and mine to stop worrying, but I doubt anything I say will settle our moms."

"How much have y'all been gossiping about me?" I asked, fighting a laugh.

"Do you honestly think we've talked about anything else, dumbass?"

Now she sounded like Logan too. "Let's get out of here. There are a dozen guys in my house who probably have questions for me."

We stood, but instead of leaving, she pulled me into a hug. "I know I just gave you a hard time, but Logan would be proud of you, Aiden. Pissed that you haven't let him go. But so proud."

I kissed the top of her head. "Not as proud as he'd be of you."

She let out the sob I knew she'd been holding since we got here, and I let the guys work without me a while longer until she'd cried enough for us both.

Chapter Twenty-Nine

Lauren

My heart pounded against the sign pressed to my chest. This was it. Once I put this piece of cardboard in the window, everyone would know. I'd put it off long enough. My real estate agent had been on me for days. I'd chosen someone I didn't know in Jericho and insisted he didn't put the listing online until I gave him the green light. Not that I'd change my mind. I just needed time to brace myself for the onslaught of questions. Or worse, silence.

People were nice here, but by now the entire town probably knew about the baby and my lack of maternal interest. Aiden may have kept his mouth shut, but all my friends knew I was pregnant and didn't want to be a mother, which meant Rose knew, which meant her friends knew, and so on. Deadbeat moms were judged harsher than deadbeat dads. The good people of Peace Falls would probably be relieved to see me go.

I turned the "For Sale" sign to face the street and propped it in the front window. It immediately fell over, scaring Medusa and Desdemona, who were curled together sleeping in the Hot Summer Reads display. I tried propping the sign again, and it fell over again.

I headed for the self-help section, not because I liked irony, but because it was the closest to the front. I was sandwiching the sign between the glass and a motivational text when Aiden's truck pulled to a stop in front of the café.

He climbed from the driver's side and walked around to the passenger side but froze when he saw me in the window. By the look on his face, he hadn't expected to see me, which was understandable at four-fifteen in the morning. His eyes lowered from mine to the sign, then to his boots. His chest moved rapidly, his hands balled at his side.

I was about to open the door and tell him to leave when he ripped open the truck's passenger door and grabbed a stack of printer paper and ink cartridges from the seat. He set them at my front door and left without sparing me another look.

I waited until his truck pulled away to gather the office supplies from the welcome mat. All this time, he'd been the one making donations to the career center. I'd never limited the number of pages people could print for free, yet I'd never once had to shell out money for supplies. Because he had.

I never questioned why the paper never ran out or how the exact cartridges arrived exactly when I needed them. I received thanks every day from people who used the printer. Gratitude I didn't deserve since all this time his quiet generosity had kept the center running.

I closed my eyes, willing myself not to cry. I should be happy. Yet again, Aiden had proved himself to be a good man. I should be relieved, knowing my child would be guided by someone who did things for others without expecting anything in the return. Heck, he'd gone out of his way to prevent anyone from knowing. Until recently, he'd been a regular. He could have dropped off supplies when he came in for his coffee.

But would I have accepted them? The part of me that worked so hard to be kind might have. But the part of me that bantered with Aiden, that pushed him away whenever he got too close, that woman would have thrown reams of paper in his face.

I took a steadying breath. It no longer mattered. Someone else would own Karma soon. The career center could be nonexistent by the time the baby arrived. At least Cammie and Wyatt already had full-time jobs elsewhere. I'm sure anyone in town would be happy to hire them for part-time work if the new owner didn't keep them on.

I expected a flood of calls and texts as soon as Wyatt saw the sign and the note I'd left on the counter, so I quickly grabbed a blanket and a few books and set off to spend the morning anywhere but Karma.

As expected, my phone started blowing up with calls from Wyatt just as I pulled into the lot at the Sawtooth Ridge trailhead. Rowan and Cammie started calling and texting soon after. I put my phone on silent, but I didn't turn it off since I needed the flashlight as I picked my way down the quarter-mile path to the first outlook.

Reason 1,002 why I shouldn't be a mother: Thinking it was a good idea to stumble through the dark woods predawn while pregnant with only a cell phone, a blanket, and my car keys to protect me from predators, animal or human. Not my best idea.

I hated hiking, but even I could appreciate the beauty of the mountains that surrounded Peace Falls. I wouldn't have many more opportunities to enjoy them and felt compelled to watch the sunrise from the ridge. Not to mention, none of my friends would think to look for me on a trail. I pushed down all thoughts of the life I was leaving behind and focused on my next step on the uneven path. When I reached the first overlook, I shone my phone around a large rock, hoping to scare away any slithering things before I plopped down on the blanket and waited for the sun to rise.

I put my hand on my tiny bump as the sky sparked red, then orange, before easing to soft swirls of pink. "You'll love living here," I said. "It doesn't matter what season, it's always beautiful. And you'll have so many people who love you. You already do."

Tears stung the corners of my eyes, but I blinked them back. "I hope you know I'm one of them. It might not seem like it, but I'm letting you go because I love you so much. I know you'll be ok because your dad—" The words stuck in my throat, but I swallowed and pushed down the sadness clawing me inside. "Your dad will know how to be a good dad because he has a good family. The kind who like each other enough to spend time together beyond Thanksgiving and Christmas. The kind of family you can count on, always. I'm sorry I couldn't give you that."

The sun burned across the ridge, illuminating the forest behind me. It'd be blinding soon. I thought of turning my back to it, but even with the blanket, the rock wasn't the most comfortable place to sit. I waited long enough for the light to reach the path before I headed back.

I planned to spread out on the soft grass in a park in Jericho and read for the rest of the day. I knew I couldn't avoid my friends forever. I also knew they'd worry if I didn't at least send proof of life. I had no less than twenty text messages when I arrived at the car. I wanted to ignore them all, but just as I was typing a group text to my friends, a message came in from Poppy.

> *I can't believe you pulled this shit the day before Rowan's surgery*

"What?" There's no way I'd been that selfish, right? I checked the date on my phone and sure enough, it was the day before my best friend's spinal operation. It's official. I was a terrible person.

> *Please tell her I'm OK and not to worry*

> *Tell her yourself. In person. Like a decent friend*

I blew out a breath.

*I'm not joking, Lauren. Get your ass to her house.
She needs you*

No she doesn't. She has you

*Fine. I need you. Rowan's crying nonstop and I
don't know how to help her*

My chest squeezed. Rowan had been a wonderful friend to me, the best I'd ever had. Poppy might be blunt, but she was incredibly sweet and caring with the people she loved. If she felt helpless, Rowan must be really bad. Of course, they were both wrecks. They'd probably been upset about the surgery before I pulled a disappearing act.

I'm on my way

Bring junk food

I smiled despite the ache in my chest. Rowan did like a good sugar binge while she worked through her feelings. I backed out of my parking spot and headed for the main road. It was barely past six, so my options were limited. I realized the pharmacy where I'd taken my pregnancy test was the closest, so I headed that way.

Melissa smiled at me when I slipped through the automatic doors into the bright store lights.

"Hi," she said. She glanced at my stomach, and her smile grew. "How are you doing?"

She remembered me. Of course she did. How often did people find out they were pregnant in the employee bathroom, then vomit into the bushes by the door?

"The second trimester has been a little better," I said, walking toward the drink cooler. I got two sodas for the Stevens sisters and a lemonade for myself before heading to the candy aisle. I grabbed Kettle chips, candy bars, and Rowan's favorite sour gummies before putting everything on the counter.

"I remember the cravings," she said, eyeing my selections.

"Honestly, I haven't craved anything other than a day without puking. My friend's having surgery tomorrow, and I'm taking her something to cheer her up."

Melissa smiled at me again. "I can tell you're going to be a great mom."

No, I wasn't. I hadn't even remembered Rowan's surgery. Poppy had been the one to tell me to get junk food. I gave Melissa a tight smile and nodded.

Her hand hovered over Rowan's gummy worms, but she stopped and studied me. "You don't believe me, do you?"

What was this, a pharmacy or a therapist's office? I didn't need to get into my shitty past and all the reasons I'd be an unfit mother with a relative stranger. I could have just shrugged or waved off her question, but instead I let the foster kid shine through my eyes, the fuck-around-and-find-out kid who got me through each day before I moved to Peace Falls.

Melissa's eyes widened, but she shook her head and laughed. Laughed. "You got the mama bear part down. Ain't nobody messing with your kid."

"Excuse me?"

She was still smiling when she put the last of my items in a plastic bag and slid them across the counter. "You know how I know you'll be a good mom? You're worried you won't be. Which means you'll work hard to be the best you can. Believe me. I was only sixteen when I had my daughter. Everyone expected me to be a terrible mother, myself included." She pulled her phone from her pocket and showed me the photo on her home screen of an adorable little girl with brown pigtails and a huge smile. "I don't always get it right, but I always try."

"She's beautiful," I said, swiping my card and trying not to cry.

"Thank you," Melissa said. "Go on, Mama Bear. Everything will be OK."

I wasn't expecting life advice with my snacks, but I thanked her and headed to the parking lot. Everything would be OK because I was leaving.

When I arrived at Rowan and Cal's house, Poppy was pacing the porch in nothing but an oversized black t-shirt that probably belonged to Theo. Her pixie cut stood in all directions as she tore down the sidewalk in her bare feet toward my car.

I braced myself for the wrath of half the Stevens Suicide Squad (aka whichever two of the Stevens siblings were going apeshit on behalf of the third), but instead of yelling at me, Poppy pulled me into a hug, squishing the plastic bag between us.

"Why?" she asked. A one-word question with so many answers.

Why? Because I can't watch Aiden and our child be a family without me. Because I hate myself for not being the person I want to be. Because it's easier to run away than face the truth that I will never be good enough.

"Is she inside?" I asked instead of answering.

Poppy stepped back and nodded. "You know I'd punch you in the tit right now if you weren't pregnant."

"If I weren't pregnant, you wouldn't need to," I said, walking past her. "But feel free. I don't think a tit punch would hurt the baby, and I deserve it."

"Son of a biscuit, Lauren," she said, hurrying after me. "Is this what pregnancy hormones do to a person, or have you been hiding your crazy this whole time?"

"Both," I said, knocking on the front door.

Poppy took the bag from me, opened the door, and walked in. "Good luck," she said over her shoulder.

I took a breath and went in after her. Rowan flew off the couch where she'd been huddled with Cal, her face tear-stained and swollen, and tackled me in a hug. I waited for her to say something. Anything. But she just held me tightly.

"I'm sorry," I choked out.

Rowan didn't answer. She just squeezed me harder.

I'm not sure how long we stood like that before I wrapped my arms around her waist and fell apart. She loosened her grip to rub my back while I cried on her shoulder. Unlike Brandi, I wasn't concerned about snotting up Rowan's old-lady floral pajamas, so I let it all out. At some point, she maneuvered us to the couch. When I finally looked up, Theo, Poppy, and Cal were standing together, staring at me. Cal looked like he wanted to murder me, but Theo and Poppy had teared up.

"I'm sorry," I told them as well. For so much. For making them worry today. For leaving them. For breaking Aiden's heart.

"You're a coward," Cal said.

Poppy and Theo glared at him, but I nodded.

"Um, I'm not sure that's helpful right now, Caleb," Rowan said, her voice tight.

Cal kept staring at me. "He's worth the risk. You know he is."

Which was exactly what I'd told him about Rowan when he thought he couldn't have a serious relationship. "But I'm not."

Everyone looked confused except Cal, who appeared equal parts pissed and sad.

"I can't be a good mother. Aiden will end up hating me, more than he does now."

"He said you were the love of his life," Theo said, softly. "Pretty sure that means he doesn't hate you."

My stomach dropped like I'd just plunged down the world's tallest rollercoaster. "He did not say that."

"He did," Cal said.

Rowan and Poppy looked at their partners and then at each other as if to confirm that they were both learning this information together. Theo and Cal were in for it later.

I blew out a breath. "It doesn't matter. He wants the baby, and I can't be a good mother."

"You keep saying that," Poppy said, narrowing her eyes. "But how would you know? I would have noticed if you'd had a kid before."

"What'd I miss?" Cammie said, throwing open the front door without knocking. Her long blonde hair was dripping wet and had soaked the shoulders of her pink scrubs. She came to a halt when she saw Cal, Theo, and Poppy lined up like a firing squad.

"Aiden is in love with Lauren, but Lauren would rather skip town than be a bad mom, which doesn't make a lick of sense to me," Poppy said.

"That's because you never had a bad mom," Cammie said, flitting past them to take a seat on the couch next to me.

"I still say it's bullshit," Poppy said, crossing her arms. "Lauren is the most nurturing person I know."

They all hummed in agreement, even Cammie, who I'd thought might be on my side, whatever that meant.

"Don't leave," Cammie said, taking my hand. "Because if you do, the people who hurt you, who made you believe you can't be whatever you want to be, win. Don't give them that power."

"You don't know what you're talking about," I said, pulling my hand away. "You have no idea why I'm leaving."

"Because you're scared," Cal said.

Rowan glared at him.

"Of course she's scared," Cammie said, twisting to shoot him a glare as well. "Before you moved here," she said, turning back to me, "you bounced around foster homes because your mom couldn't get it together, and your dad's been MIA your whole life. Maybe your mom used. Maybe she hit you or neglected you. I bet you've been yelled at, smacked, and/or touched in places you don't want to talk about. Not just by your mom or her boyfriends or your foster parents, but by other kids in the system. You probably did some things you aren't proud of just to get through it and because of all that, you think you're incapable of being a good mom."

My mouth fell open. Had she hacked the CPS database? "Did you research me?"

Rowan sucked in a breath, and I realized I'd just confirmed at least some part of what Cammie had said.

She nodded. "I have the same trust issues you do. For a lot of the same reasons. When you offered me the job at Karma, I poked around. I don't know everything you've been through, and honestly, I don't want to know unless you want to tell me. Because when it comes down to it, none of it matters. Unless you let it. You can be a great mom, Lauren. Heck, you already know all the things not to do."

Rowan let out a sob and put her head in her hands.

"Cam," Cal said, hoarsely. "I'm not sure we all needed to hear that."

He looked shattered. They all did. Poppy had her head buried in Theo's chest. Theo's olive skin had paled to a shade lighter than Poppy's.

Cammie shrugged. "Normally, I wouldn't spill someone else's secrets, but Lauren's about to make the biggest mistake of her life unless we stop her."

Rowan grabbed my hand, but kept her face buried in the other. I'd never seen her cry so hard. Not when she came back to Peace Falls after her first marriage failed. Not even when Cal broke her heart.

"Hey," I said, putting my arm around her. "It's OK. Breathe, Rowan."

"No, it's not," she said, her head snapping up. "I'm crying because of things that happened to you before I knew you, and you're trying to comfort me. How could you possibly think you don't have the compassion, the love to be a mom?"

"Well," I said, looking to Cammie to back me up. She lifted her eyebrows as if to say, "I told you so."

"I promise to tell you if I ever see you being a shitty mother," Poppy said, her voice cracking. "We all know I don't have a filter."

Theo kissed the top of her head. "And love you for it."

"She has a point, you know," Cammie said. "Every one of us would stop you from being a bad mom. Be honest, you love this baby?"

I nodded.

"How do you feel about Aiden?" Poppy asked softly.

"Poppy," Rowan hissed. "One problem at a time."

"Is it even a problem if she loves him back?" Poppy snapped.

Everyone turned and stared at me. I twisted my hands in my lap, avoiding eye contact with them all. "Having a family with Aiden is more than I've ever let myself imagine."

Rowan started rooting around the plastic bag by her feet and yanked out her gummies. "First things first," she said, around a mouth full of candy. "Call Wyatt and tell him to take down that sign."

"Rowan—"

"Don't mess with me, Lauren," she said. "I'm twenty-four hours from someone fiddling with my spinal column."

"Fine." I pulled my phone from my pocket and gasped when I saw the text from my real estate agent.

> *Received offer at 10K over asking. Text me ASAP to accept*

"What?" Rowan asked, her cheeks stuffed with candy.

I held up my phone.

Everyone read the text message and started talking at once.

"It doesn't matter if someone made an offer. You can back out," Rowan said.

"Did you sign anything?" Cal asked.

"Is Karma made of gold?" Cammie asked. "I thought you put the sign up today. It isn't even seven."

Poppy laughed so hard she snorted. "He bought the building."

"Who?" Theo asked.

"Aiden," she said, then smacked her hand over her mouth.

"What makes you think that?" Cal asked.

Poppy shook her head. "Nope. Not going there."

I locked eyes with Poppy as Theo and Cal tried to pull more information from her, and I knew without a doubt she was right. Aiden had put in an offer for Karma, my business, my home. "Guess he wants me gone."

Everyone stopped talking.

Poppy walked across the room and kneeled in front of me. "He wants to give you whatever you want, Lauren. Time to figure out what that is."

CHAPTER THIRTY

Aiden

I'D NEVER SEEN CAL so nervous. Not before our state championship game and not before his wedding. He stayed with Rowan until they rolled her to the operating room, then settled in the waiting area with the rest of us.

Settled wasn't the right word. He'd had his head in his hands, gripping his hair for the past ten minutes. Not that anyone looked relaxed. Theo held Poppy's hand while she bounced her knee and stared at a blank wall. Chris paced the room with Rose, shooting nervous looks at Poppy, Cal, and the door where nurses and doctors popped in and out to update other families.

I'd googled Rowan's surgery—artificial disc replacement—and knew we had at least a couple hours to go. Way too long to leave Cal alone with his thoughts. I might be a dick for thinking it, but I was relieved to have something to distract me from the storm in my head.

When I saw Lauren with the "For Sale" sign yesterday, something in me broke. Until then, I'd held out hope she'd come around and realize how much she wanted the baby, and, OK, me. So I did what any man hopelessly in love with a flight risk would do. I put an offer in on the building. One she couldn't refuse. Why? Because if I owned Karma, she could always change her mind and come back to me. I hadn't heard a peep. The offer expired tonight at midnight, and I hadn't received a single call or text from her real estate agent. I didn't know how to read the silence.

I still hadn't decided if I wanted to see Lauren if she joined us at the hospital. I felt raw, like my body had been scraped down to the nerves. Focusing on Cal had helped. I needed to keep myself distracted, which come to think of it, was exactly what Cal needed too.

"I sued your parents," I said.

He lifted his head from his hands and stared at me.

"And Theo's."

By now, I had everyone's attention. After Poppy texted me to confess her slip up yesterday, I figured I had to come clean. Telling them both now was either an asshole move or an act of kindness. "I had a ton of medical bills after the accident that my parents couldn't afford."

"Aiden—" Cal started.

I held up my hand to stop him. "The suit was for more than the medical bills though. I ended up getting enough to start my business, so everything I have now was built on money I took from your parents."

"Their car insurance," Cal said. "Not them."

Theo nodded.

They didn't look surprised. If anything, they seemed confused. "Did you know?" I asked.

"Yeah," Cal said with a shrug, like his best friend sued his parents every day.

"We both had to give depositions," Theo added.

"Your parents left right after the case settled," I said to Theo.

His eyes widened. He unfolded his long frame from his chair and crossed the narrow waiting room to me. "You think they left because of that?"

"I think it was the nail in the coffin, yeah."

Theo rubbed his forehead and blew out a breath. "Damn it, Aiden. Please tell me you haven't been feeling guilty this whole time?"

I squirmed on the plastic chair next to Cal, who for the record, was no longer yanking out his hair. Now he was looking at me like I'd said the stupidest thing he'd ever heard.

"Told you they wouldn't care," Poppy said.

"You knew about this?" Theo asked her.

Great. Now I'd started a fight between Theo and Hell Cat. "I made her swear not to tell either of you. She only found out when I bought the bakery building."

"You bought the whole building?" Cal asked. "Didn't you buy Theo's house around the same time?"

I shrugged.

"He's loaded," Poppy said. "He also paid a lot more for that villa in St. John than he led everyone to believe and a bunch of other stuff."

"And all of that was because of the money I took from their parents," I said to Poppy.

"Their insurance," Cal and Theo said at the same time.

Rose stopped pacing and started shaking her finger in my face. "Aiden O'Malley, any money you received paled in comparison to what you lost. The fact you used it to build a life for yourself shouldn't make you feel an ounce of guilt. Not a smidge."

"Yes ma'am," I said because I sure as hell wasn't going toe to toe with Rose. Not when her daughter was in surgery. Not ever. She'd raised three of my favorite people, mostly on her own. The woman could say just about anything to me, and I'd listen.

"Have you only been friends with us because you felt guilty about the money?" Cal asked without lifting his eyes from the floor.

"What? You're joking, right?"

"It's a fair question," Theo said, shoving his hands in his pockets.

"No," I said, standing. "That's—Why would you even think that? I love you idiots like family. The only reason I never mentioned the settlement before was because I thought you'd both hate me."

"Are they always this dramatic?" Rose asked Chris.

"Most of the time they're chill, but they have their moments."

"You're such an idiot," Theo said, pulling me into a tight hug.

Cal joined him and the three of us hugged it out right in the middle of the hospital waiting area.

Something crashed in the hallway. When I broke away from the guys, Cammie was guiding Lauren to a nearby chair over a pile of plastic containers on the floor.

"Cal?" Cammie choked out, looking terrified.

He and I both rushed over. I gripped Lauren's shaking hand right before Poppy shoved Cammie aside to grab the other.

"Rowan's fine," she said. "They were in their feelings about something else. She's OK."

Lauren burst into tears. "I thought something terrible had happened," she said. "And I wasn't here in time to see her before she went back."

Cal and I exchanged a guilty look before Lauren's words sank in and he seemed to remember where he was and why. He glanced at the clock on the wall and back at me. "Thanks, brother," he said, gripping my shoulder. "I needed to get out of my head."

"Anytime," I said.

I let go of Lauren and stood with Cal, but she grabbed my hand. She wasn't in any danger, just upset. I could leave. I should leave. But she'd reached for me, and her hand felt so good in mine. I slid into the seat next to her. Cal, Poppy, and Cammie collected the food containers, which had somehow stayed closed, and carried them deeper into the room where the others sat watching us.

I couldn't take my eyes off Lauren while she worked to regain her composure. She had on a billowy green dress that hugged her full breasts and fell all the way to her sandal-clad feet. Even with the loose fabric, I could make out the slight bump in her midsection. Stunning didn't begin to describe how she looked. She'd always been gorgeous, but seeing the changes to her body, knowing she was growing my child, took her beauty to the next level. She'd also worn her hair loose, cascading past her shoulders in gentle waves that begged to be touched.

"Did you put in the offer to buy Karma?" she asked once she was calm.

"I did."

"Do you want me to leave?"

The rest of the group pretended to search through the food selection, but they were all listening. I might be willing to air my dirty laundry to take Cal's mind off Rowan, but not Lauren's. I squeezed her hand and lifted my chin towards the group.

"They know everything," she said. Doubt that. When I still didn't say anything, she studied my hand, running her graceful fingers across every callous, like she was memorizing each one.

"I never told them," I said, my heart thudding hard in my chest.

"I did. Everything. Even the choice I gave you."

"That wasn't a choice."

"You're right," she said, running her fingers along a groove on my palm. My body reacted to her touch, and I hated myself for still being drawn to a woman who didn't want me the same way I wanted her. "Why did you offer to buy Karma?"

At the rate my heart was going, they'd need to wheel me into the back with Rowan soon. "Because I wanted to give you the option to change your mind."

"What if I have?" she asked loud enough for the entire room to hear.

Everyone was lined up on the other side of the room, staring at us while they ate. Even the couple who'd been waiting for updates on their son's tonsillectomy were enjoying French toast sticks and the show. No one had the decency to look away when I caught them watching. "I'd say I'd love to talk about that later."

"OK," she said in a voice so small I wanted to wrap my arms around her and pull her onto my lap.

But I couldn't let my feelings for her get in the way of making the best decisions for my kid. I gave her hand a squeeze, stood, and crossed the waiting room.

"Save any for me?" I asked, eyeing the spread of scrambled eggs, bacon, and French toast sticks. Cammie and Lauren had gone all out, but despite asking the question, my stomach rolled too much to eat.

"Rowan's going to be so pissed she missed that," Poppy said before shoving a strip of bacon into her mouth.

"Just so we're clear," Theo said, "I'm getting an impartial realtor to value what the house is worth to rent or buy. No more of this 'construction inconvenience crap," Aiden. I mean it. You don't owe me a thing."

"Fine," I said, grabbing a plate and dumping a piece of French toast onto it.

"Um, just so we're clear too, Rowan and I can't afford higher rent yet," Poppy said. "But we'll raise it as soon as we can."

I blew out a breath and nodded. I didn't need their money, but they needed to know our friendship wasn't built entirely on guilt.

Cammie took her plate over to sit with Lauren, and I plopped into the chair she'd left beside Cal. "She came today," he said so low only I could hear. At least someone in this messy group knew how to whisper. "It's a start."

"She came for Rowan," I whispered back, dropping my plate onto the table beside me and knotting my hands together. I couldn't look at Lauren without wanting to go to her, so I stared at my hands and did my best to distract Cal until a doctor pushed through the door calling his name.

"It went well," she said, smiling. "She's in recovery now. I can take one of you back."

Rose jumped up and ran toward the door before stopping. "I'm not her one anymore, am I?" she said, turning to face us.

"I'm Rowan's PT," Cal said, shooting the doctor a look.

She smiled. "I'll brief you about the surgery while I escort you both to the back."

"Hope you don't have plans this week, Chris," Poppy said, standing on her tiptoes to loop her arm around her brother's shoulders. "Mom's going to need to smother her baby boy with love and affection after that."

He let out a sigh but nodded.

"Well," Cammie said in a voice even higher than her usual chirp. "I'm headed out now that we know Rowan's OK. Anyone want to leave with me, Aiden?"

I guess it made sense I'd go. Cal didn't need me anymore, and Rowan had a line of people waiting to see her. My crews could certainly use my help. "Yeah, sure."

"Come on, Lauren," Cammie said, pulling Lauren from her chair and walking her toward the elevator. "You rode with me."

"I could give her a—" Theo started before Cammie shot him a death glare. She punched the button for the elevator. When the door slid open, she motioned us in and then waited until the door closed, leaving her in the hallway and us inside the car alone.

"Subtle," I said, trying not to laugh.

Lauren gave me a small smile but stayed quiet the entire ride down. OK, this was going to be awkward as hell until we addressed how exactly she'd changed her mind.

"Would you give me a ride to Karma?" she asked when we reached the hospital lobby.

"Sure. I need to stop by my house first, so I can change before I head to work. It's on the way." My house wasn't on the way. It wasn't even a slight detour, but I wanted as much time with her as I could get. Lauren knew the way to Karma as well as I did, but she nodded and followed me to my truck.

I opened the passenger door and held out my hand to help her up. She gripped my fingers and climbed into the passenger seat, only letting go when I did. Part of me wondered how long she would have let me stand by the truck, holding her soft hand in mine, but I was resolved to talk things out before we let things get physical. No sense torturing myself with the feel of her warm fingers curled with mine.

"How have you been feeling?" I asked as I turned out of the parking lot. A nice safe subject. She was pregnant with my kid. She'd been sick. It was the thing to ask. I think. Had she changed her mind about relinquishing her parental rights or having the baby at all? Even with Rowan's surgery, I assumed the others would have clued me in if the latter were the case. But what if she hadn't told them?

"OK," she said, twisting her fingers in the skirt of her dress.

My stomach and lungs felt like they'd knotted together. Doubt that was possible, but it sure felt like it. I physically couldn't dance around this conversation any longer, but I also couldn't think of how to ask about the baby. "Has the morning sickness gotten any better now that you're further into your second trimester?"

She let out a breath, and I glanced from the road long enough to watch her rest her hands on her lap. "OK."

"OK," I said. A word had never felt so inadequate.

"How's the renovation going?"

I didn't want to talk about tile choices and plumbing. I didn't care what the house looked like. I just wanted to know if she was still pregnant and planned to stick around.

"Everything should be done by the time the baby arrives."

"That's nice."

"For fuck's sake," I said, slapping the steering wheel. "What are we doing, Lauren?"

"I'm trying to work into the conversation," she said, eyes blazing. "It's called small talk."

That's my girl. I just had to get her good and pissed. "Consider it done."

"I was trying to apologize to you properly in a way that didn't sound like it was coming out of left field."

"Since when have we ever done anything proper?"

"Seriously, Aiden," she said softly before reaching across the wide cab to rest her hand on my arm. "I'm sorry for so much. I've made everything difficult for you."

I shrugged. "You're the one throwing up every day. I should apologize to you, but I'm not sorry. I mean, I'm sorry you're sick. But I'm not sorry for getting you pregnant."

"You have nothing to apologize for," she said, pulling her hand back and placing it on her stomach. Thank fuck. I fought the urge to reach across the truck and place my hand on her midsection too.

We pulled up to my house, and I shut off the engine before turning to face her. When she didn't speak or turn to look at me, I figured I had to be the one to get this conversation going. "Tell me how you changed your mind."

"I still don't know if I can be a good mother, but I want to try," she said, her eyes glued to the house. "I want our baby, and I want to explore having a relationship with you. I'm terrified of being a mother, of my feelings for you. But I want to try."

I scrubbed my hand down my face and blew out a breath. "I'd like to give you all that, but if I'm being honest, I don't trust you not to bail."

She nodded and finally turned to look at me. "That's fair. What do you need from me?"

I need you. I need to wake up every morning tangled with your body. I need to know that my entire heart is safe in you. That you want me and our baby so much, you have zero thoughts of ever leaving. "If we're doing this, you're living here."

"After everything I've pulled, you still want me to move in with you?" she asked, her eyes wide.

I shook my head, stabbing my heart in the process. "Not like before. It's just the only time I don't worry about the baby is when I'm with you."

"Oh," she said in a small voice. "You want to keep an eye on me."

It would be so easy to tell her the truth. That, yes, I didn't worry as much when I was with her because I didn't have to rely on what someone else told me. But also because spending time alone with Lauren gave me a peace unlike any I'd ever felt. "I want to make sure you're all right."

"You could install a couple ring cams at Karma."

This wasn't going well. Now she thought all I wanted was an incubator for my child. "But then I wouldn't be with you. And I want to be with you. I just need to take things slow."

Because I'm so in love with you, and I don't know if you'll ever feel the same for me. Because it hurts to be with you, but it hurts more to be without you.

She gave me a sweet smile. "Do you have time to show me what all you've done inside?"

"For you, Princess, I have all the time in the world."

Chapter Thirty-One

Lauren

THE MORNING AFTER ROWAN'S surgery, Wyatt was already behind the counter when I came downstairs to open the café.

"You're here early," I said, giving his shoulders a squeeze.

He nodded and kept measuring grounds for the next pot.

"I owe you an apology and an explanation," I said.

His hand stilled mid scoop. He finished dumping the grounds into the filter before turning to face me. He looked tired, which was understandable given the hour, but the dark circles didn't bother me as much as his blank expression. He had his walls up, something he'd never done before with me. I couldn't blame him, but the lack of warmth in his eyes cracked my heart.

"I'm sorry," I said as my throat clogged with emotion. "I did pull back from our friendship after you quit. I was protecting myself without even realizing it, but I never meant to hurt you."

"I know," he said, gently. "But you scared the shit out of me with that note. I thought I'd never see you again."

He looked devastated, which made me feel even worse about how I'd treated him.

"Honestly, I was crying so hard when I wrote that note, I can barely remember what I said. I'm sure it was terrible."

"Mostly just a lot of apologizing. I'd show you, but I threw it in the dumpster with the 'For Sale' sign." The corners of his lips quirked up and some of the tension in my chest eased.

"Good. That's where it belongs. I have no plans to leave Peace Falls, and I promise I'll be a better friend from now on. Assuming you still want me in your life after what I pulled."

He shook his head and chuckled. "You're annoyingly easy to forgive."

I hoped that was true. Not only with Wyatt, but with all my friends. I knew earning Aiden's forgiveness would take more than a simple apology, but in time I'd show him how serious I was about staying, and maybe, just maybe, building a family together.

"So, we're good?" I asked, opening my arms.

Wyatt stepped forward and wrapped me in a tight hug. "Just don't go Houdini on me again."

"I promise," I said, stepping from his embrace. "And to prove how serious I am about fixing our friendship, I want you to take over the search for your replacement here. Post the job wherever you think best. Hire whomever you think will work out. Because I want what's best for you."

"Same," he said, his eyes brightening with that indescribable quality that made me trust him immediately. "Which is why I intend to hire two full-time employees. Assuming you can afford it."

"I can. I was just—"

"Scared?"

"Yes," I said, taking a deep breath. "I still owe you an explanation for why I acted the way I did."

Wyatt shook his head. "No, you don't. You can tell me anytime you want, but not today. Not when you think you owe it to me."

"Are you sure?" I asked, sounding far too relieved. It's not that I didn't want Wyatt to know about my childhood, it's just that I'd never found the words to talk about it with anyone but Aiden. Even then, I'd blurted out fragments because something like rain boots triggered a memory.

"I accept your apology, Lauren. Now let's get moving, or we're in for some grouchy customers who have to wait for their caffeine fix."

"There's something else. Are you free Sunday after closing?"

"I am," he said carefully. "What do you need?"

"A friend," I said, "who can lift heavy objects." Because even though I knew moving in with Aiden was the only way for us to move forward, the thought of leaving my tiny apartment filled me with the same fear I had every time I shoved my belongings into garbage bags to hop to another foster home. "I'm going to ask Cammie too."

He smiled at me. "Sure. Whatever you need."

After the early morning rush, I made my way to the hospital to visit Rowan. I'd seen her briefly after I left Aiden's yesterday, but she'd been on too many painkillers for a serious conversation. When I arrived in her room, she was propped on her side, tucked between two mountains of pillows. Rose had filled the tiny room with so many flowers, I fought the urge to sneeze.

"Hey," Rowan said, when she spotted me in the doorway. "I was hoping you'd stop by. I made Cal go into the office, but now I'm bored out of my mind."

"This should help," I said, placing a new release from her favorite romance author on the bedside table next to several cards, one with an intricate design that had to be handmade by Poppy. "How are you?"

"I felt worse after the accident."

And yet she hadn't told me about it until after she'd been released from the hospital. I'd been angry and hurt that she didn't lean on me then, which was exactly how she probably felt now.

"Aiden wants me to move in with him," I said, because apparently the only way I could talk about difficult topics was to shout them out of nowhere. "Not move in, move in. At least not now. I don't know if we're together or not. He just wants to make sure I'm not running again. But he also said he likes being around me. And moving in together makes sense, especially after the baby is born, but I'm scared to move. Which I know is stupid since I put the whole damn building up for sale."

Rowan nodded and winced.

"I'm the worst friend ever," I said, collapsing into the chair by her bed. "On top of everything I did this week, you're clearly in pain, and I'm rambling about my problems."

"Stop it," she said in a tone I'd never heard her use before. She sounded so much like Poppy, I glanced behind me to make sure it was just the two of us in the room.

Rowan held out her hand to me, and I took it. She gave my fingers three quick squeezes and one long one, our secret handshake from middle school, the one that said, "You're my best friend. I got you." I returned the handshake and settled back in the chair, clutching her hand like a lifeline.

"Now tell me why you're scared."

"Because the apartment is the only place I ever lived where I felt safe," I answered in a quiet voice.

Rowan's eyes filled with tears, but her voice was steady when she spoke. "It makes sense you'd be nervous to leave, especially to move in with someone you have a complicated relationship with. Have you told Aiden you're scared?"

I shook my head. "Moving in together shows Aiden he can trust me to stay. Honesty, I can't picture a better place to raise the baby, so I know it's something I need to do. I don't want my past messing up my life any more than it already has, but I'm terrified."

"When are you moving?"

"Sunday."

"Oh." She looked slightly alarmed, which made my heart pound.

"You think it's too soon?"

"No. I just realized I won't be able to help you. I'm out of commission for a while." She motioned to the wall of pillows between us, like she needed an excuse for not lugging my crap from Karma to Aiden's. "But if you're afraid, I say you're smart to do it as soon as you can. Don't overthink it."

Rowan was a planner to a fault. She probably knew what she'd be having for dinner a week from now. Scratch that. She'd probably made all her meals for the month and frozen them since she knew she'd be recovering from surgery. "How many pain meds are you on?"

"Just enough I'm not crying. Trust me, they aren't impacting my thought process at all. You said having a life with Aiden and the baby was more than you'd ever let yourself imagine. So don't bother imagining it. Just live it." She gave my hand a hard squeeze. "But Lauren, you have to be honest with him. If you're afraid, tell him. And you have to be honest with yourself about your feelings for him. Aiden and the baby aren't a package deal. You can just be co-parents."

"I think I might be falling for him," I said so quietly, I could barely hear myself.

"I think you already have," she said with a small smile. "Either way, you should call your realtor and have the listing for the building taken down." She cocked her eyebrow at me.

I felt my face heat. I had asked Wyatt to get rid of the sign, but I still hadn't officially removed the listing. I told myself I just dreaded talking to the realtor after ignoring his incessant calls and texts. He'd likely be pissed because of all the work he'd done for nothing, but really, I was keeping my exit plan open. Rowan didn't say anything. She didn't have to. We both knew I was hedging. The fact she'd taken the time post-surgery to look up the listing proved she understood me better than anyone.

After the silence stretched between us, she gave my hand a final squeeze and dropped it. "Love of his life, Lauren. You're either all in or not at all."

Chapter Thirty-Two

Aiden

I'd used low-emission paint in Lauren's room, but a slight chemical scent lingered. I opened all the windows and put a box fan in each, hoping to suck out whatever fumes remained.

"Looks great in here," Kayleigh said, standing in the doorway with her arms full of the curtains she'd just ironed. "Is the paint dry enough for these?"

"Yeah, I finished up yesterday. I didn't think it'd still smell. Is it safe for her to sleep here tonight?"

"Absolutely not," Ciara said, walking into the room after Kayleigh with her own armful of fabric. "She'll throw up for sure."

"Yeah, it's best you wait at least seventy-two hours," Maddie said, joining the conversation with a stepstool in her hands.

Guess I was sleeping on the new couch tonight. Until I knew Lauren was here to stay, I needed to keep some distance between us. I grabbed the stool from Maddie, placed it by the window facing the front yard, and climbed up. Kayleigh handed me the first curtain.

"Is it safe for her to be in here at all?" I asked while I straightened the fabric. "She wanted Cammie and Wyatt to help her move, and the only night all three of them aren't working is today. I told her that Theo and I could handle it, but she insisted."

"Can you blame her?" Fiona asked before taking a huge slurp from the straw in her oversized travel cup. "She's meeting all of us."

"You probably shouldn't be in here either," I said, glaring at her. "And y'all all know Lauren."

"Relax, Aiden," Fiona said, resting her cup on her huge stomach. "I just wanted to see how the room turned out. I'm going back downstairs to organize your kitchen."

"Well?" I asked, more nervous about my interior design skills than I'd ever been in my life. "How does it look?"

I'd painted the room a soft yellow and picked out navy curtains with a swirly design that reminded me of one of Lauren's dresses. I looked around and realized the color combo reminded me a little of Theo's dated bathroom. "Fuck. I should have asked her what color she wanted the walls to be."

Ciara shrugged. "Probably. Too late now. You can always paint over it later."

Kayleigh shot her a mom glare. Ciara returned it to her.

"I think it's gorgeous," Maddie said, stepping between them. "The white headboard and dresser go great with everything, and the bedspread ties it all together."

Because Lauren wasn't moving in. Not really. After she'd confessed how scared she was to leave her apartment, I'd told her to keep all her furniture there and just bring whatever clothes and things she needed. That way, she could nap in the apartment during the day and go back anytime she wanted. I knew it was a necessary compromise. I still hated it.

It didn't help that her building was still for sale. The day after she told me she wanted more, Sam came across the online listing while searching for flip projects. When he showed me, I assumed her real estate agent was taking his sweet time removing it, but each day the listing remained felt like a stab to the gut.

I'd done everything I could think of to make her room as comfortable as possible, but it was giving guest room vibes. A small, idealistic part of me hoped that's what it'd become because Lauren and I would end up sharing my room. Even so, the impersonal feel of her current space in my house wasn't helping ease the gut-twisting fear that she'd bolt and take my heart with her.

"I still don't understand why she's sleeping in here," Ciara said, handing me the next curtain.

"You of all people should know how much bed space you need to get comfortable when you're pregnant," Fiona said, rubbing her lower back.

"Out, Fi," I said, pointing to the door.

"I'm going," she said, heading down the hall. "Someone has to make sense of your kitchen cabinets."

"They looked fine to me," Maddie said with a shrug.

"She's nesting," Kayleigh said. "Don't try to understand. What time are you leaving to help Lauren pack up, Aiden?"

"I'm not," I said, carrying the stool to the other window and ignoring the looks between my sisters and Maddie. "Wyatt is borrowing Theo's truck and loading it. They should be here soon."

"What did you do to that woman?" Ciara asked, putting her hands on her hips. "She doesn't even want you to help her move in?"

"Knocked her up. Thought that was pretty obvious."

"Does she even want to live with you?" Kayleigh asked.

"Not really," I said, fumbling with the curtain rod, so I didn't have to see their reactions.

"So why would she?" Ciara asked.

"Ladies," Everly said, busting into the room like an angel of mercy with her arms full of more curtains. "I need to talk to Aiden about a permit issue before Lauren gets here, and Fi could really use your help downstairs."

By the looks they gave Everly, none of them believed her. They still left us alone.

"Perfect timing."

Everly smiled. "Figured you'd need reinforcements. How you holding up?" she asked, handing me a curtain.

I blew out a breath. "Honestly, I feel like a piece of shit for making Lauren move in with me."

"Pretty sure you can't make that woman do anything," Everly said, smoothing out the fabric I'd just hung. "But it's definitely a 180 from terminating her parental rights."

"Which my family can never know about," I said in a low voice. "Or about the whole adoption fiasco."

"No shit," Everly said, pinning me with a glare.

"I'm sorry, Ev," I said, climbing down. "I know you're a professional. I'm just nervous my sisters will grill Lauren when she gets here."

Everly shrugged. "Of course they will."

"You're not making me feel better."

"Just being realistic. We'll find out soon enough," she said, pointing out the window to where Theo's truck was pulling to a stop in front of the house. Lauren's sedan followed close behind. "And don't worry about Lauren. I have a feeling she can hold her own with this group."

I was surprised when Theo and Poppy climbed from the truck and walked to the back. Wyatt, Cammie, and Lauren joined them from the sedan.

"Better get down there before your sisters and mine realize they've arrived," Everly said, handing me the last curtain.

I threw it over the step stool, and Everly and I booked it downstairs, her to either tell my sisters or delay them.

Poppy grinned when she saw me. "Nice place you've got here, Stud Man. Hope you don't mind we dropped in. Theo wants to show me the wall where the mural's going."

I raised an eyebrow at her, and she smirked. Theo might show her the wall, but that wasn't why she came.

"When Rowan heard all your sisters would be here, she insisted we came to make sure Lauren didn't feel outnumbered."

"Pretty sure you're more his friend than mine," Lauren said, nudging past Poppy with the suitcase she'd taken to St. John. She looked stunning with her checks flushed, her lips slightly parted.

"Let me get that," I said, reaching for the suitcase. "Please," I added for good measure.

Kayleigh burst through my front door and down the porch stairs before Lauren answered me. My other sisters and Logan's were close behind.

"It's so good to see you," Kayleigh squealed, wrapping Lauren in a tight hug. "You look gorgeous. Doesn't she?"

Maddie, Fiona, Everly, and Ciara all agreed in chorus and took turns smothering Lauren with hugs.

"All that moving sure made us thirsty," Poppy said, working her way into the circle of women who'd surrounded Lauren. They scattered like dandelion seeds in the wind with promises of lemonade and sweet tea.

"Your family needs to work on boundaries," Poppy said, glaring at me.

Lauren laughed. "I'm a hugger, Poppy. That didn't bother me at all."

Thank fuck for that. I loved my family, but they could be a lot for some people.

"Sure made me uncomfortable," Poppy said, lifting the suitcase and carrying it toward the house.

"Hey, A," Theo said, walking past Lauren and me with a box in his arms. "Room across from the nursery, right?"

"Yeah. I'll grab a box or two and be right in."

"Nonsense," Cammie said, walking after him with a lamp in one hand and a stack of throw pillows tucked under her other arm. "Take Lauren inside to visit with your family. We can handle the rest. Can't we, Wyatt?"

"Sure," he said, flashing her a big smile as he hefted a large box from the back of the truck. He lifted his chin to me in greeting as he passed and quickened his pace to catch up with Cammie, who was holding the screen door open for him with her hip.

"Don't overdo it, Wyatt," Lauren called after him. "You haven't had dinner yet."

Why this woman ever thought she didn't have what it took to be a mom was beyond me. "You know I make him move shit all day when he's on job sites, right?"

"You know he's diabetic, right?" she said, turning to face me.

I loved riling this woman up, getting her so good and pissed her perfect mask slipped, and I got a glimpse of the spitfire beneath. But now wasn't the time. I wanted her to feel at ease living with me, not braced for combat.

"I didn't know until recently," I said, taking all the snark from my voice. "I promise to keep an eye on him whenever he comes back."

Lauren nodded. "I better grab something."

She started toward the truck, but I placed my hand on her arm to stop her. With a house full of well-meaning friends and family, it might be hours until I got a moment alone with her. She looked up at me and my stomach dipped. I was so screwed. Earlier this week she'd shredded my heart, and all I wanted to do was wrap myself around her like a barnacle and beg her to stay.

I pulled my hand away and shoved both in my pockets to keep myself from reaching for her again. "Thank you. I know this isn't easy for you. I just wanted you to know how much I appreciate it."

"Aiden, I—"

"Get inside out of the heat!" Ciara hollered from the front porch. "It's not good for the baby."

A flash of terror crossed Lauren's face, but I just started walking with her toward the house. "Don't mind Ciara. She's the drama queen in the group."

"I heard that," Ciara said, putting her hands on her hips.

"Women have babies in places a lot hotter than this," I said, glaring at her.

"I can see how flushed Lauren is from here."

Now it was my turn to give Lauren a terrified glance, but she was smiling at my sister. "I'm fine. Really."

"Nonsense," Ciara said, looping her arm into Lauren's. "Everyone should move while they're pregnant. It's one of the few perks. You can relax while everyone else happily carries your stuff."

With that, she guided Lauren into the house, and I headed to the truck. I climbed into the bed for one of the few remaining boxes as Theo came back through the front door.

"Is there more in the car?" I asked him.

My stomach sank when he shook his head and gave my shoulder a reassuring squeeze. I passed Cammie and Wyatt on the way to Lauren's room, where Poppy was fussing with the curtain I hadn't hung.

"I love the color you picked for the walls," she said.

"I screwed up," I said, putting down the box. "Making her move in with me right away."

"No, you didn't," she said, hopping down from the stool and coming to stand beside me. "Lauren needed a kick in the crotch after the crap she pulled. I'd have made her wear an ankle monitor."

"She should have at least waited and moved in a week from now. She can't sleep in here for a couple more days. The paint's still letting off fumes."

"Smooth," Poppy said, trying not to laugh. "Nothing like the old 'the paint's still toxic play' to get a woman in bed with you."

"I'll be sleeping on the couch." I must have let a fraction of the hurt I'd been hiding show because Poppy about knocked me over with the hug she gave me.

"Just stop pretending to be an asshole," she said into my t-shirt. "She'll come around."

Theo clomped in with his combat boots, followed by Wyatt and Cammie, but Poppy stayed snuggled against me. "This is the last of it," he said. "Want to look at the nursery wall?" he asked Poppy.

She gave me a final squeeze and followed him across the hallway. After Wyatt and Cammie set down the last of Lauren's things, she grabbed my hand and tugged me toward the door. "Let's get downstairs before your sisters scare the living daylights out of Lauren."

Cammie shouldn't have worried. Lauren was sitting on the new couch with a frosty glass of lemonade in her hand, surrounded by my sisters and Logan's, a dimpled smile on her face.

"We had a terrible time potty training him. He'd pee anywhere but the bathroom," Kayleigh said, and I cringed.

"Remember that time he peed in the front yard when it snowed?" Fiona said. "Mom made me shovel more on top of it so the mail carrier wouldn't see."

"Did they tell you I was two?"

Lauren looked up at me, her eyes sparkling. "Three."

"Two and a half," I said, glaring at Kayleigh.

"You were three and a half when the snow thing happened," Kayleigh said, taking a sip of her own lemonade. "I was being generous."

"Don't," Lauren said. "I want to hear every embarrassing story you have."

"Oh, having you in the family is going to be so much fun," Ciara said, wrapping her arm around Lauren's shoulders and giving her a squeeze.

"Ciara," Fi snapped. "She hasn't even unpacked yet *in the room down the hall from his*. Don't scare her off."

"She's the mother of my niece or nephew. That makes her family, no matter what happens with them," she said, motioning between Lauren and me.

Lauren's reaction wasn't the panic I expected. Instead, she flashed a smile at Ciara that lit up her entire face. "Thank you for making me feel so welcomed. All of you," she said, taking the time to look each of them in the eyes.

Fiona teared up, which wasn't out of the ordinary with her pregnancy hormones. Ciara quickly launched into another embarrassing story about me before the waterworks started in general, and soon everyone was laughing, including me.

Eventually, Cammie squeezed my arm and gave me a reassuring smile. "Well, we better head out," she said.

There were several protests from my sisters, but Wyatt and Cammie managed to leave with Poppy and Theo after the latter came downstairs. My sisters dipped a few minutes later but not before hugging Lauren several more times and exchanging phone numbers with her.

"Sorry about that," I said, closing the door behind Kayleigh after she'd turned on my oven for the first time and put in the casserole she'd made.

"Don't be. They're a lot of fun." Lauren stood and stretched, her shirt riding up to show the swell in her midsection. I wanted to run my hands across her soft skin, to feel every curve her body had made to accommodate our growing child. "I assume you never told them about my plans to give up the baby?"

I shook my head. "Only Everly, and she'll never breathe a word to the others."

"Thank you," she said softly. "I better start unpacking."

I looked away from her and cleared my throat. "Maddie thinks you should stay in my room for a couple days while the paint smell in yours clears. I'll take the couch. I just need to grab some of my stuff from the room, and then I'll take over whatever you need from yours."

"Aiden," she said, gently, walking to stand so close I could feel the warmth from her skin. I wanted to hold her so badly it hurt. "We can share a bed."

I shook my head, and she reached out like she was going to touch me. I bolted up the stairs and into my room, where I grabbed shit at random from the bathroom and closet before dumping it in my gym bag. She was still in the living room when I returned, staring out the window at the field beside my house with her hands cradling her bump. A rich smell of tomatoes and garlic seeped from the kitchen.

"You hungry?" I asked. "Don't tell the others, but Kayleigh is by far the best cook in the family. Smells like it might be her eggplant parm pasta bake, which would be a crime to miss."

Lauren turned from the window and gave me a small smile. "Sounds great."

We ate at the breakfast table, our conversation polite. We both had seconds. It made me hopeful the worse of Lauren's HG had passed. I loaded our plates into the dishwasher while Lauren wrapped up enough leftovers for another dinner.

"Is it OK if I see my room now?" she asked as I dried my hands.

"Should be. I have the windows open and fans running."

I followed her upstairs and down the hall. She smiled as she stepped through the doorway into her room. "This is so pretty."

"I can hang anything you want on the walls."

She looked around and nodded. I wondered if she'd brought anything to even put on the walls. "All I need for now is my suitcase," she said, pulling up the handle.

She took a deep breath and looked me in the eyes. "I never owned a suitcase before Rowan gave me this one. I moved all my things from foster house to foster house in black trash bags until I moved in with my grandpa. It's why I was protective of the suitcase on our trip."

"Fuck," I breathed out before I could stop myself. Good thing I hadn't tossed the thing in my truck like I had mine and everyone else's.

She shrugged. "I don't like talking about my life before Peace Falls, but I realized you should know the big stuff, so you can understand why I acted the way I did."

The eggplant parm twisted in my stomach, but I nodded. "Let's sit on the window seat in my room. You probably shouldn't be in here too long." And I might need to be sitting down for whatever I was about to hear.

I rolled her suitcase down the hall and took a seat, giving her as much space as possible on the cushion. She put her hands on her lap and took a steadying breath.

"I don't know where to start," she said, tucking a strand of hair behind her ear.

"What happened that made you think you couldn't be a mom?" I asked. The question had haunted me from the moment Lauren said she wanted to put the baby up for adoption.

"OK, we're getting right into it." She rubbed her hands along her leggings. I wanted to hold them, but I pressed myself tighter to the wall. "My mom never wanted me. I wasn't planned. My dad stuck around through her pregnancy but left soon after I was born. She resented having to take care of me alone, so once she thought I was old enough to take care of myself, she'd leave me in our apartment to go and party with her friends."

"How old did she think was old enough?"

"Four or five."

Shit. I'd never been alone a minute in my life I didn't want to be. "How long would she leave you?"

"At first just a few hours. Then overnight. By the time I went to school, she'd leave me days at a time. Honestly, I didn't mind. I have very few memories of her when she wasn't high or looking for a fix. It was even worse when she had a boyfriend. Some were OK, but some weren't."

"How so?" I asked, my blood pressure rising.

"Some hit. Some were too nice, you know."

No, I didn't, but I could imagine, and the things I imagined made me feel sick.

"Child services got involved from time to time, and I'd go into the system. The foster homes were like Mom's boyfriends. Some were OK, but some weren't. "

"Were you ever—" Fuck, I was a coward. I couldn't even get the words out. This time when she reached for me, I let her take my hand.

"Assaulted, yes. Raped, no."

I dropped my head into the hand that wasn't holding hers.

"I fought my way out of a few close calls," she continued. "Like I told you before, I did some things when I was younger that I'm trying to atone for. I lied, stole, and hit."

I lifted my head and placed my hand on her face. "You did what you had to do."

She nodded, her eyes going glassy for the first time in the conversation when I let my hand drop. "Things got better when I moved here. My grandpa wasn't the warmest guy, but he was reliable. Truth is, I didn't mind. I've always been afraid of love. Every time Mom found a new guy, she'd hand him her heart, and when things ended, she'd be worse off than before. The foster cycle would start again until she pulled herself together, but she never stayed single long."

I wanted to hold her so badly, to tell her that not all love harmed. That I loved her and always had. I let go of her hand, stood, and began pacing.

"I'm so sorry for everything I put you through," she said, her voice breaking. "I was terrified I wouldn't be able to love the baby like I should. But I want to try. Say something, Aiden. Tell me what you're thinking."

I took a deep breath and locked eyes with her. "I know you'll love our child exactly as you should. I didn't question it before, but now that I've heard what you've been through, I know you'll be the best damn mom in the world because you're strong and resilient and so incredibly kind." She stood, and I backed toward the door. "I should let you rest."

"Stay," she said, her voice so sweet I almost broke every promise I'd made to myself and our child.

"Slow," I said. "Spend some time with me before you decide if you want to be more than co-parents."

She nodded, but the pain in her eyes made my chest ache. "Night, Princess."

I carried my duffle bag to the hall bathroom and took a quick shower before changing into gym shorts. When I was ready for bed, Lauren was already asleep with the door to the hallway open. I watched the steady rise and fall of her chest, relieved she'd spread out so much there wasn't space for me to crawl in beside her. Eventually, I switched off the bedroom light and made my way downstairs to break in the couch.

CHAPTER THIRTY-THREE

Lauren

THE FIRST FEW DAYS living with Aiden passed in a blur. Before I knew it, I'd unpacked everything I'd brought to the house and been added to the O'Malley sibling group chat. Between exchanges of who was bringing what to the 4th of July picnic and subtle teasing about Ciara's potato salad, Aiden's sisters asked questions to pull me into the conversation. By the time we got to his parents' house for the party, everyone treated me like I'd been part of the group for years. Most of his nieces and nephews recognized me from story hour at Karma and were beyond excited to learn they were getting yet another cousin. The youngest even kissed my tiny bump, which was apparently something he did regularly to his mom, Fiona, who was due in September.

Though I felt much better in my second trimester, looking pregnant meant everyone from the mail carrier to the Torid Tuesdays Book Club thought I was working too much. Cammie insisted I end my days when she came in, if for no other reason than she was tired of hearing customers fuss. I typically arrived at Aiden's house before him, but the massive summer storm soaking the area must have shut down his worksites. I parked behind his truck and hurried through the rain to the porch.

"Hey, Lauren," he called from the back of the house as soon as I opened the door.

I kicked off my wet shoes, hung my keys on the hook Aiden installed for me, and headed to the kitchen. I found him leaning against a counter full of groceries, studying a piece of paper. His hair was still damp from the shower, and he'd changed from his work clothes into a pair of gym shorts and a t-shirt that molded to his toned chest. I wanted him to cross the kitchen and kiss me hello, but he simply looked up from the paper to acknowledge me.

"Making dinner?"

"Trying," he said, setting the paper on the counter. "At least I hope so. I grabbed a frozen pizza just in case."

"Smart." Between his mother, his sisters, and Rose, we'd had enough casseroles to get by since I moved in. I usually ate before Aiden, but he'd made a point of finding me wherever I was after he'd heated up his food in the microwave. It was as if he couldn't stand the idea of eating alone.

"It seems pretty straight forward," he said. "Dump all the ingredients on a sheet pan and put it in the oven." He pulled open the drawer under the stove and took out a baking sheet and a skillet. "But what the hell is a sheet pan? A sheet is flat and pans usually have edges. Neither of these looks like they'd work."

"I don't cook," I said, stepping closer. "But I've seen Rowan use a cookie sheet with edges. I'm guessing that's a sheet pan."

He nodded as his phone rang with a video call.

"Have you cut yourself or caught anything on fire yet?" Kayleigh asked as soon as he answered. "Hi, Lauren," she added, waving at me.

"Hi," I said, trying not to laugh. Aiden operated a successful business that regularly required the use of heavy machinery, yet his big sister had called to make sure he was OK making dinner. I'd never experienced that level of care and concern as a child. Rose came the closest to filling the maternal role in my life now, but from what I'd seen, each of Aiden's sisters were more of a mother to him than my mom had ever been to me.

"I feel better knowing you're there, Lauren," Kayleigh said.

I held up my hands. "The closest I come to making a home cooked meal is reheating what someone else cooked."

Kayleigh rubbed her forehead. "It's OK, we have a while before the baby eats solids. How far along are you in the recipe?"

"Far enough to know I don't have a sheet pan," Aiden said.

"Yes, you do. Ciara bought you one. I watched her put it under the stove."

He showed her the drawer, and she sighed. "Fiona is the worst nester," she mumbled. "Look around. It's there somewhere that Fi thought made sense."

We finally found it in the pantry holding an assortment of plastic containers arranged in an impressive pyramid.

"Did you get the parchment paper I told you to buy?" Kayleigh asked, having stayed on the call the entire time we looked for the pan. "The precut sheets?"

Aiden nodded and showed her everything he'd laid out on the counter. "Thanks for the recipe. I've got this."

Kayleigh bit her bottom lip. "Maybe you should call me later to make sure the chicken's cooked."

Aiden let out a huff. "I grill chicken breasts all the time. Don't worry. I'll be sure it's only a little pink in the middle." He ended the call, but his phone rang again before he could put it down. He smiled and typed a text.

I hadn't seen him smile much since I'd moved in, and I was no doubt the reason. He had his guard up. He was attentive, caring even, but cautious. "Can I help?" I asked.

He placed his phone on the counter and gave me his full attention. "I was only teasing Kayleigh. I won't serve you undercooked chicken. You can go upstairs and rest. You must be tired."

I was, but the last thing I wanted was more time in my room alone. Apart from the first couple nights I slept in Aiden's bed, I hadn't been sleeping well. The mattress in my room was comfortable, but I had a difficult time shutting off my mind. I tossed and turned, replaying all the ways I'd hurt Aiden and wishing he was curled around me. More than once I thought of walking down the hall and sliding into bed with him, but he wanted to take things slow. The least I could do after all the pain I'd caused was respect the pace he set. But that didn't mean I couldn't try to speed him up by spending more time together. "I'd like to help. If that's OK."

"Yeah, of course," he said, running a hand through his damp hair like the thought of an extra hour with me had rattled him. "We better start by washing our hands. Kayleigh wrote it in all caps on the top of the recipe."

"I adore your sister," I said, walking to the sink.

A soft smile crossed his lips. "Yeah, she's pretty great. Overbearing sometimes, but she means well."

I flicked on the faucet and started washing my hands. "You're lucky to have her."

"I know," he said, joining me at the sink. "I won the family jackpot."

The words had rolled out of his mouth like he said them all the time, but as soon as he spoke them, his eyes widened.

"Lauren—"

"I couldn't have picked a better family for the baby."

His eyes softened. "They're your family now too. You're in the group chat. That's our version of initiation, and you earned it in record time."

My chest filled with warmth. The O'Malleys had gone out of their way to make me feel welcomed. "Must be all the good karma I've been working on."

"Or mine," he said softly.

Talk about taking the top prize. I'd won the one-night stand, accidental pregnancy jackpot. Less than four months ago, Aiden and I couldn't be in a room together without fighting, and now I wanted to spend every moment I could with him.

He soaped his hands and put them under the water I'd left running. It was the closest we'd been, physically, in days. I let my hands drip dry into the sink, soaking in the comfort of being near him again. I could feel the heat from his body and practically taste the spicy scent of his soap. Too soon, he stepped away and grabbed a dish towel that he handed to me.

"Ready to do this?" he asked.

"I am."

We muddled through slicing three peppers, two onions, and a pair of portabella mushroom caps. They weren't pretty or even, but they were sliced and in a large plastic zipper bag waiting to be seasoned with the chicken.

"I bought tenders, so we don't have to cut up raw chicken," Aiden said. He reached for the package of meat on the counter with a grim look on his face.

"I hate touching raw meat," I blurted out. "It's one of the reasons I don't cook. It's gross, and I can never eat it after it's cooked if I touch it when it's raw."

His blue eyes sparked with amusement. "Same. But I've gotten used to it. I was just thinking that I didn't want you anywhere near raw chicken, but I didn't want to piss you off by asking you to let me handle it."

"Handle away. In fact, I'll turn my back until it's in the bag with the vegetables." His lips quirked but stopped short of a full smile. I spun around and kept rambling. "I promise I'll get over it. After the baby's born, I'll handle raw meat like an adult, but my stomach still isn't 100% all the time, and I'm pretty sure I'd gag right now if I tried."

"The chicken is safely in the bag," he said a moment later. "Mind turning on the sink for me and squirting some soap on my hands?" The man was not messing around with salmonella, and I felt confident he really could cook chicken safely.

As he washed up again, I grabbed the recipe and studied Kayleigh's neat handwriting. "Looks like we just need to add the garlic oil and spices."

"Way ahead of you," he said, pulling a packet of fajita seasoning from a drawer. "I figured we could take a short cut."

"You had that in the drawer because you knew Kayleigh would video call at some point, didn't you?"

He shrugged. "I figured it was likely."

I looked at the collection of spice bottles on the counter and shook my head. "You already bought everything. We might as well follow the recipe. She took the time to write it down so neatly."

He looked over my shoulder at the careful script and frowned. "Fine, but we're using the premade salsa and guacamole I have in the fridge. We can try her recipes for those once we master fajitas."

"Deal," I said, and my stomach grumbled loudly.

He raised his eyebrows at me. "We might need to dig into the chips and dips before dinner. It'll be a while since we forgot to preheat the oven."

Shoot. We'd missed the first step after "WASH YOUR HANDS." "We're really bad at this, aren't we?"

"Everyone makes mistakes," he said, his eyes serious and fixed on mine. "That's just part of trying."

He wasn't talking about dinner. I wanted to assure him I was trying. I pictured myself as a mother, as a part of his family, but the image remained hazy in my mind. Golden and dreamlike. Too good to be true. I wanted to apologize again for all the ways I'd hurt him and still could.

I hadn't told the realtor to take the listing offline. No one had made an offer after Aiden's expired, and I honestly didn't want one. But I still wasn't confident I could be the person Aiden and the baby deserved. I figured if I wasn't meant to stay in Peace Falls, the universe would send me an offer I couldn't refuse.

Instead of admitting my doubts to Aiden, I set the temperature on the oven. We measured spices and oil before he sealed the bag and shook everything together. When he dumped the food onto the parchment-lined pan, it smelled so good my stomach grumbled again.

"Take a seat," he said, pointing to the table and benches built into one of the kitchen's corners. "Food is on the way. I even got microwave queso, but if you value your life, best keep it a secret."

While dinner cooked, we sat across from each other eating tortilla chips and talking. As he'd done every night since I moved in, he asked me how my day had gone and told me about his. Sitting at the table he'd built, pulling chips from the same bag, I finally understood why he'd sought me out every night with his leftovers. I'm sure he'd grown up having family dinners, and even if I'd already eaten, he was continuing the tradition with me.

I'd never shared the smallest moments of my life with someone day after day. Mom didn't care, and Grandpa wasn't much of a talker. My friends were always there for me, especially for the big stuff, but I wasn't calling Rowan daily to tell her that one of my suppliers had switched my order for caffeinated and decaffeinated beans. While the kitchen filled with a delicious smell, we kept talking. The conversation might have seemed mundane to him, but the realization that I could do this every night for the rest of my life made it feel extraordinary to me. Before I knew it, the timer beeped.

Aiden's eyes widened. "Shit, we were supposed to make rice and beans."

I smiled at him. "Like you said, everyone makes mistakes when they're trying. Plus, we took down an entire bag of chips. I'll be good with one fajita."

"Let's see how we did," he said, finally giving me a full smile.

I cut one of the chicken tenders in half, snapped a picture, and sent it to Kayleigh before we sat down again to eat the first meal we'd made together. It was without question the best fajita I'd ever had.

Chapter Thirty-Four

Aiden

I DIDN'T THINK IT possible, but watching Lauren charm every member of my family and coming home to her each night made me fall even more in love. She fit into my life as if we'd been together for years, yet two weeks after she moved in, I still didn't trust her to stay.

I swung by Karma to confirm she was there any chance I reasonably could without looking like a complete stalker. My crews had never been so caffeinated, which considering the number of projects we were juggling came in handy.

An electrical issue at one of my sites this morning had kept me from making any coffee runs. Despite texting back and forth with Lauren throughout the day, a knot formed in my stomach on the drive home and tightened until I saw her beat-up sedan. I pulled in behind it and let out a relieved breath as I turned off my truck. She hadn't left. Yet.

I opened the front door to a delicious smell. Given our busy schedules, Kayleigh had come through with countless slow cooker recipes. I'd dropped a roast and some vegetables in the crockpot before I left for work, but something else mingled with the meaty scent filling the house.

Learning to cook with Lauren had been surprisingly fun. We made meals together whenever I wasn't working late, but every night, regardless of the time, we sat down together to eat and talk.

"Close the door before you let the cat out," Lauren shouted from the kitchen.

"Cat?" There hadn't been a cat in the house when I left this morning, but I quickly shut the door. Good thing too, since Dido shot down the stairs and straight for my legs. She wound around my ankles, purring loudly.

I picked her up and walked to the kitchen where Lauren was pulling a tray of dinner rolls from the oven.

"Those look great," I said, giving the cat a scratch behind the ears.

Lauren smiled at me, and my heart skipped a beat. I was so fucked if this woman bailed on me.

"Rowan's recipe. Hope you don't mind," she said pointing at Dido. "A few of the regulars started calling her Hissy. I thought she might be happier living here since you're the only person she likes, but if you want me to take her back tomorrow, I will."

Dido looked up at me with her big green eyes then rubbed her head on my beard. Fucking adorable. "You can bring all the cats here if you want."

Lauren shook her head. "It'd be too hard for Medusa to learn a new place, and she and Desdemona are a bonded pair."

"I'll run out and get a litter box before I shower," I said, ignoring the hunger pain that'd replaced the nervous ache in my stomach.

"I got a new one earlier today. Wyatt loaded a bag of litter into my car but made me promise I'd wait for you to bring it in. There's food out there too."

"I'll grab them now," I said, holding the cat toward her. Dido hissed at Lauren, and I tried not to laugh. "I'll put her in my room while I carry everything inside."

Lauren nodded and started placing the rolls into a napkin-lined basket. I went upstairs to my room but came to an abrupt stop by the bathroom door. Dido meowed, and I looked down at her. "You living here is a good thing, right? It means she's settling in. You don't think she's leaving you with me before she skips town?"

This woman had me so twisted, I was seeking reassurance from a cat.

Dido protested when I shut her in the bathroom. Hopefully, I could unload the car before the feline unleashed her revenge in there. I might be her favorite human, but she had a solid mean streak.

When I got downstairs, the front door was wide open, and Lauren's keys were missing from the hook where she kept them. I hustled outside and found her rooting in her trunk.

"I got it," I said, coming up beside her and grabbing a jumbo bag of kitty litter.

"I was thinking," she said as I started toward the house. "Instead of buying a new glider for the nursery, we could use my grandpa's leather recliner. It rocks, and it's super comfortable. And it reminds me of him," she added softly.

I put the litter back in the trunk. I wasn't having one the most important conversations of my life while holding a bag of clay pellets destined for cat crap. "Anything else you'd like to bring here?" I asked, my stupid heart pounding in my chest. I'd never been so eager to move shit in my life.

"There's a few prints that would look nice in my room, and I think my jewelry stand could go in the corner. I can't fit into most of my clothes now, but I'd like to bring over the rest of my shoes and accessories."

"Are you sure you want to move more of your stuff here?"

She gave me a confused look. "I'll put everything in my room except the recliner. I promise not to clutter up your house."

I blew out a breath. It was time to ask Lauren what I'd been dying to know for weeks. "Since the building is still for sale, are you sure you're here to stay?"

Her eyes widened. "You knew about that?"

I nodded.

"Why didn't you say anything before?"

It hurt to look at her, so I stared across the field to the barn, sending up a silent plea to Logan to help me find the right words. "You said you wanted more. I'd give you everything, but it's your choice. It has been since the first time we were together."

"Aiden," she said, placing her hand on my arm. Her fingers were warm and soft, yet painful. The possibility of her leaving was like a hot iron branding her touch on my skin. "I told the realtor to remove the listing this morning."

I snapped my gaze back to her. She looked sincere. She'd moved in the cat. She was making plans for the nursery. I wanted to wrap my arms around her and never let go, but I couldn't ignore the fact she'd kept an exit open. If I touched her, we'd likely end up sleeping together, and I couldn't complicate things between us until I felt certain she was here to stay. "Thank you," I said, grabbing the litter again.

"I want everything too, Aiden," she called after me.

I smiled but didn't turn around. "Glad we finally agree on something, Princess."

CHAPTER THIRTY-FIVE

Lauren

I STOOD IN THE middle of the nursery and admired the changes. I probably should have waited until after we found out the sex of the baby tomorrow, but I woke up determined to decorate. On one wall, Theo had painted
a gorgeous mural of lush leaves and bamboo dotted with white frangipani
flowers and bright orange flamboyant blooms. The neutral green Aiden
had chosen for the rest of the room felt soothing, exactly as a nursery should
be, but apart from the crib and changing table that Aiden already had when
I moved in and my grandfather's chair, the room was empty.

I thought I'd miss living in my apartment or resent Aiden every time
I drove the ten minutes into town before the sun rose to open Karma. I
didn't. Instead, I imagined my child running through each room downstairs, feeling safe and loved. Once I'd settled into my room across the hall,
I made regular visits to the nursery, imagining how it could look when
finished.

Today I stopped imagining and let Cammie and Wyatt train Karma's
two new hires alone, so I could spend a few hours shopping. I found a plush
green-and-white blanket to toss over the recliner. I also found a simple ivory
rug, a color I knew I'd regret eventually, but couldn't resist because of how

soft it felt. I wanted the baby to have something cloud-like for tummy time. Moments after I unrolled the rug, Dido had stretched out on it and fallen asleep. She's much calmer living in the farmhouse, though she still only tolerated me. I've been kind of jealous of all the affection Aiden has lavished on my cat. She purrs the moment he walks in the door and follows him everywhere he goes when he's home. She had it bad for him. I could totally relate.

Since Theo had done such an amazing job with the mural, I didn't think the room needed anything else on the walls. Instead, I focused on finding curtains for the large window and lamps. Then I checked in at Karma and filled a couple canvas bags with my favorite children's books. I still needed to find a dresser and a bookcase, but I'd made serious progress in one afternoon.

The front door slammed closed, and Dido startled awake.

"Hey, Lauren," Aiden called, kicking off his boots.

The cat let out a meow and shot off toward the sound of his voice.

"Hi," I said, feeling guilty as usual that he'd probably raced home to confirm I was here.

"I'm jumping in the shower," he yelled, not bothering to stop by and see me first. Hearing me was enough.

After three weeks of living with Aiden, I'd learned a few things. One: He always sang in the shower. Two: his song selection and mood were so aligned I could predict what kind of day he'd had at work before I saw him. Three: I've never wanted to shower with someone so badly.

Unfortunately, he hadn't touched me. Not once. Which meant my vibrator and I had spent a lot of time together, usually while Aiden showered. Yet again, my room shared a wall with his bathroom, so I could hear every note, every splash, and easily imagine him naked under a cascade of water.

Horny didn't even begin to describe the longing I felt for him. But it wasn't just sex I craved. For the first time in my life, I wanted to cuddle. I blamed the pregnancy hormones.

Instead of torturing myself listening to him shower, I settled in the recliner. As soon as I stilled, the tiny flutters began. Rowan, Poppy, and Cammie had all tried to feel the baby move by placing their hands on my stomach, but so far, no luck. I couldn't wait to see how much the baby had grown in the ultrasound and feel it move inside me while I watched it move on the tiny screen.

I grabbed a book off the floor and started reading out loud, rubbing my stomach with my free hand. When I looked up from the last page, Aiden stood in the doorway in a t-shirt and a pair of gray sweatpants that hung low on his hips. I sucked in a breath. It was as if the longing I'd felt for him each day had settled in his eyes.

He cleared his throat and shoved his hands in his pockets. "I like what you did in here," he said, stepping inside the nursery. Dido followed him and started rubbing her face against his legs.

"I kept the receipts in case you didn't."

"Nah, it's perfect," he said, looking everywhere but at me. "We can go together to find a dresser this weekend."

"And a bookcase," I said, motioning to the pile of books on the floor.

"I can build a custom one once we have the rest of the room figured out."

"That's so sexy," I said, which was not at all what I meant to say. "Sweet. That's so sweet."

He smirked at me, finally. I'd missed that smirk. The playful banter between us. "I liked the first version better."

"Never took you for a tease," I said, trying my hardest to sound casual when all I wanted to do was rip off his clothes.

He lifted his eyebrows and smirked again. "That's because I've never been one."

"So," I said, placing the book on the floor and rising from the chair. "You're saying if I told you I wanted to have sex right now, you'd be down for it?"

He shrugged. "Sure."

If it wasn't for his eyes, I'd think he'd just agreed to scratching-an-itch intimacy. But there was so much more than heat in those deep blues: hope, fear, maybe even love.

"But not in here," he said as I started toward him. "I'll fuck you in any room of the house except this one." He backed out into the hallway without taking his eyes off me.

For some reason, that made me laugh. "So you'll put your penis inside me while the baby is in me, but you want to keep the nursery pure?"

"I didn't say it made sense." He turned and ripped off his shirt as he walked to his room. Dido followed behind him with her tail stub held high, flashing me her butthole. I scooped her up, placed her outside Aiden's bedroom, and shut the door. She let out an indignant yowl in the hallway.

"She's really going to hate you now," Aiden said without turning around. The muscles in his back bunched as he tossed his shirt on the floor and slid off his sweatpants, leaving him gloriously naked.

I took a moment to enjoy the tight curves of his ass before removing my own clothes and standing beside him. We were both completely naked, staring at the bed, but neither of us made a move to touch the other.

He reached out and took my hand, his touch almost hesitant. He swallowed hard, his eyes still on the bed, and my heart ached. He wanted me. His thick erection left no question of that, but I'd hurt him. Sleeping with me again was a leap toward something more between us or a heap more heartbreak.

"Can we cuddle first?" I asked. "I've—" Wanted you every day. Been letting myself fall for you. "I've missed you."

He squeezed my fingers and guided us both to the bed. He placed his rough hand on my stomach, pulled me close, and nestled his face into the curve of my neck. His wet hair cooled my heated skin, but the scratch of his stubble woke every nerve in my body. As soon as he'd molded his front to my back, the ache in my chest eased, but the ache to feel him inside me intensified. I pressed my legs together for some relief. He lowered his hand from my stomach to my throbbing center.

"The great thing about cuddling," he said, sliding a finger against my swollen clit, "is we can get started on that orgasm count." I arched, rubbing against his erection. He let out a small groan, and I placed my hand over his.

"The first time, together," I said, twisting to face him.

"Good thing you have a hair trigger," he said with another smirk. "And good thing I just jacked off in the shower thinking of you."

He kissed me, gently at first, but then we both gave in to the hunger that had always been between us. He took his time, easing into me inch by inch, his lips never leaving mine. We rocked against each other, our bodies moving together in a slow dance of pleasure. I fought my orgasm until I couldn't. "I'm going to come," I said, breaking our kiss for the first time.

"Look at me."

I shattered as he held my face, his eyes locked with mine. He pulsed inside me, finding his own release as we clung to each other. He brushed the hair from my face, then rubbed his thumb across my cheek.

I loved him. I wanted to tell him, but part of me still worried I'd never be enough. My eyes filled with tears as he placed a gentle kiss on my forehead. I wrapped myself around him and spent the rest of the night telling him with my body all the words I was too afraid to say.

Chapter Thirty-Six

Aiden

Lauren looked terrified as we drove to the ultrasound appointment. After last night, I thought we were headed in the right direction, but she fidgeted with her braid and avoided eye contact like she wanted to bolt from the truck.

"What if I hurt the baby?" she said when I pulled into a parking spot at her OB/GYN's office. "I changed the cat litter several times before you told me not to. What if I made the baby sick, and it didn't grow correctly, and it's all my fault?"

"Hey," I said, taking her hand. Her palms were sweaty, which made my blood pressure shoot up. "The doctor tested you for toxoplasma. You're fine."

"What if the test didn't pick it up? Or what if I did something else wrong? I didn't know I was pregnant right away. We drank in St. John, and I drank wine with Rowan after, before I knew. And I wasn't on prenatal vitamins. No telling what my folic acid levels were."

I unbuckled my seat belt and slid across the bench seat to gather her in my arms. She was shaking, and I felt like the world's biggest dumbass for not just asking her earlier what was wrong. "I'm sure the baby is fine, but if not, we'll handle it. Worrying won't change anything." She let out a stuttering breath and nodded.

"Just promise you won't hate me if something is wrong. I swear I've done everything I thought I should once I found out about the baby. Except read those papers from the doctor. I should have. I just didn't know about the cat litter and—"

"Princess," I said, taking her face in my hands. "I promise."

"OK," she whispered.

I wanted to tell her I loved her. That a part of me had loved her since that very first night when we curled together on her crappy sofa and talked for hours. But I didn't know when she'd be ready to hear it, if ever. I placed a gentle kiss on her lips, and she took one more deep breath before opening the truck door.

I hurried around to help her down, and thankfully she let me. We held hands the entire time we waited to be called back. I had to let go while she climbed onto the exam table, but she held her hand out for mine as soon as she was settled.

"Ready to get started?" the ultrasound tech asked. She wasn't the same one from our last visit, but she hadn't called us Mom and Dad. I bet Lauren had some interesting notes in her chart.

Lauren nodded and the tech squirted gel on her belly and started moving the wand around. The moment the baby came into view, Lauren squeezed my hand.

"Is the baby OK?" she asked after the tech had taken some measurements, the panic clear in her voice.

"Your doctor will review any findings with you later, but I can tell you the sex."

I cleared my throat, and the tech glanced at me. "I know you can't tell us anything but maybe a nod or a blink. She's really anxious."

The tech smiled, then nodded and blinked.

Lauren practically melted onto the exam table with relief.

"Would you like to know the sex?"

"I kind of would," I said, looking down at Lauren. But her eyes were fixed on the screen. She nodded, transfixed by the baby's tiny movements.

"It's a boy," the tech said with another smile. "Congratulations."

My throat pulled so tight I couldn't speak.

"Logan." Lauren took her eyes from the screen to look at me. "We should name him Logan, unless you think his sisters want to use the name."

I looked back at the screen where my son was alive and well, then back at the woman who I loved despite all reason, and lost it.

"I'll, um, give you two a couple minutes," the tech said, placing the wand by the machine and leaving the room in a rush.

I laid my head on Lauren's chest and cried for the best friend I'd lost. It gutted me that my son would never know Logan, but in that moment, I finally felt at peace with all the twists and turns in my life that had brought me to this exact moment and the incredible gift I'd been given.

Lauren ran her fingers through my hair, but otherwise let me cry myself out. When I finally lifted my head, she smiled at me with shiny eyes. "I figured out your nickname."

"Woman, if it has anything to do with what you just saw, keep it to yourself."

"Oh, it has everything to do with what I just saw," she said with a devilish smile.

Great. Guess I was going to be Crybaby or Kleenex Man for the rest of my life. "Fine, hit me."

Her eyes softened. "My Love."

My chest filled with warmth, but also a tinge of fear. "Please tell me you're not being sarcastic right now."

"You have the biggest heart of anyone I know. I've tried to fight it, but it's useless. I love you, Aiden O'Malley."

"Good," I said, taking her face in my hands. "Because I love you too, Princess."

I was still kissing her when the doctor came in to resume the ultrasound and confirm the baby looked healthy.

"Do you want to tell everyone it's a boy?" Lauren asked as we walked to the parking lot.

"Sure, you handle our friends. I've got my family and Logan's. I'll ask about the name."

We both typed out messages before I started the truck. The entire drive home, our phones pinged. The smile on Lauren's face made me feel seven feet tall, but when we pulled in front of the house, I knew I needed a minute with Logan.

"I'll be in soon. I have to check something in the tree house."

My phone chimed again, and I passed it to her. "Mind taking that inside? The passcode is your due date if you want to see if Logan's family wrote back about the name."

"Damn it, Aiden," she said, swatting my arm as tears leaked down her face. "I held it together the whole time in the office."

I chuckled and climbed out of the truck. After I helped her down, I brushed the moisture from her cheeks before resting my forehead on hers. "I love you so much, Lauren. I've wanted to tell you for a while, but I didn't want to scare you off."

"I'm not going anywhere," she said, wrapping her arms around my waist and resting her head on my chest. "I love you and our baby more than I ever thought possible."

I lowered my mouth to hers and kissed her until she was breathless. "Go," she said, pulling away before we got too heated to stop. "I'll be waiting."

Once I'd made sure she got inside safely, I crossed the dirt road and the freshly mowed field to the tree house.

Theo and Poppy delivered the statue earlier in the week. It sat beneath the tree, covered with a tarp for the big reveal we had planned for the anniversary of the accident. Since Lauren had been staying with me, I'd tinkered on the tree house whenever I had the urge to touch her, which was often. I'd finished up everything in record time.

I climbed the ladder and took a seat on the couch, admiring my work. It was admittedly a little overboard for a tree house. The windows were actual windows instead of cut-outs in plywood like our first tree house. The walls were insulated and finished with white shiplap. I'd gone back and forth between reclaimed wood or laminate for the floor, before remembering the first was prone to splinters.

"Who'd have thought we'd have a tree house this nice, Logan," I said.

I'm not sure how long I sat there, remembering him and the childhood we'd shared before I finally said out loud what I'd been thinking since the moment Lauren said his name. "I don't want to let you go, but I want to move on. I wish I could bring the best of you with me and leave behind all the regret, the anger. I'd appreciate if you'd help me out with that."

"You sure he didn't already?" Cal asked.

I jumped and may or may not have made a noise that sounded like a scream. "What the fuck, man? You about gave me a heart attack. Why'd you sneak up on me?"

He shrugged and took a seat beside me on the couch. "Seriously though, what are the chances you and Lauren would get drunk enough to sleep together one time and make a baby?"

He had a point. "Not that I'm not thrilled to have the shit scared out of me, but what are you doing here?

"Lauren asked us over. When she said where you were, I figured it was time I saw this place. It's incredible. Way nicer than that pile of wood in your parents' backyard."

"Don't knock that pile of wood. It's the only reason I ever camped out after the neighbor's dog bit my leg. The tree house was Logan's idea, of course."

Cal's mouth fell open. "How did I not know that?"

"My sisters don't even know. We told them we wanted space away from them, but really, I was scared to sleep on the ground."

"Are you two done with your manly bro bonding yet?" Poppy shouted from below. "Theo's on his way, and I'm not sure how he's going to handle this without you."

"Don't get your panties in a twist, Hell Cat," I yelled.

"Don't talk about my fiancée's panties," Theo yelled from a distance.

Cal and I laughed and took turns climbing down the ladder. More cars were pulling up to my house, including Fiona's minivan and Everly's SUV.

Theo stood between Rowan and Lauren, escorting them both through the shorn field.

"I told you to wait," Cal said, sprinting off to help his wife. "Not that I don't trust you, Theo."

"Never doubted it," he said, slapping Cal's shoulder after he took Rowan's arm.

"I hope you don't mind," Lauren said, smiling at me. "I thought maybe we should celebrate with everyone."

Theo walked her all the way to me like some father of the bride before pulling Poppy to his side.

"Everyone?"

Lauren shrugged as a pack of my favorite kiddos tore across the field and went straight for the tree house.

"Wait," Kayleigh yelled after them. "I hope you weren't planning a ribbon cutting or something." She wrapped Lauren in a hug before greeting me, while Ciara helped a very pregnant Fiona across the field. They both pulled Lauren into crushing hugs as well. Good thing I'd kept my mouth shut about the whole adoption thing.

"Hey," Everly said, walking up with Maddie, their parents, and mine. Logan's mom grabbed my hands. "We'd be honored if you named your son Logan."

"You're sure," I said, looking at Mr. and Mrs. Hendricks. They nodded, both beaming.

My parents hugged Lauren like they hadn't seen her in years, not weeks, and rubbed her stomach. Poppy was right. Zero boundaries. Once she'd freed herself from my parents, Lauren put her arm around my waist and smiled up at me. "You sure this is OK?"

"This is perfect," I said as children's laugher trickled down from the tree house.

"You know," Everly said, looking at the tarp-covered statue. "We're all here now. Well, everyone except the guys."

"I've already got them on a video call," Fiona said. "The two that matter, anyway." She held up her phone and her husband and Ciara's waved at everyone.

Kayleigh shot Fiona a look but didn't disagree.

"If I'm being honest," Theo said. "I never thought the anniversary was the right day to honor Logan."

"So, we're going with a random Tuesday?" I asked.

Maddie shrugged. "Why not? I mean, you're naming your kid after him. The tree house and statue are great, but we all know Logan would have thought having a namesake was a bigger deal."

"You OK?" I asked Theo.

"Yeah," he said, and I actually believed him.

"Let's do it then," Cal said.

"Kids, get your butts down here," Kayleigh hollered.

A chorus of complaints echoed, but one by one, my nieces and nephews joined us in a circle around the tarp-covered statue. Lauren squeezed my hand, and I moved behind her so I could place my hands on her bump. Fine, and so I could bury my face in her hair if I lost it again.

Theo unfastened the tarp, and he and Poppy each took an edge. She looked up and frowned. "Where's my brother when I need him?"

Theo laughed and motioned for Cal to take her place, and together they lifted the tarp and flung it to the ground.

A life-size statue of Logan stood beneath the tree house, an exact replica of the picture someone had snapped of him when we won state. I recognized the moment. Logan leaping in the air with his arms stretched wide in celebration, a huge smile on his face.

"Who's he hugging?" my niece Aubrey asked.

"Life," Theo said.

Aubrey tilted her head and shrugged.

One by one, each of us stepped closer to admire Theo and Poppy's work before my mom said we needed to make s'mores. Fiona texted her husband, who arrived with a bag of groceries and a case of bottled water right before Ciara's husband pulled up with enough pizza to feed everyone. Before I knew it, we'd built a small fire by the tree house and were roasting marshmallows as the sun set.

When Lauren settled on my lap to enjoy her second s'more, I pulled her close. "This has been the best day of my life," I whispered in her ear.

"Mine too," she said, laying a chocolate-scented kiss on my cheek. "So far."

EPILOGUE

Lauren

I WOKE TO AIDEN singing a lullaby, his voice low and soft. My eyes fluttered open, and I found him sitting in the chair beside the hospital bed with the baby swaddled in his arms. When he saw me, he smiled. The baby let out a little cry, and I quickly propped myself up.

"I was trying to let you sleep," he said, laying the baby gently in my arms.

I glared at him. "You nurse when the baby is hungry. You know this."

He placed a lingering kiss on my forehead and all my irritation melted. "I also know you pulled an all-nighter in the delivery room."

The baby let out another cry as I lowered my hospital gown and positioned us to nurse.

"That's a solid latch," Aiden said, nodding his approval.

I tried not to laugh. "Did you ever think you'd say something like that while staring at my naked breast?"

"After last time, yes," he said, running his hands through his hair. It still caught me off guard sometimes when I saw his wedding ring. When I was a girl, never in my wildest dreams would I have imagined myself happily married to anyone, let alone someone like Aiden O'Malley.

It had taken a while for me to agree, not because I didn't love him, but because I didn't want anything to change. I reasoned having a child together bound us tighter than a few words and a piece of paper, but eventually, I realized those words meant something to me too. That I was his forever, and he was mine.

We stared at the baby together, falling in love with every eyelash and sweet feature. Dark circles bloomed under Aiden's eyes. He had to be exhausted as well, but the smile hadn't left his face since he held the baby in the delivery room.

"That is a good latch."

"You're a pro," Aiden said, leaning closer to us both.

"She isn't."

He smiled at me. "She has an excellent teacher."

Not a day went by when Aiden didn't reassure me I could handle whatever challenges motherhood threw my way. "What time is Cammie coming?"

"Any minute now," he said, glancing over his shoulder at the closed door. "When the baby started fussing, I knew you'd be up soon and texted her."

"I'm so excited. And nervous. What if Logan doesn't like her?"

Aiden shrugged. "He won't. Not all the time. And that's perfectly normal."

As usual, Aiden soothed my anxiety with a few words. It took two years before I was comfortable enough to consider having another child. It only took Aiden a month to get me pregnant again.

"So," he said, taking the hand I wasn't using to hold our daughter. "We should decide on a name before Logan meets his little sister."

"I know it's your grandmother's name, but Siobhan is so hard to spell. Imagine her as a preschooler trying to write that out. I doubt Logan could even pronounce it."

"Look at that latch. Our girl is a fast learner. She'll master all those vowels in no time. And so what if Logan can't pronounce the name now? I love when he messes up words, don't you?"

He had me there. Three-year-olds had the best interpretations of things. "What's Grams's middle name?"

"Caoimhe."

"Um, no. Sorry, My Love."

He laughed. "Well, we could name her after the best mother I know."

I nodded. "Amanda works, but isn't that Mandy's full name? Having the same name as your cousin doesn't feel right."

His eyes softened, and he gave my hand a squeeze. "I meant you, Princess."

The universe had really delivered with this man. It got easier and easier to pay the good karma forward as I settled into my beautiful life with him. Difficult spelling aside, Aiden's grandmother would adore having a child named after her, and though I knew he'd accept whatever I suggested, Aiden loved the name. "Siobhan Lauren. That way, she could go by Lauren if she wants."

The baby gave a contented sigh, which made Aiden and me both giggle. Guess that settled it.

Aiden flipped a burp cloth over his shoulder and reached for the baby. "Let me burp her before she goes into a milk coma, so you can try her on the other side."

I'd already fallen for Aiden before Logan was born but watching him be an amazing father deepened my love. Who knew watching a burly guy make baby food could be a turn on? Siobhan let out a gurgling sound, and Aiden glanced over his shoulder.

He handed me the baby and took a deep breath.

"Did she even spit up?" I asked, moving the baby to my other breast. Aiden's weak stomach remained his only paternal kryptonite.

"No, but that sound." He shuddered.

Unfortunately, my HG had made an encore appearance with this pregnancy. Aiden and I had both lost a considerable amount of weight during the first trimester.

"You handled spit up fine with Logan," I said.

"Eventually. Give me a week, woman. I just need a little exposure therapy again."

A soft knock sounded on the door and we both yelled, "Come in."

Cammie stood in the doorway with a pair of tiny hands wrapped around her leg as my little guy hid behind her.

"Hey buddy," Aiden said, crossing the room. Logan immediately let go of Cammie and ran to his father, his light brown curls bouncing with every step. "Ready to meet your little sister?"

Logan nodded. I kept my eyes glued to him while they approached the bed. The baby was still nursing, something Logan understood well from watching Rowan with her infant daughter Dahlia.

I'd prepared for him to be shy, even fearful. But the look of pure love on his face when he saw his little sister for the first time took my breath away. Aiden lowered Logan onto the bed, and he quickly nestled in beside me.

"I missed you so much," I said, kissing the top of his head and breathing deep the smell of his tear-free shampoo. I didn't think my heart could love anyone else the way I loved my son, but one look at my daughter, and I understood love wasn't finite. It didn't have to be given in scraps and fragments. It could grow and compound beyond anything I ever thought possible.

"She's pretty like you, Mommy," Logan said with a huge smile that looked so much like his father's but with my dimples.

"Her name is Siobhan."

"Sissy," Logan said, leaning closer to place a gentle kiss on the baby's forehead.

"That works," Aiden said, winking at me.

"Oh my gosh," Cammie said, putting down her phone and wiping tears from her eyes. "That was the cutest thing I've ever seen, and I got it all on video." She walked closer, her face full of warmth.

Siobhan had no idea yet how much love surrounded her. She had so many cousins, both by blood and friendship, that she'd always have someone to play with. She'd bounce from home to home not because she was placed there, but because everyone in her life would open their doors to her with the same love and acceptance as Aiden and I opened ours.

"When can I have a brother?" Logan asked.

I shot Aiden a glare, and he held up his hands. "I swear I didn't tell him to say that. You know I'd like to fill every bedroom, but we can't even try for six weeks."

I gaped at him. He couldn't be serious. We'd never actually discussed how many children he wanted. I'd asked him to let the universe guide us as we went, and he agreed. "Four kids?"

He smirked at me. "Nah, kids don't take up much room. Eight ought to be enough."

If I wasn't holding our children and still sore from giving birth, I'd have gotten out of the bed and into his face for the mother of all arguments. Which usually led to exactly the thing we couldn't do for six weeks. Sometimes, I think he nettled me just to get us revved for makeup sex.

"You do make really cute kids," Cammie said. "And Poppy's due in five months. If you got to it, they'd be in the same class at school."

Really, Cam? "Spoken like a woman who's never pushed out a nine-pound baby."

She shrugged. "If anyone could do it, you could."

And despite how I started in life, and how hard it was for me to accept being a mother the first time, I believed her. I still wasn't having eight kids.

Epilogue II

Aiden

We had four, just like I'd always wanted.

More from Hannah

Can't get enough of Lauren and Aiden? Sign up for my newsletter for a bonus epilogue of the day they become parents.

Visit https://dl.bookfunnel.com/5x1v3y9okn

If you enjoyed *For You I'd Bloom*, you'll love the rest of the Peace Falls Series.

Book 1: For You I'd Break Available Now

Book 2: For You I'd Mend Available Now

Book 4: For You Always Available July 7, 2025

LETTER TO READERS

Dear Reader,

Let me start by saying thank you to all the amazing foster parents in the world. I'm constantly in awe of the individuals who open their homes to kids in need. While Lauren's story paints a bleak picture of the system, I'd be remiss not to acknowledge the effort, expense, and love so many foster parents provide. It's truly remarkable, and you have my upmost respect and gratitude.

I hope you enjoyed the final book of the original Peace Falls trilogy. Don't worry, I'm not leaving Peace Falls for a while, but when I started my journey as a romance author, I intended to tell the stories of three men who'd survived a tragic accident together but needed to find love to move forward with their lives.

A loss like Logan's never truly heals. Time passes and life happens, but the absence remains because love is infinite. No one can replace the ones we've lost. Still, there's beauty in the bittersweet life after.

And gratitude. I'm grateful for every day I'm given, for each opportunity I've been granted, and for all the people who have so graciously given their time to read these stories. I hope they've brought you the same joy they've brought me.

Thanks for reading!

Hannah

P.S. Please keep in touch! For news and exclusive content visit https://hannahjordanauthor.com and sign up for my newsletter.

f facebook.com/hannahjordanbooks/

instagram.com/hannahjordanbooks/

Acknowledgements

To James Carpenter and Gerri Mahn for hyping me up when I need it and mercilessly tearing my writing apart the rest of the time. To Claude and Melyssa, thank you for your invaluable feedback and continued support. A special thanks to Kaytalin McCarry for your beautiful cover designs. Finally, to all my family and friends who have embraced my new career, thank you. For a time, I thought I'd never tell any of you that I'd written a romance novel, let alone three. I'm incredibly grateful I did. Your enthusiastic support has meant the world to me.

ABOUT THE AUTHOR

HANNAH JORDAN GREW UP in the Blue Ridge Mountains of Virginia but moved to South Jersey after falling in love with her complete opposite. She's got all the advanced degrees of a "serious" fiction writer but only smiles when she's writing romance. She lives with her husband and two daughters in a picturesque town outside Philadelphia where she enjoys reading in all genres, especially the spicy ones, and confusing people with her half-Southern, half-Northern accent.